REST EASY

REST EASY

WARONA JOLOMBA

wattpad books **w**

wattpad books **W**

Content Warning: underage drinking, underage drug use,
maternal death, domestic abuse,
sensitive familial relationships, racial insensitivity

Published in Canada by Wattpad Books, a division of Wattpad Corp.
36 Wellington Street E., Toronto, ON M5E 1C7

www.wattpad.com

First Wattpad Books edition: October 2021

ISBN 978-1-98936-595-3 (Trade Paper original)
ISBN 978-1-98936-596-0 (eBook edition)

Library and Archives Canada Cataloguing in Publication information
is available upon request.

Printed and bound in Canada
1 3 5 7 9 10 8 6 4 2

Cover design and illustration by Chelsea Charles
Typesetting by Sarah Salomon

For my little sisters. Shoot for the stars.

PROLOGUE

Summer, 1972. Bakersfield, California.

"I wrote a list, even though it won't be a huge shopping spree. Just a few necessities." Violet unbuckled her seat belt. Her husband lowered the volume on the radio, watching her as she brought down the mirror above her head and hastily powdered her face, spraying some perfume afterward.

"Didn't know the supermarket had a beauty pageant aisle." He chuckled.

"So just to make sure: fruit to fill the bowl, some bread and milk, diapers for Charlotte, some cigarettes, and salmon for tonight's meal?" She looked over at Charles once she'd finished applying a rose-colored lip tint. The toddler gargled and mumbled incoherently to herself in the back seat.

"Yeah. Oh, and get us a bottle of wine. Your choice. We can

celebrate my promotion, after dinner. Watch a film once Charlie's in bed. Drink up." He rubbed her left thigh, and she smiled at him softly, bringing her hand to his cheek.

"Congratulations, honey. I'm so proud of you. I can only hope for the same kind of fortune for me, one day," she said.

"Don't hope. *Expect* it. It will come, I promise you that." Charles knew how much her poetry meant to her, and it broke his heart to see her still struggling to get it out into the gargantuan, chaotic, fickle world. She had been writing for as long as he had known her, needing to work three jobs, and still being turned down at every agency, her work given little attention in poetry journals. It almost finished her, once upon a time. She almost gave up on herself, on everything. *Almost*. Her husband was getting what he wanted in life: a good job, a baby, a wife, and she was a ball of static energy, her efforts being wasted, her poems piling up in their house like a mountain she couldn't climb. She still had so much to give to the world, she was sure of it. It was just a question of figuring out how.

Violet leaned over to kiss her husband. He counted its duration: four seconds, approximately. "I love you," she said, and kissed him again. This time, two seconds. When he turned to face the windshield, she kissed him on the cheek, quickly, in an almost juvenile fashion. Three kisses.

"I love you too," Charles said.

Baby Charlotte started laughing at something imaginary in the back seat. Violet got out of the car and strode through the parking lot, toward the glass doors of the local supermarket. Her strawberry-blond hair swayed and bounced along with her peppy gait, and her skirt fluttered in the gentle wind outside. She clutched onto her handbag like a rich schoolgirl with a Chanel purse, and she suddenly looked eight years younger. It was like he saw a spark of energy in her, and it warmed his chest. *She's okay,* he thought. *She will get what she wants in life. She'll be fine.*

That was the last time Charles ever saw his wife.

1

THE RESTLESS

Dee Warrington could not sleep. And he felt like letting his ex-girlfriend, Vanessa, know about it. He was itching to fill up the emptiness inside his chest, the cavity that grew mercilessly, a black hole feasting on light. He hadn't wanted her so much since the last time they were together. So at 3:22 a.m., while his heart refused to drum a lax cadence, he scrolled down through his phone's contacts until he saw her name. His thumb hovered over the Call button as he held his breath. Before he could talk himself out of his decision, he pressed it. To his surprise, she answered the phone.

"Hey, Dee. What's up? Is everything okay?"

"You're still awake?" he asked, trying hard to mask his triumph at the sound of her voice.

"Yeah. I have a Spanish final tomorrow. Cramming, you know. I was just about to sleep. What's going on? Are you okay?"

"I'm fine. Uh, actually . . . I—I'm just having trouble sleeping."

"I gathered that. Did something happen? Is Dylan home?"

"No. He went out. I've been studying for the history final. I know I'm going to fuck it up, though. Mrs. Meyers' voice is so whiny. I just zone out."

"I don't think you can really blame Mrs. Meyers' voice for your grades."

"No shit, Vanessa." He gulped another shot of his brother's whiskey as he sat upright in bed, looking out his open window. There was not even a slither of a breeze, and the air felt stifling.

"Sorry. Um . . . why are you calling me? We haven't spoken in weeks."

"I don't know. I can't sleep. It's been really bad lately. I'm scared." He paused, sighing, trying to keep himself together. "This house is so empty. I can't handle it. I don't like it. I don't know who else to talk to. I just knew you'd understand."

"Of course I understand. Yeah, I do." She spoke as though she was convincing herself. He sensed hesitance.

"I really miss you," he mumbled. Their relationship had ended just after their one-year anniversary. The cavity in him was taunting him as it grew, and he thought he might just die. He knew he'd feel better in a few months, but that didn't matter in that moment. Hopelessness never pointed you to the future.

"Okay. I'll come over," Vanessa said. Another surprise. Dee wasn't expecting such a statement from her, but then he didn't know *what* he'd expected.

"You sure? It's dark out."

"It's a five-minute drive. I'm a big girl. I'll bring my bag and my toothbrush so we can just leave for class in the morning."

"What are we gonna do?" he found himself asking.

"I don't know. What do you *want* to do?"

"Uh . . . I don't know. I mean . . . wait, no. There's something I have to talk to you about."

"There is?"

"Yeah. Something I think you really ought to know."

"Right, okay . . ." Vanessa responded, her voice thick with intrigue and suspicion. "I'll see you in ten, then?"

"Sure. Sure. I'll see you soon."

His palms were instantly clammy once she hung up. He didn't know if he was ready to see her up close, even though he thought he was. He had started off pathetic around her when they first met—a skittish mess, hiding his nerves behind flirtation and cheap jokes. Now he was feeling skittish again, but on a whole new level. In the worst way.

◆

A half hour later, he got a text from Vanessa, who was waiting at the front door. He had been hastily tidying his room, shoving stray clothes under his bed and into his closet, clearing his desk, switching on his bedroom fan to dispel the warm stuffiness in the air. He finished the whiskey and drank a glass of water to compensate for his ever-intensifying intoxication. Vanessa knew he wasn't sober the second she saw him. She smiled softly, taking a deep breath before planting a kiss on his cheek. He led her into the living room, where cans of beer littered the coffee table.

"Dylan pregamed with some of his friends. Do you want a beer or something?"

"It's nearly four in the morning, Dee. We have class at nine."

"One drink won't kill you."

Vanessa shook her head. "I said I can't. God, you're like the devil on my shoulder."

"Okay, okay, whatever. How about a smoke?"

She looked to the floor, then back to him. Tilting her head back, she sighed. "I guess. Just a little bit."

Dee smiled. "That's more like it. Let's go upstairs. The stuff's in my room."

Once they got there, Vanessa sat on his bed and he went to his desk to roll up. His lamp was situated in front of him, silhouetting the back of his head in a soft incandescence. He played music on his speaker, something hushed and melodic.

"Did you join the pregame?" she asked him.

"No, I didn't. I just stayed in my room. Listened to some music until they left for Phoenix. I know he won't be back until, like, tomorrow evening."

"You mean *this* evening?"

"Tomayto, tomahto."

"So you've just been by yourself, huh?"

"Yeah. Lonely." He turned to look at her, licking the joint closed. He sealed the end up and shook it, not once unlocking his gaze from hers. Her stomach flipped. He was beautiful, and that was what she hated the most. He had always looked like a girl, with hair three times longer than her own, so long it almost reached his waist. She remembered the times she used to braid it, on quiet nights in. "Shall we?" he asked, getting off his chair and sitting next to Vanessa on the bed.

"What was it that you wanted to tell me?" She watched him take a long toke. He held it in for a few seconds, furrowing his brows at the heaviness in his chest, before blowing out a cough.

"Uh . . . I can't remember."

"You can't remember? It sounded important."

"It probably wasn't if I can't remember it."

"Come on, Dee. You're holding back, I can tell."

"I just wanted you to come over. I didn't want you to change your mind." He passed the joint to her, then picked up his phone to change the song. "Freudian" by Daniel Caesar started playing.

"You don't have to lie to get me to come over. I said I would."

"Remember how much we loved this album?" he said, lying back on his pillow. "How we'd make out to it, like, all the time?" He looked at her, smiling.

"I remember. It was nice." She killed the joint after taking a few puffs, leaving it on an ashtray on the bedside table. Then she lay on her back and turned her head to face him, their eyes level. Her heart was hammering ferociously, and she could hear the blood rushing in her ears. She turned on her side and placed a hand on his cheek. They were kissing each other before they could even register it.

Their hands slid all over, fingers slinking and climbing under T-shirt, bra, boxer shorts, panties, like they were desperately clawing for something within each other, holding onto skin and fabric like it was keeping them from falling over a precipice. The last time they were together felt like eons ago, but it also felt like it was just yesterday. Their love existed outside of the confines of time, or space, or rationality.

Each kiss carried a sprinkle of hatred. Hatred toward one another for taking advantage of the other's vulnerabilities; hatred of themselves for letting themselves be taken advantage of. Still, Vanessa held onto Dee, kissing his neck, kissing his shoulders, draping her leg over his, holding his chest against hers. He had shattered her heart, yet he still got to have her, whenever he wanted.

All he had to do was call her at stupid-o'-clock in the morning, and she'd be there. She resented him for it. He knew it was easy for her to come to his aid. He had been through a lot the past few months. He had been through a lot his whole *life*. She was the lucky one, the one with the functional family and the money and the opportunities in life. He wasn't. There had to be a compromise, and it was right there, in each other's arms.

Vanessa got on top of him, gazing into his eyes. She leaned down and kissed him again, and he suddenly froze. Something had changed; the mood had shifted. His grip had softened, and he wasn't moving.

"Are you okay?" she asked, her breathing heavy.

"Wait, wait—stop. Please get off."

"What's wrong?" She moved away, a wave of mortification crashing over her.

He sat up with eyes watering, lips creased into a frown. He was crying. "I can't do this. I'm sorry."

"What the fuck, Dee?"

He sat up, staring into nothingness. The silence cloaked the room for what felt like an eternity. "This isn't your fault. You *know* it isn't."

"This is about Karina, isn't it?" Vanessa's voice wavered. "That's why you can't sleep with me. God, I feel disgusting." Holding back tears, she moved to the end of the bed and grabbed her sweatpants.

"Vanessa, I . . ."

"It *is* about her? Fuck. I'm such an idiot."

"No, you're not. I'm the stupid one. You did nothing wrong."

"Why didn't you just call *her* over instead? Maybe you would actually have enjoyed yourself."

"Vanessa. It . . . it didn't happen. I'm telling you. She made it up."

"Oh yeah? Tell that to all of junior year, who found out before I did. Tell that to Karina, who literally *told* me it happened. I'm sick of this bullshit."

Dee sighed, defeated. "This wasn't a good idea."

"Exactly. I need to go."

"No—don't. I meant . . . us making out and shit—*that* was a bad idea. But I don't want you to leave me here alone. I can't sleep. I don't know what to do."

"I'm not going to sing you a lullaby or rub your back. You need to learn to deal with this. I can't always come to the rescue." He watched her put the rest of her clothes on and slide into her sneakers. She'd normally steal his hoodie, but she didn't this time.

He got out of bed and searched for his pants in the dim light. "You're right. I'm sorry."

"Stop saying sorry. I'm leaving now. It's ten past four. I'll see you tomorrow." She sniffed, wiping her wet eyes.

"You mean today." He smiled pathetically. She didn't react. Just grabbed her phone, slung her bag over her shoulder, and left his bedroom. Dee got an hour of sleep before his alarm went off.

◆

Dee walked into his first class half an hour late. Vanessa was sitting on the left side of the room, as she always did. She looked up, sinking into her seat. He glanced toward her for a millisecond before traipsing to his desk in the newfound silence that saturated the room. His teacher called him out, asking him why he was late.

"I missed my alarm clock. My bad." He shrugged.

"That's not good enough. You should have informed the school before you got here."

"Well, I didn't," he said, rubbing his eyes, still burning from lack of sleep.

"Do you want to pass this class? Do you actually *want* to make it to senior year?"

"Oh my God. I said I was sorry I'm late. Can we just get on with the lesson?"

"That's my call to make."

"Okay. I guess we won't, then."

"Is that another detention you're asking for?"

Dee threw his head back, frustrated. "*Yes*, Mr. Bernardo. I would *love* another detention. It would be my *honor*." A couple of students snickered at his remark. Vanessa looked down at her desk, wishing she could dematerialize.

"You're not helping yourself out here," the teacher responded, pulling out a slip from his desk and writing on it. "I know you're much better than this. *You* know you are. Please start acting like it."

Dee spent most of the lesson with his head on the desk, somewhere between reality and a dream state. He could see Vanessa from where he sat, and he could tell she was trying to avoid looking at him. Still, when everyone emptied out into the hallway after class, she stayed and waited outside for him.

"Mr. Bernardo giving you another speech in there?" she said when he entered the hallway.

"As per usual. Next Tuesday I have to spend lunch in his office. Exciting times."

"You'll survive." Vanessa shrugged sympathetically.

"I hope so. He also made me sign up for this dumb volunteer

program over the summer. I'd rather blow my brains out than do that, if I'm honest."

"You're so dramatic. It wouldn't be the worst thing in the world."

"Not until the worst thing in the world ceases to exist." Dee smirked, then looked at the ground. "Aren't you gonna be late for second period?"

"Ohh . . . yeah. I wanted to ask if we could talk at lunch? Just for a second." She looked at him, crossing her arms.

Dee stared at her. "Yeah, sure." Kids in the hallway stared at them; this was the one thing he hated about dating Vanessa Bailey. Everyone knew, and everyone cared. Everyone talked. He treated the gossip as static noise, but when it got too loud, all he wanted to do was hide. So when he met her later, they found a discreet place on the school grounds to try and hash things out.

"You good?" Vanessa asked.

"I'm fine. Kinda hungover. It was worse in the morning."

"Yeah, I felt cruddy this morning too." Vanessa looked at the ground. "Sleep deprivation isn't ideal."

"Tell me about it. And hunger. Damn, I could murder a burger at Benno's right now. Think I'm gonna head there soon."

"Can't even wait until you're a senior for an off-campus pass, can you?" She shook her head.

"When have I ever waited for anything?" he responded, grinning. They both looked out into the distance. Then Dee crouched beside the brick wall of the school gymnasium and lit a cigarette—they were still on school grounds and he couldn't afford to get caught. He offered one to her, and she accepted, sitting next to him. He helped her light her cigarette as they leaned back on the wall. They both took long drags.

"I didn't last long, trying to quit," she said.

"Just be like me. Don't quit. Then you won't disappoint yourself when you cave."

"Good one." It seemed like they were trying to avoid the real reason they needed to speak. It was easier pretending small talk was the right way forward. But it wasn't; it never was. A group of girls walked past, ogling the couple like they'd just witnessed something scandalous. Dee wiped rhinestones of sweat off his forehead.

Vanessa sighed, looking at him. "Look, Dee. We need some time apart. For real this time. No more calling me up in the middle of the night. It kind of defeats the purpose of a breakup."

"Okay. Cool."

"I want you to be all right. I want to know you're handling things well. You know, without your . . . with everything at home. I still care about you."

"I don't need you to. I know shit's hard for me right now, but I really don't need your pity."

She frowned. "*Pity*? That's what you think this is? I care about you, and you think it's pity?"

"Whatever it is. Care, pity, worry, I don't know. I don't need it."

"I just want you to be happy! To be at peace. It's just you and Dylan. You have your friends. You'll always have me, as a friend. But right now . . . it's too soon. We need time to move on. But I don't want you to head for a downward spiral."

"Okay."

"Okay? That's it?"

"The fuck do you want me to say?"

"Oh forget it." She stood up and crushed the rest of her cigarette with the sole of her shoe. "Just get back to me when you've gotten your shit together, okay?"

He rose, looking out past the football field. In the distance, he could see someone he recognized—a girl from his math class. The girl briefly looked at them as she strode past, her frizzy blond hair bouncing along with her gait.

"Thanks for the pep talk," he muttered cynically. "I guess I'll see you around, then."

"Bye, Dee," she responded. As she walked away, the cavity in his chest throbbed. He was certain that nothing would ever shrink it. It would grow to immeasurable dimensions, and one day, he'd be swallowed whole.

2

RED & BLUE

South Harlow High was a small school with an alloy of kids from varying socioeconomic backgrounds. Situated west of the well-to-do Smithson suburb, it was initially a private school until locals began lobbying for free access for the neighboring New Eden residents, who had to commute farther for public education. Perfectly situated near desert terrain, national parks, and reservations, Harlow was framed by a highway that connected it to Tucson and Phoenix. It was a municipality that oozed capitalism, consumerism, and ridiculously sky-high property values. But in every pretty city was a low-income community, and New Eden served as that neighborhood. When Mayor Robert Bailey campaigned to lift the tuition for anyone living within a three-mile radius of the school, he was praised by the town for successfully implementing the local access scheme, and became revered and respected overnight. Harlow loved him and everything he stood for, and his children looked up to him. His eldest son, his youngest daughter, and his middle daughter, Vanessa.

She was the most popular girl at South Harlow, famous for throwing unforgettable parties at her Smithson mansion, or flying her friends out for vacations at her summer home in Los Angeles. Her status around school made her the talk of the town at all times, and when the news hit that she and Dee Warrington were officially over, a magnifying glass was put over the pair as the rumors swirled.

Naya Stephens was no stranger to the gossip, and when she observed the pair talking to each other behind the gymnasium after weeks of giving each other the cold shoulder, she couldn't help but speculate as to what it could mean. Were they trying to revive things? Maybe air out their grievances? Either way, her curiosity was fleeting, because there was always a couple in junior year embroiled in relationship drama, and the school would rotate between them like they were weekly episodes of a TV show. As she walked across the school's campus to the library steps for lunch, Naya sighed, feeling sleepy from the heat, praying that the Girls were situated somewhere in the shade. To her relief, they were—she spotted them huddled inside the perimeters of the building's shadow as they talked and ate. She approached them, swinging her hot-pink Fjällräven Kånken backpack from her shoulder and pulling out a sandwich. Just as she sat down, Amber Harper looked out into the distance, shielding her eyes from the sun. "Ugh. Brother incoming," she said, rolling her eyes. Her coiled brown hair was up in a loose ponytail, and the baby hairs along her nape were damp with sweat.

"Yay!" Tori Richards beamed, standing up as Tyler approached. "Hey, boo!" She was still wearing her indoor volleyball uniform, a luminescent red against her deep-brown skin. On a cooler day, she'd probably be reprimanded for walking on school grounds with that much leg on display, but on this one, most students had opted for minimal clothing. Boys were walking around with their shirts hanging from their pant waists. And if the teachers punished every girl they saw wearing Daisy Dukes, there'd be a whole army of detention attendees.

"What it do, ladies?" Tyler greeted the Girls. Tori embraced him while Amber grimaced behind them, melodramatically miming putting two of her fingers down her throat. Jasmine Collins and Evie Anderson giggled, and Naya looked on as she ate her lunch.

"I'm fine now that you're here," Tori crooned, kissing him before unlatching herself and sitting back down on the steps.

"You know, I'm all for the abolishment of capital punishment, but I'll make an exception for PDAs. It's so fucking gross," Amber said.

"Jealousy is a disease, little sis. You'll find yourself a boo one day. Don't sweat it," Tyler responded.

Amber frowned. "The day I call anyone 'boo' is the day I lose my dignity. And for the last time, being born three minutes after you does *not* make me your 'little sis.' Get a grip."

"I'm just kidding. Has anyone seen Dee?" Tyler asked, spinning his cap around his index finger.

Amber rose to grab it from him, fanning herself with it. "We're surprised he isn't with you right now," she said.

"He ain't responding to my texts or calls. I don't even know if he's here today." He scratched the back of his head.

"He's none of our business, Ty. He's not gonna be here. Not without you, anyway. Can't you spend one lunch break without him?"

"I think I saw him on the way here." Naya spoke, and everyone turned toward her. "He was talking to that girl. Vanessa Bailey."

"Oh, word? This ain't good news." Tyler shook his head.

"There's a reason he's not answering your texts," Tori said, sighing. "He's up to no good. It's wild that he even has the gall to go back to his ex." Considering Dee and Tyler were best friends, Naya found it interesting to see how much Tyler's sister's friends would lay into him. Then again, the Girls weren't exempt from the hearsay; they fed into it just as much as everyone else.

"It looked like they were arguing," Naya said. "I don't know. I wasn't watching them superhard or anything. But they didn't look happy."

"What could they possibly have to argue about?" Tori rolled her eyes. "Talk about beating a dead horse."

"Cut him some slack, y'all," Tyler responded. "He's going through it. I wouldn't exactly say this has been a great year on record for him. If he's still hung up over her, it's whatever. He'll move on eventually."

"Why don't you set him up with one of us?" Jasmine piped up. "Maybe we could do a cute double dating thing. You and Tori, Dee and, ideally, me. Actually, I don't know if I could handle the inevitable heartbreak—Karina Fitzgerald probably wouldn't be the only girl he'd hook up with behind my back." She leaned back on the steps, elbows propped behind her. Her black box braids flowed past her shoulders, accessorized with silver beads. She studied her nude acrylic nails, recently shaved down after a caution from her chemistry teacher that their previous length violated health and safety rules.

"Yikes." Amber shook her head. "I'd also rather that didn't happen. It's bad enough having my brother steal my best friend from me. I don't need another one of his goons all up in my friendship group."

"Wait . . . my memory's failing me." Tyler wrinkled his forehead in feigned rumination. "Was it you or me that broke sibling code first?"

Evie, Jasmine, and Tori laughed as Amber frowned. "It was *one* time, and I'm not in love with any of your clown friends. I learned my lesson," she said.

"*I* haven't yet." Jasmine smirked. "Levi and Dee . . . they could both get it. Tyler, do you know if Dee has a type? Is it just white girls, or is he down to broaden his horizons a little?"

"I ain't answering none of that." Tyler glanced away. "Anyway, I'm heading back to the Guys. Thanks for nothing. Oh, wait— thanks, Naya. Looks like the new girl is the only helpful one here." He smiled before turning and walking away.

"Tell Levi I said hello!" Jasmine yelled once he was a few feet away.

Evie laughed, repeatedly flapping her tank top to cool herself down. "Jesus. It's so hot today. Shit's fucking up my edges." She patted her head, attempting to stop her curls from breaking through her hair gel.

"It's a hundred and twelve degrees. I feel like I'm evaporating," Jasmine mumbled. Though the incessant glare of the sun was a given in their town, the heat waves never ceased to take everyone by surprise. An hour earlier, someone in Amber's gym class had fainted on the football field, prompting the principal to send out a PSA on staying hydrated throughout the day.

"Tell me about it," Naya replied. "I put on so much sunscreen today but I'm probably still going to look like a lobster in a few hours." She looked down at her sandals and shifted her foot slightly, noticing the deviation in hue where her skin was exposed.

"That's crazy. You're braver than our troops for moving to Arizona with skin that pale." Evie laughed. "I used to think that I didn't need sunscreen when I was a kid. I thought it was, like, physically impossible to get a sunburn. Granted, I haven't had a sunburn yet, but I'm not tryna age like leather. You got any of that good stuff on you right now?"

"Haha. Texas was the same, so I'm pretty used to it," Naya said. "And yeah, *everyone* should wear sunscreen. Anybody can get skin cancer, after all. I left the good stuff in my locker, though— sorry. I can give you some after lunch if you want."

"That'd be great, thanks. Speaking of hot—let's go back to Dee. Jasmine kind of has a point." Evie grinned.

"Please love yourselves, girls. He's a hot mess," Amber said.

"Exactly. *Hot*. And just because you and Ash didn't work out doesn't mean all of your brother's friends are out of bounds." Jasmine's remark was met with a sardonic sneer from Amber. "Hey, Naya. What do you think of him? Are we wrong here?"

"I don't really know. I've never even talked to him before," Naya responded.

"Damn, you've been here for eight weeks and you haven't formed an opinion. I love that, but I'm not talking about his behavior—that's . . . up for debate. I just mean his *looks*."

"I don't know." Naya shrugged. "He looks kind of intimidating." In class, Naya would witness his nonchalance, riveted by it. When he was once called out for his failure to hand in an assignment, he'd retrieved the untouched papers from his bag and started filling them out, right there and then, without saying a word.

Everyone burst into fits of laughter and the teacher was losing his mind, but Dee didn't flinch, even when threatened with suspension. It was absorbing, trying to figure out what was going on inside his head.

"Right. He's hot in a you-wouldn't-want-to-admit-it kind of way. And hell, if the hottest girl at school found him attractive once, so can I," Jasmine said.

"All right, cut it out. No more talk about Tyler's friends. Is anyone going to Erin Giardino's party tonight?" Tori cut in.

"I am," Amber said.

"I didn't get an invite," Evie said in a huff.

"You don't need an invite. There's not going to be a security guard at the door," Amber replied.

"I wouldn't put it past anyone who lives in Smithson. But whatever, I guess I'll crash it. Naya, you coming?" Evie turned to her.

"You can count me out. Pigs will literally fly before my parents let me go to a party."

"Girl, how many parents actually *let* their kids go to parties? Just go."

"It's not worth the hassle," Naya said.

"I don't get it." Amber narrowed her eyes. "Your parents are superstrict, superreligious, but you're *openly* bi? And they know?"

"It's complicated. Cliché, I know, but it is."

"How are you going to spend this whole summer if you can't branch out a little?" Jasmine asked.

"It's cool. I signed up for the school's volunteer program to get me out of the house." Naya shrugged.

"Cleaning up someone's barf in Silver Rock Plaza for free is not quite what I meant by branching out."

"Well, there is that famous saying—it's not about the barf cleaning, it's about the friends you make along the way." Naya smirked. Though she was semi-joking, Naya genuinely hoped the program would be worthwhile. She had already started looking at potential colleges to attend, and she knew that her résumé had to be more than perfect. Putting herself up for an extracurricular activity when she didn't have a worthwhile sport or hobby to carry her into a scholarship was just the long game, a part of her desire to break free from small-town life. She had considered spending all of her pocket money on a top-grade sewing machine so she could teach herself to make new clothes over the summer, but the thought of spending her days indoors and by herself as the sun blazed was less than inviting. And considering she knew her parents like the back of her hand, she didn't have the energy to try and circumvent their overbearing dominion over her social life. So cleaning barf in Silver Rock Plaza might just be the compromise she would make.

"Wholesome," Jasmine said with a laugh. "I'm actually working on a zine this summer, if any of y'all wanna contribute. My uncle's got a cool photography studio downtown, so if y'all are free, we can set something up. I'm still tryna figure out what to call it—the zine, I mean. I'll get there eventually. If you want a break from barf, you're free to join." She smiled, looking at Naya.

"Thanks. I'll consider it."

The Girls broke into a new conversation, giving Naya the chance to recede. She thought about Jasmine's question about the evasive and misguided skate fanatic with a penchant for classroom dramatics and no patience for authority figures. He was not much for smiling, but when he did, the expression turned him soft, wiped away his ever-furrowed brows, and painted his face with a certain femininity to match his long, dark hair. But somehow he still gave nothing away, and there was only so much judgment she could place on someone who she had never uttered a word to.

◊

"What happened at lunch, man?" Tyler asked Dee as they walked in the direction of their neighborhood after school. Although they usually walked with their group of friends, Dee'd been held back by a teacher for a few minutes after class for another stern talking-to. So the rest of the Guys had got a head start while Tyler idly waited around for him.

"I was speaking to Ness."

"So I heard."

"How did you even find out? Shit spreads so fast here, man."

"One of Amber and Tori's friends told me. Naya."

"Naya?"

"You know her, man. The new chick? Blond afro, kooky out-fits? But anyway, you gotta fill me in. What were you and Vanessa talking about?"

Dee bit the inside of his cheek. "I fucked up last night."

"You called her, didn't you?" Tyler shook his head.

"I did more than call her. I invited her over. Sort of. Well, any-way, she came. It didn't end well."

"This is worse than I thought. She's got you cuffed. You're the next light-switch couple."

"The next what?"

"On and off, like a light switch."

"No, it's not like that."

"Then what's it like? No feelings? No strings?"

"It's dead, man. We spoke about it at lunch. She basically dumped me for a second time."

"I know it must suck. Exes are exes for a reason, my guy. It's just like a fuck-ton of baggage. Kinda like an airport with a carousel full of unclaimed suitcases. And it keeps going around and around, never ending. Damn, that was mad deep. I think I should become a poet." Dee almost smiled. "But seriously, this isn't a good situation. I will say it took a lot of willpower for Tori to get over her ex before she got serious with me. It's like a supernatural force, right? It's like you're possessed."

"Something like that. Fuck knows what it is."

"Time is the best healer, my friend. How's home? Is Dylan still partying all the time?"

"Pretty much. I barely ever see him around. He's clearly the legal guardian of the year."

"Damn. He's got big shoes to fill, though."

"I mean . . . he got me out of that suspension, in his defense."

Tyler laughed. "That was hilarious. He didn't give Principal Smith *any* mercy. I think the whole school could hear him yelling."

"'Do you know what my brother's been through? And you're gonna give up on him!?'" Dee laughed, mimicking Dylan's tirade in the office on that day. "It worked, I guess. But it's not gonna work forever. If I get kicked out and have to spend all day at home, I'm gonna lose my mind."

"You know we're always at No Man's. If you're climbing up the walls, just join us. We can go there right now, shoot some hoops. I think Ash and Wallis are there."

"Thanks. I'm supertired, though. I need to catch up on some Z's. If you're still there later, I might join."

"Okay, cool. Let me know. And don't sweat the Vanessa thing. Summer break's around the corner. More functions equal a higher chance of finding someone new."

"Ain't that right. Anyway, I'll see you around." Dee bumped shoulders with his best friend before they diverged paths on their neighborhood's street corner.

◆

Lately, Dee's dreams had been haunting him. The worst ones were the good ones: the ones where his mother was still around, dancing in the kitchen or smudging sage around the house. The place would be full of candles, and she'd be meditating in the living room or singing to herself. He'd dream of the times when they'd drive out to the desert and watch the stars, and she'd speak out to their ancestors or try to predict their future. Those were the dreams that felt real, tangible. He could smell the sage like it was burning under his nose, and he'd wake up still smelling it. He still saw her in his dreams. Sometimes sitting in the back of Dylan's teal-blue pickup truck, smoking or playing guitar. Sometimes with a beer, or dancing with the red-and-blue vista as her backdrop. Sometimes sleeping soundly in a maxi-dress, an aged brown leather jacket with fringed sleeves draped across her back. Always alive.

Dee was awoken from the couch a couple of hours into his nap by the arrival of his brother and a group of his friends. His grogginess was wiped away at the realization that they were all at varied levels of intoxication, Dylan predictably the most drunk of them all. His girlfriend, Mia, seemed to be the only one who could stand up without swaying. She, like Dylan, was decked out in bold neo-traditional tattoos. Her hair was dark and wavy, her eyes a jarring green against her olive skin. Dee was sure he'd heard that she was South American, but he couldn't remember exactly where she was from; he had never bothered asking. Dylan and Mia had spent the last seven years in a light-switch relationship that put whatever Dee and Vanessa had to shame.

"Hey! It's the little broski! Say hi to my brother, Dee," Dylan slurred. The other men and women laughed and waved, greeting him as he stood up to leave the room. "Hey. Where you going? Don't you wanna join us?"

"I'm good, thanks." He walked briskly into the kitchen to grab a glass of orange juice, and he could hear his brother continue to drunkenly yell his name.

"Come on, Dee. Join us! Get your ass over here."

Gritting his teeth, Dee hesitantly walked back into the living room. "What the fuck do you want? It's nearly ten thirty. I'm going to bed."

"Oh come on. We all know you ain't sleeping until four in the morning. Sit your ass down and hang out with us."

Dee looked at the strangers in his house, lounging around all over his mother's possessions like they owned the place. "I said I'm going to fucking bed."

"Dylan, let the kid sleep," Mia snapped. "He was literally passed out on the couch when we got here. Pack it up."

"Don't be a fucking buzzkill. That's my brother—you ain't gotta tell me nothing about him."

"Y'all look nothing alike," one of his friends piped up. "You don't even look like cousins. Y'all blood brothers? He adopted?"

"He's my brother-from-another-mother. His mom was this hippy chick from the rez. Bless her soul."

Dee turned around and walked away, the sounds of their continuing conversation trailing behind him. "Living on that government check, I bet. The Indians have it easy these days," another voice flippantly blurted. Everyone laughed, and Dee could feel his blood boiling. He found that comment nowhere near funny, because it was nowhere near the truth. "Shit for brains," he muttered to himself on his way to the kitchen.

Ever since his brother had moved down to Harlow to take care of him, his house barely felt like his own anymore. Every other evening there'd be the odd stranger in his living room or kitchen, doing rails off the table or making rude, drunken remarks that Dylan always seemed to just egg on. Dee would spend his time hiding out in his room until the house was empty again, making sure to avoid the disorderly guests until their departure. Most of them worked with Dylan at the garage in town, where he'd got a job as a local mechanic for a generous wage. Dee's car—the same one he'd spent months saving up for, and the same one his mother had contributed a month of her shop's profits toward— was damaged by Dylan in a minor crash a week after her funeral. It was taken to the garage, where he promised to fix it, but when he started carpooling with coworkers and hijacking the rusty pickup he lent Dee to use as a temporary mode of transport whenever he felt like it, Dee knew it would be a while before he got his car back. Even though Dylan was entrusted with the responsibility of looking after him, it seemed like it was the least of his concerns.

Leaning over the kitchen counter, Dee checked his phone, finding a couple of missed calls from his friend Ash and a message from Tyler. He also saw a text from an unknown number, which he was too curious not to read.

Thank you for showing an interest in our Summer Volunteer Program at South Harlow High! We will be in touch soon.

—The Extracurricular Leadership Faculty

This is an automated text. Please do not reply.

He sighed, remembering the deal he'd shortsightedly agreed to in order to dash from Mr. Bernardo's classroom. They had his contact details. It didn't matter—he wasn't going to participate. Picking up trash from the streets of Harlow or feeding homeless people hot soup for three months was not for him. Of course, he had better things to do—like partying, doing drugs, finding rebounds, and hanging with his friends at No Man's Land, the abandoned community pool turned skate park that served as the border splitting the New Eden and Smithson neighborhoods. From there, Dee could see the towering mansions that loomed on the other side of the wired fence, and he thought back to how he'd once caught a glimpse into the pretty part of Harlow—the part he'd never quite related to—when he was still dating Vanessa. But now, he was planning on spending his time attempting switch heelflips, smoking with his friends on the benches, and hanging around in the confines of his world. Of course he wasn't going to volunteer, and lose his summer to philanthropy and altruism. He deleted the text and threw some leftover pizza into the microwave.

3

SALVATION

Naya arrived home in the afternoon to find her mother watering flowers on the front lawn. She looked up from the bed of fuchsias and shielded her eyes from the unrelenting sun before turning off the hose. "Hey, Yaya. How was school?"

"It was fine. I had a biology final today. I think I did well."

"That's what I love to hear. Honey, you're a little pink. Did you check the forecast before you left the house? The sun's quite intense today. You could've done with one of your UV shirts."

"I'm not going to turn into a pile of dust in the sun, Mom."

"Okay, okay. I'm just looking out for you."

"I know, I know."

She went inside to the kitchen where she stood for a moment, taking in the coolness of the air conditioning. Then she took out a bag of chips from the pantry and sat on a stool, eating them slowly. She put her earbuds in and played her favorite song that week, "C U Girl" by Steve Lacy, and thought about the party that her friends were attending that evening. The bud of resentment in the pit of her stomach began to sprout; in her sixteen years of life, she had never been given the go-ahead to socialize at events that weren't church-related, and she knew that things weren't going to be any different in a new town. Still, she decided that she might as well test the waters; being told no would be the worst-case scenario, which was already the default. After hesitating, she yanked her earbuds out and left her phone on the kitchen counter before walking back outside.

"Hey, Mom. Do you need any help with the flowers?"

"I'm fine, darling. I'm almost finished, actually."

"I can help. It'll be done quicker."

"Are you sure? It's hot out here."

"I said I'm fine. It'll only take five minutes."

Her mother paused before nodding. "Okay. If you insist. Could you grab the watering can over there? Just keep the hydrangeas and the ice plants wet for a couple minutes." She turned and stooped down, patting the moist soil beneath some newly planted flowers.

"Okay. Uh . . . by the way, I was invited to a birthday gathering this evening. I was wondering if it's cool for me to go?"

Her mother stared at her. "Who invited you?"

"My new friends. Tori, Amber, Jasmine, and Evie."

"Is it any of their birthdays, or someone else's?"

"It's a classmate's." Naya frowned, already knowing where her mother was going with her line of questioning. "Why does it matter whose birthday it is? That's not the point. Can I go?"

"You say 'gathering.' That's code for party, correct? Because if that's the case, no. You have a curfew for a reason."

"I can come back before curfew ends. Just a couple of hours, Mom. Come on."

"That's how it always starts," her mother said, shaking her head. She turned the hose off and stood with her hands on her hips. "It's just one party for just a couple of hours, and before you know it, you're intoxicated, knocking on the door at three in the morning. Forget it, Naya. You'll have your chance for parties. Right now, you've just got to focus on excelling at school. You have finals."

"I can manage my work. I don't need to be babied. I can work hard and I can also have fun."

"There are plenty of other ways you can have fun, baby. I've invited you so many times to the youth choir here and you always turn it down. The kids there are lovely. You'd expand your social circle if you gave it a try."

"Mom. Stop acting like that's going to make a difference to anything. We up and leave from one judgmental community to another and you think the problem's solved."

"This new church is nothing like Ampleforth. They're much more accepting."

"If God really cared, he'd make sure all churches were." The moment Naya blurted out those words, her heart stopped. Letting her mom know she doubted her all-knowing, all-seeing, all-loving deity was not going to help her cause. "I'm sorry. I didn't mean to say that."

"Naya Grace. We are not in Ampleforth anymore. We're here. We're still children of God. If you want to come to church, you're welcome to. Nobody is going to turn you away. You have to stop holding grudges."

"I don't know, Mom. It's kind of hard to not hold a semblance of a grudge when I don't know if I'll ever get to see Haley again."

"Please . . . Naya. This has nothing to do with Haley. We don't need to go there right now."

"It has *everything* to do with her." She put down the watering can and walked toward the house, blood boiling. "By the way, I signed up for volunteering. I hope that's good enough for you."

In the months since moving to Harlow, Naya had been desperate to turn over a new leaf, to try to forget about the small Christian community she was raised in. She tried to forget about her scrutinizing extended family and all the church members who'd turned their backs on her and her parents when she came out to them. She tried to forget and move on, to find a new place in the world for herself. The shame she once felt might have dissipated, but the discontentment stuck with her, filling up her home like a mist. She tried to forget a lot of things, but she would never forget Haley Fawcett, the girl who changed everything.

An hour later, her father returned from work; her mother was making dinner downstairs. The last thing she felt like doing was interacting with her parents, knowing that her friends were all getting ready for a fun night out and she wasn't. Before she could stalk their Snapchat stories and wade into a pool of self-pity, she received a text notification from her school about the Summer Volunteer Program, and she sighed. She was not anticipating a lively summer, but to her, anything was better than the alternative—being locked within the prison walls she called home, or being constantly reminded of a God whose presence she had never felt.

◆

Dee was called out of math class the following Monday morning and sent to the Extracurricular Leadership Faculty office, along with the new girl. The second he'd heard his name called and found that he wasn't in trouble, he knew what it was, and he wasn't happy about it. By the looks of it, she wasn't so happy either.

"My name is Naya. Not Neya, or Nadia, or whatever else you want to confuse it with. It's Nah-yah." She sat up straight, staring the head of the Extracurricular Leadership Faculty in the face with a deadpan expression of impatience.

"I'm sorry about the misunderstanding. Your last name is still pronounced Stephens, right?" The man chuckled awkwardly. Dee eyed both him and the girl, arms crossed and leaning back as far as he could in his chair.

"And Dee Warrington. Welcome, both of you. How are things going?" the man asked, trailed by a cringeworthy silence. The name tag on his desk read MR. WALTERS. Dee thought to himself that he looked like a Walters, with a first name like Bartholomew, or Edgar, something like that. It was the mustache that had planted the assumption. "All right, I'll just cut to the chase." He gathered a few papers in front of him, straightening them out in his hands. "Your names are on the Summer Volunteer Program list. It appears you expressed an interest."

"Bullshit."

"Language."

"I just let my English teacher put my name down so I could get out of detention," Dee said.

"Is that so? Hmm. What about you, Naya?"

She shrugged. "I just want to do it. That's all."

"Well, this program is usually for struggling students, or those who need to improve their educational credentials before college. You've had straight As since seventh grade, according to your previous school's transcript; your track record is impeccable. Are you just a naturally studious and proactive kid, then?" He smiled.

"Sure." She felt the boy next to her perk up when he heard this information. He was staring at her. But this wasn't new; he always did. As did most people, especially because she was the new kid. Also because she wore things like mustard-yellow corduroy flared pants and flower-embroidered denim blouses; oversized sweaters with block colors and metallic silver Birkenstocks; lime-green marble hoop earrings that looked handmade; gold-rimmed spectacles that seemed like they should have been paired with a zigzag on her forehead, Harry Potter–style; and bright-red lipstick and indigo eyeshadow, a contrast against her pale skin and blue eyes. Tori and the girls who had recruited her as a newfound member of their group were all African American, with varying hues of skin tone, and different curl patterns and hair colors. Naya was Black, yes, but with her albinism, she often perceived that others saw her as the subject of some experiment, a test-tube baby created by Nordic scientists with the Aryan gaze in mind.

Mr. Walters turned to Dee. "I know you're not going to be keen on this, but you shouldn't knock it just yet. There is so much you could do for this community. Even if just for a few weeks."

"Ten weeks isn't a few weeks."

"Even if just for a couple of months."

"Almost three."

Mr. Walters pursed his lips, clutching tightly to his patience. "Here's the thing. I called you both here at the same time for a reason. The SVP is only running with pairs or groups this year. Last year was our first ever, and we logged the results. It showed that those entering into the program solo were *five times* more likely to drop out, or not even make it past this meeting." He held up a hand with his five fingers splayed for emphasis. "But those who were in groups of two or more had a much higher chance of seeing the whole thing through to the end. And they had more fun too. So the idea is that everyone is given a partner or a group to carry out their weekly volunteering activities with. Now, you were two of the last few people to sign up. Naya, because you're new, and Dee, because it was done apparently . . . against your will. Everyone has been grouped and assigned their tasks, barring the pair of you. Meaning that if one of you drops out or refuses now, you'll leave the other one on their own."

Dee scoffed. "Why can't the other one just join another group?" He didn't want to say her name, and he was already starting to feel guilty about his suggestion.

"Does this look like a mix-and-match to you?" Mr. Walters chortled. "Your late registration meant you missed out on the switch-up period, which ended last week. You unfortunately don't have much choice. You either stay or you leave this poor girl to do all the volunteering by herself." He frowned awkwardly at Naya.

Dee was cornered. For a moment, he resented her and her weird yellow pants, her gold-rimmed glasses, and her frizzy red-blond hair. *Stop making me do good things just because you're a good person. I didn't ask for this. I'm a shitty guy; just let me be shitty.*

"I'd like to know now, before I continue, if you want to stay and proceed with the program, Dee. I don't want to keep you any longer. So are you up for it?" Mr. Walters asked. Dee winced, trying harder and harder not to answer the question. He stayed quiet, hoping that would do the trick. "Okay, let's try something else.

If you don't get up and leave within the next ten seconds, I'll take that as your full consent to participate."

He was frozen from then on. All he had to do was glance over at Naya, who sat staring at the floor, twiddling her thumbs and wagging her feet either in impatience or apprehension. His chest tightened, and he realized something. He was compelled by the sudden overwhelming feeling that he couldn't just abandon her. He had no clue whether she truly cared, and he knew she'd go on with the program anyway, but he'd feel like a jerk for leaving the room. He sighed, sitting forward, dropping his head toward the ground, resting his elbows on his knees as his hair tumbled out in front of him. He didn't leave the room.

"Your ten seconds are up. I'll take that as a yes!"

Naya felt like she'd coerced the boy into joining her, and that wasn't a nice feeling. She also didn't want to spend time hanging out with someone who clearly didn't want to hang out with her. But she also knew that there was something else about the boy that wasn't revealing itself. There must have been a reason he didn't refuse in the same way he ardently protested when the teacher requested action in class on a regular basis. That behavior came naturally to him, avoiding things he didn't like; she had noticed over the past few weeks how good he was at that. He could have easily left the room, but he didn't. And she wasn't sure whether to be grateful or pissed off at that fact, because maybe his tendency to reject orders was also the same reason he hadn't budged.

Naya and Dee swapped looks. She was intrigued by his dark and restless aura—he gave off an intense violet purple. That's how she felt around him. Ten weeks partnered up with him could either be a nightmare or a daydream. Or both.

Mr. Walters commenced typing something into his computer and stared at the screen for a few seconds. "Everyone has already been allocated their activity and locations in different places around Harlow, and there is one location left. You two will be working at the Salvation Hill Nursing Facilities."

"Where's that?" Naya asked.

"It's a nursing home, ten minutes south of Smithson. It's the farthest location we have—a twenty-minute drive from here, a little out in the desert. Probably an hour's walk. Watch out for rattlesnakes!"

"I don't have a car. I can't drive," Naya responded. "Is there any other way I can get there? Public transport?"

"I drive," Dee said, quickly and quietly. She turned to him. "If you live close enough . . . I guess I can drive us both there . . . or whatever." He couldn't believe he was saying this, though he had not explicitly refused to partake in the program. He didn't ask for any of it, but it was happening.

"Problem solved!" Walters chirped. "This is our only meeting. The next step is a training day with the staff at the nursing home in a couple of weeks, once junior year is over. As far as I know, you'll be assigned to look after certain residents for a few hours, twice a week. Most likely through activities like reading them books and playing board games, doing errands like getting them food from the café, things like that." Dee's chest sunk at the last part of the sentence. Twice a week. Two times. That meant ten weeks and twenty visits. It felt like a prison sentence. "I don't want to keep you guys any longer, so I'll just give you these leaflets that have a bit more information about Salvation Hill. Give them a good read. Visit their website, drive down there to gauge the place before your first visit. Good luck!"

◆

After their math class, Dee attempted to rush to lunch. Naya stopped him.

"Are you sure you want to do the program?"

"Yeah, whatever. Just reading books to old people. I can do that."

"I just want to make sure you won't drop out."

"So what if I do?"

"Look. Are you doing it or not? Because you already said you would."

Dee paused. "I will."

"I don't believe you."

"You don't know me. I'm not a liar."

"Breaking a promise isn't *exactly* lying."

"When did I promise anything?"

Naya held out her pinky finger. He just stared at it, dumbfounded by her speedy yet nonchalant reaction. She looked around the hallway, whistling as she waited for him to link up his finger with hers. "You're not serious." He frowned.

"I don't joke about pinky promises."

He had the urge to burst out laughing, because he realized that she was funny. Odd, but funny. He shook his head, linking pinkies with her. "I don't break promises."

"Great." She beamed. "I know it's still a while away, but I need to know that I can trust you with help whenever I need it. You know, so I can ask you stuff about the program. We could DM on Instagram?"

"I barely use it." Naya already knew this, after spending her first few weeks searching any new names being bounced around her at school. She'd looked up her new friends, as well as her friends' friends, and her friends' boyfriends' friends. It didn't take her long to realize Dee wasn't active on social media. But she went along with the notion that she had no idea, so she didn't seem like a stalker.

"Hmm, okay. Snapchat?"

"Nope."

"Geez. Well, this is weird. I don't know, then." She shrugged.

"I have . . . a phone. I have a phone number. You can have that, you know."

She raised her eyebrow and shrugged her shoulders. "Well, if you *insist*. Flirt." Shaking her head, she whipped out her smartphone and planted it in his hand, letting him fill in his contact details. "Okay. I'm going to text you now so that you can save my deets. Wait." She did. His phone buzzed, and he saw the notification pop up on his screen.

Wassup, punk?

He smiled, looking at her. He answered her text.

Who you callin a punk? Punk.

She laughed. "Geez, stop with the flirting. Save my number. I'll see you around." She skip-walked in the direction of the library.

He didn't know what he had signed himself up for, but it certainly wasn't to spend his summer with a girl he barely knew. Though he didn't have anything to lose—no more than he already had. Setting off to meet his friends at lunch, he decided to keep quiet about the volunteer program. He always hid the worst secrets in his brain, away from everyone else. But he cherished the days when he'd had benign secrets to conceal, just little beans of harmless gossip. Like this one. He wouldn't even reveal anything to Tyler until after the first day of the program, he decided.

Salvation Hill would be his secret, and so would Naya Stephens.

4

YISKA

Whenever Dee had trouble sleeping as a kid, his mother would always run him a hot bath and make him something warm to drink before bed. She was like a magician or a good witch—one with an array of herbal remedies and soaps—and the house would be saturated with sleepy smells and sounds that could knock someone out for a millennium. When she was discharged from the hospital eight years ago, she was adamant about starting her life over in the best way. She quit her day job and began selling homemade soaps and dermatological treatments that were well received in the South Harlow communities. Dee had clear memories of walking door-to-door through the pretty suburbs with his mother, promoting her products on hot weekend afternoons, interacting with the flashy residents and their pampered dogs on their marble patios. Eventually, she did well enough to be able to set up a small shop downtown, which she decided to name Yiska.

That was what she'd first called Dee as an infant, as he had always been restless. Back in those days, when she was still studying for her high school diploma from home, she would be up all night with him wailing in his makeshift crib, inches away from pulling her hair out. She called him Yiska because he was like a nocturnal creature, spending the light of day in a deep slumber and fully animated at night. Only every so often would his circadian rhythm align with the earth's rotation—this was rare until he got a bit older. Through the years, whenever he would fall into a diurnal pattern of rest and emerge sleepy eyed from his room at three in the afternoon on a Saturday, she'd roll her eyes and tut and tell him, "You need to sleep along with the rest of us—not when the night has passed. Yiska, you're missing out as life goes on without you. Rest easy, sleep calm, close your eyes when the moon is up. Don't let the night swallow you whole."

His childhood nickname had two meanings: the literal one, and the metaphor. The night was the dark, the place that people didn't want to live in. When it was over, light would shine upon everyone who needed it the most. The pained, the paralyzed, the drained, the worried. *The night has passed, the day is new, we need not worry, we can rejoice without fear.* His mother always reminded him of the silver linings and the lanterns that shimmered along the horizon, right at the opening of the obscure tunnel. When she died, the night seemed like it was here to stay. Dee spent every living moment in it, waiting for the light to come back. The night was here, and it was never to leave, and all Dee could do was traipse mindlessly through it like a transient in an infinite dusk.

Her soap shop was closed down shortly after her death. Dee sometimes stood outside the glass doors, peering in at the blank walls and dreaming of the days when he'd found solace in the little world his mother had made for them. By now, he could walk straight past it without looking, but it always called to him. The rustic-style sign that once hung above the store beckoned to him like his mother used to: *Yiska*. He could act like the shop never existed, but it always reminded him that it did, that *she* did, and the tight, tugging feeling in his chest was never going to subside. He just needed to bide his time and wait patiently for better days to come.

◊

"You doing this Good Samaritan shit on your own?" Dylan asked him a few days after the Extracurricular Leadership Faculty meeting, as they ate Chinese food in the living room. Seeing as he'd saved Dee from getting kicked out of school, Dee thought it was worth showing him that his help had paid off somehow— though it wasn't like it made a difference to his brother whether he participated in acts of goodwill or not.

"The what?"

"The nursing home thing."

"Salvation Hill."

"Same difference. Something biblical."

"No, I have a partner." Dee pretended to watch TV, twirling his chow mein around his fork before taking a bite. "Everyone is assigned a partner or a group."

"Huh."

"Yup."

"Dude or girl?"

"Girl."

"Heck yeah! Maybe she'll blow you in the reading room every now and then, if you're nice." Dylan laughed before dipping a chicken ball into sweet-and-sour sauce and scarfing it down.

"Dude."

"What? How else are you gonna get over Cher Horowitz?" Dylan once told Dee that he thought Vanessa was superhot but also way too into herself, which was partly true and partly false. She liked to keep up appearances, but she wasn't a mean girl, nor was she completely conceited. Dylan never called her by her real name, always something alluding to what he saw as her vanity.

"Jesus. That's not what all girls are for."

Dylan shrugged. "It was a joke."

"You must have been the one who put Dave Chappelle out of business."

Dylan laughed. "Funny."

Dee didn't know what to make of his brother sometimes. He never seemed to react appropriately to things. The only time he had seen him display poignant emotion in recent years was at Dee's mother's funeral, where his face was hard as stone and his eyes glinted with moisture. He'd got blackout drunk that evening and spent most of the night crying, but once the day was new, he went back to acting like everything was hunky-dory. He'd barely consoled Dee after his loss, just treated him like a college roommate that he didn't know on a personal level. Sometimes he'd bring out a benevolent side, making Dee a nice breakfast or giving him cash so he could go out and do whatever he wanted with it. But the fact of the matter was he didn't know how to look after his kid brother. It was a duty bestowed upon him by his trusting stepmother, and it was a promise he knew he had to keep.

All the previous years, Dee had been the one leaving the house and going to wild parties and gatherings, but he'd always come home to a place of solace and tranquility. Now the walls were caging high tension, deafening music, and drug-fueled chaos, and he had to accept that this was going to be what life was like, at least for a while. Spending a few hours reading books to old people became more enticing as he toyed around with the idea; he could bask in a certain quietness and solace that his friends or his brother couldn't feed, and that his heart needed.

◊

Later that afternoon, Dee decided to join his friends at No Man's Land and was surprised to see that he wasn't the last one to arrive for once.

"Where's Tyler?" Ash O'Brien asked as Dee sat beside him, dangling his legs off the edge of the skating pool.

Jamal Wallis's speaker was perched a few feet away, blaring songs from the Guys' collaborative Spotify playlist as he attempted a frontside 180 inside the pool. "Probably with Tori," he responded.

"Fuck Tori, man. He was supposed to get here a half hour ago." Ash frowned, running a hand through his straw-blond hair.

"He's obsessed with her," Dee said. "I wonder what *that* feels like."

"Don't sweat it, man. Heartbreak isn't unique. We're all gonna go through it one day." Ash nudged him.

"Heartbreak? Give it a rest."

"Just saying." Ash shrugged. "Gotta go through the motions."

"Is that what you told Amber last summer?" Dee smirked.

"It was never that deep," Ash said defensively.

"It was deep enough for Amber to break the sibling code," Dee said, referring to the twins' pact to never get with each other's friends. Once Ash and Amber had crossed the line between the Guys and the Girls, Tyler took it as the green light for him to get to know her best friend, Tori, the Queen Bee of the Girls, the pretty ringleader, the volleyball ace—the girl he'd always secretly liked. At the start of junior year, he'd decided to shoot his shot, detouring to the Girls' hangout spot by the library steps to converse with his sister's friends, and the rest was history. Though Amber and Ash had never made it past a one-night stand, it was still a topic of conversation nearly nine months later.

"That shit wasn't a big deal," Ash said with a chortle. "And I was fucked up at that party, man. Amber was too." He shrugged. "Wasn't like we were thinking straight."

"Yeah, that's why you didn't go for round two." Wallis laughed. "Hooking up with your homie's sister is never a good idea."

"Dude, she was all over me. I was just being generous."

"Like charity work, huh?"

"Your words, not mine." Ash held his hands up. "Besides, I was still fucking with Selina back then. I didn't want things to get messy."

"That was a busy-ass summer for you, huh?" Wallis laughed again. "Meanwhile, all I got was some weak top from Meg Yates. It's hard out here in these streets." He shook his head.

"Girls can smell desperation a mile away, Wallis. At least cover that shit up with some decent cologne," Ash said, bringing out a chuckle from Dee. Ash turned to him. "I'm right, aren't I?"

"I'm not saying nothing. I'm not a pickup artist," Dee responded, amused.

"It's still a mystery to me how you ended up with a dime piece for a whole damn *year*, if I'm honest. No offense."

"None taken," Dee said, lighting a cigarette. "It's a mystery to me too."

"I still remember when you told us you made out with her at Jamie Zhang's party. Nobody believed it. Shit was stranger than fiction."

"Makes sense to me," Wallis interjected. "She was probably getting tired of being hit and quit by the senior football team. She wanted to try something different."

"Look, I know we're not together anymore, but cut that shit out," Dee said. "That was just a rumor, I told you that."

"You mean like how Karina was just a rumor, too, right?" Ash laughed.

Dee clenched his jaw. "Don't bring her up, Ash. I'm not in the mood." Before the breakup, Karina had sent Vanessa a DM on Instagram saying it was her duty to let her know what had happened between her and Dee, that she couldn't just stay quiet about it. Vanessa had sent Dee a screenshot of the message, and from that moment on, he knew he was royally screwed. Once the Guys had caught wind of the drama, any conversation about Dee and Vanessa always diverged into locker-room talk about Karina, and Dee was sick of it.

"Okay, okay. Touchy subject, my bad." Ash reeled back, surrendering his sly digs.

"Yo. Why don't you try your luck with the Girls now that you're single?" Wallis chimed in.

"I'm good," Dee said, flicking away his cigarette butt. "I don't need to follow in Ash's footsteps."

"I mean . . . Amber wasn't a bad lay." Ash shrugged. "Maybe Jasmine or Evie ain't either."

"Once again—I'm good."

"What about the new girl? Naya Stephens?" Wallis asked, fiddling with the wheels of his skateboard as he looked up at them.

"I haven't thought about it." Dee shrugged. "I don't think that's where my mind is right now."

"Cool, but what do you think of her? Would you smash?"

"I don't see it." Ash shook his head. "She's too weird. She doesn't wanna be normal. I feel like the Girls don't get her. I know *I* don't."

"New kids always have something to prove. They always wanna stand out," Wallis said.

"Maybe that's just how she is. Not everyone's gonna live up to the Harlow girl ideal," Dee responded.

"She doesn't have to go around looking like she shops at the rainbow aisle at Goodwill. Yeah, the girls here may be plastic and pink, wearing labels and shit, but . . . there's got to be a middle ground," Ash said.

"We're all going to die one day. I don't give a fuck what people wear," Dee said.

His friends seemed sobered by his remark. "It's cool, bro. We're just teasing." Ash nudged his shoulder softly. They understood that with Dee, everything boiled down to sorrow—every rogue word or action. Things had to be judged on that basis. So "It's cool, bro," really meant *We get it. We're here for you.*

"What are people's plans for the summer? It's, like, two and a half weeks away. We need to find out where the house parties are at." Ash changed the subject.

"More like *Where's all the pussy at?* That's the real question.

My thirst levels are astronomical!" Wallis's exclamation was followed by Dee's and Ash's laughter. "I'm serious. I'll take what I can get at this point."

"Levi knows some superhot chick in Nevada he can set you up with. She's staying northwest, at her aunt's summer house," Ash said.

"Has he hooked up with her, though?"

"If he knows her, probably."

"Nice. Do I *look* like dessert?"

"Nah. You're too salty. You're a side dish. Garlic bread ass."

Dee loved zoning out around his friends, with their repartee in the periphery of his focus. They always reminded him that he was never truly alone, even if he felt it. But when he found that he was hardly throwing in his two cents or contributing anything significant to the banter, he felt that glimmer of isolation that every so often caught up with him and loomed over his head. It was a strange limbo—to feel warm around the company of people he'd been close with for as long as he could remember just as he felt the biting cold breeze hanging outside of whatever it was he was missing out on.

"Yo, Dee. Plans for summer?" Wallis addressed him, snapping him back to the now.

"Damn. I don't know. Steal my brother's drugs, host a couple of parties 'cause I'm an orphan now and I don't have a curfew, try and get over Vanessa, steal some more drugs, get over Ness some more, maybe go on a sex spree while I'm at it, more drugs, overdose on pills a week before senior year, and end up six feet under. Sounds like a plan." Ash and Wallis just stopped and stared at him. Today wasn't one of his good days; the cavity inside him was thriving.

He was not in the mood to speak anymore, instead keeping silent for the next few minutes as the conversation continued between Ash and Wallis. When Tyler finally arrived, he felt a tiny bit better, but still terrible. He couldn't shake how awful he was feeling. It was coming from everywhere, coursing through him like a heat wave. He was just a fuckup; it was genetic. With a stupid, naive, unconditionally loving woman as a mother and a violent, deplorable man as a father. He sometimes wished he could leave and go to a place where nobody knew about him. This was a place where rumors weren't spread like a school hallway–borne virus, a place where he didn't get looks for being the moody, acrimonious kid who'd broken the mayor's daughter's heart. It was filled with people who knew nothing about those he had betrayed, those he had failed to save, and those who had changed him for the worse. People like the girl from his math class. Of course, she had heard things by now, but it lightened his mood to know that there was still someone in Harlow who didn't know his deepest, darkest secrets.

5

MARIE

Dee parked his battered pickup outside of Naya's house at one thirty on the training day for the volunteer program. School was over and summer had officially begun, and this was where Dee found himself on a blazing hot Arizona afternoon. He sat and waited, checking himself out in the left side mirror. He didn't text Naya to let her know he was outside. Instead, he turned up the music in his vehicle as loud as it could go before it rattled his brains. Twenty seconds later, she emerged from her front door. She had on the gold-rimmed glasses and was wearing denim overalls with an orange tank top underneath. Her Converse were also orange, and she had sunset-colored earrings dangling above her shoulders. Everything she wore put Dee's plain white T-shirt and black jeans to shame.

"You could have called, you know."

"My phone was gonna die," Dee lied, pulling off the pavement once Naya was seated. "Didn't want to waste my battery."

Naya was firstly taken aback by the tobacco-filled aroma in the car, along with the aging smell of the leather seats. It was like it had been passed down from his grandfather or something. She asked if it was a hand-me-down. He said no, that his brother had stolen his car and totaled it, so now he was stuck with whatever hot mess this was. It was okay, though, because he liked driving out to the desert sometimes and lying in the back of the pickup, watching the sun rise or set. She laughed and said that was kind of corny; he said he didn't care. She followed up with, "Also cute." He smirked and kept his eyes on the road.

"God, I wish this thing had an aux cord," Naya said, watching the houses grow scarcer as they left the town. Monumental red rock formations took their place, spreading out toward the vista. Arizona was all Dee knew, but he loved it the way a traveler still yearned for home. There was something so sleepy and free about it, something so wild and tranquil. It was definitely home, and always would be.

"You don't like my musical taste?" Dee huffed.

"No, I love this." Tame Impala's "Expectation" was filling the air. "I'm just a bigger fan of their latest project. It's definitely way more my vibe."

"You mean the more corny pop sound they went for this time around?"

"It's not corny, and it's not pop. It's just less Beatles on LSD, and more psychedelic disco, more soul. You should embrace the synthesizer and kiss the Fender good-bye. The future is now."

"Oh, wow. Okay. Well, you're wrong."

"No. You're wrong."

"I'll be wrong while jamming to this," he said, turning the music louder. She watched as Dee bopped his head to the rhythm. *This one's a cool kid*, she thought.

Salvation Hill was a gated nursing home, situated around a mile ahead of the gas station that hung on the edge of Harlow. In contrast to the nursing home downtown, it was privately owned, housing residents mainly from Smithson. It had been renovated in recent years, and its exterior consisted of pristine white brick walls and arched doors and windows. There was a polished patio to the left of the building's entrance; and an immaculate, colorful bed of flowers that reminded Naya of her mother's flower bed at home framed the front of the building.

When Dee and Naya reached the reception area, they were greeted with hospitable welcomes from a middle-aged couple. They introduced themselves as Roy and Gita Crawford, the founders of Salvation Hill. As they exchanged handshakes, Dee couldn't help but notice the pastel-yellow walls and the slight smell of something he couldn't put his finger on. *This must be what old people smell like*, he thought. He had no reason to feel embarrassed, but he realized that he did. He hadn't interacted with elderly people for as long as he could remember; his mother was estranged from her parents, and his father estranged from his. He'd never really known grandparents the way everyone else had. He was about to be overwhelmed with a whole new type of person, one that he hadn't had practice interacting with. The old and the fragile, the wise and experienced. He didn't know much about them, directly. His little understanding of seniors was all arm's length, and now he was being given the responsibility of taking care of them.

"We honestly weren't sure if y'all'd make it." Gita beamed, leading the pair down the hallway. "Most kids aren't into this kinda stuff."

"We don't mind. We've got nothing better to do," Naya said. *Speak for yourself*, Dee told her in his head. *I've got plenty to do, but I'm sacrificing my time just for you . . . Who am I kidding? I have nothing to do, you're right. But you better be glad I joined you.*

"This is a small nursing home; there aren't that many residents. We're currently housing around twenty-five people, most of whom are in and out, and most have regular visits from family members and friends. But not everyone here is that lucky." Dee looked around. Many residents were either lounging outside or sitting in the common room. They seemed fairly normal, which was a relief. He wasn't sure what he'd been expecting—maybe half-dead people or folks in straitjackets.

They were shown around all the different rooms, including the small library and the dining area, as well as the kitchen and the staff bathrooms. They were only permitted to enter a resident's room if they were assigned to care for them. Over the course of the summer, they would be given one particular resident to work with but were still free to interact with the others.

Gita led them out to the backyard. It was huge, stretching quite far. There was a gazebo right at the end, and a small fountain in the middle. The green grass was cut so perfectly it looked like AstroTurf. There were a bunch of residents sitting or standing around in the yard. Out on the grass sat an old woman in a chair, fanning herself in the heat with her legs crossed. She appeared to be deep in thought, or really fascinated by the view of the desert rolling out into the horizon, barren and red like a Martian landscape.

"That is Marie Delden," Gita said, pointing to the lady. "She hasn't had one visitor since arriving here a couple of years ago."

"Shit. I'm sorry. I mean, heck." Dee needed to work on his language.

Naya held in a snicker before asking Gita, "Why not?"

"She's a bit of an enigma, this one. Hard to pinpoint. I mean, she does have Alzheimer's, but that's not the whole reason why she's such a mystery lady. There just isn't much we know about her."

"How did she end up here?"

"She was found living alone in a rundown house outside Harlow. She hadn't paid rent in months. It looked like she hadn't done anything in months, really. She didn't contest moving into Salvation Hill, so we took all that we could of her belongings and gave the rest away. She's been here ever since. She was the only resident that we'd been paying for out of our own pockets, while we tried to figure out if she still had any living kinfolk."

"Oh, wow." Naya gasped. "That's unreal. So she's never had even *one* visitor?"

"Well, that's sort of a lie. Around a year ago, the authorities came knocking on our door. They said they were looking for a lady who'd gone missing decades ago. We asked what they thought she'd be doing here, and they said that her social security activity had led them to us. They had a bunch of old photos of a ma'am called Violet Marie Winslow, from back in the seventies. We showed them to Marie, and her face lit up like a campfire! She told everyone that those photos were of her."

"Oh my God" was all Naya could say. Dee wasn't a thousand percent sure, but he felt like he had heard this story in the news, or overheard people mention it once. The three just stood quietly and stared at the old lady for a few seconds.

"Apparently, her husband dropped her off at a grocery store one afternoon, and she never returned. Nothing is known of her life since then. Not from our part, and not from those who were looking around for her. We couldn't ask her if we tried; her memory is real unreliable. She only tells us what she's thinking of in that current moment, and it might be gone forever within minutes."

Gita continued, telling them how her daughter, Charlotte Winslow, visited shortly after the authorities found her. Marie, of course, didn't recognize her. Charlotte was in her forties now, and she had never known her mother, as she'd vanished when she was a baby. She had children of her own, and her father had died almost twenty years previous from a heart attack, never having knowledge of his wife's fate.

Charlotte took over the monthly payments for Marie's residency, and brought in three boxes of her mother's belongings, primarily consisting of books, photos, and some old clothes, but she never returned, or even kept in contact. Gita told the pair how she hadn't dropped off much, but it was all that was left. It was a pretty sad life, in a way—to have lived, breathed, rejoiced, and cried, married and birthed, all for that to be erased and shrouded by a foggy mind that no longer fully served its purpose. Dee was afraid of what it would feel like not to be in control of your own body, and he thought of how that had been what his mother was going through for a long time, once she'd left the hospital. He knew firsthand what it was like to lose autonomy, and he wasn't sure if he was up for the challenge of keeping the mysterious Marie Delden company, watching her deteriorate in front of his eyes.

Later on, he sat on the front porch of the nursing home, lighting a cigarette. Naya could sense that his mood had shifted.

"You good?"

"Yeah. It's not that bad here," he lied. "I don't mind it."

"The Marie lady," Naya said. "You're not sure about her, are you?"

"There's nothing for me to not be sure about."

"I know. But I can tell it bothers you."

"You don't know what bothers me."

Naya kept silent for a while, staring at the ground as Dee took a few impatient puffs of smoke. "I felt kinda weird there too. I just figured you felt the same. There's something different about her, I can tell. I know we haven't even spoken to her yet, but I don't know. There is, right?"

"I don't know." Dee was shutting down, his responses becoming curt.

"There's probably so much shit she's seen in her life. Cool, amazing shit. Something memoir-worthy."

"Maybe."

Naya paused again, thinking of something to say. "We should do something cool, to pass our time here. If we're going to be stuck with that lady, we should make the most of it." She looked up at him as he stared out into the desert.

"Something like what?"

"I don't know. Try to figure out the most plausible explanation for her disappearance, and guess what she's been up to all these years. I mean, this is pretty wild. She has a completely different name, for crying out loud. There are dozens of possibilities as to how her life ended up."

"That's not gonna solve anything, though, is it?"

"Well, it's bothering *me* not knowing. And I know we'll never find out the truth, but it will give me peace of mind. I can rest easy knowing I tried to figure her out, even if she can't do that herself anymore. It'll be a nice distraction. We just have to crack the code. Play guessing games for a while. It'll make time fly by, trust me."

The pair stood quietly for a while. Naya's icy blue eyes glimmered with the reflection of the sun as she leaned over the railing of the porch.

"Okay," Dee said. "Let's do it, then."

◆

The Girls were gathered in the center of Jasmine's uncle's studio when Naya arrived later that afternoon. It was a rented space on the third floor of the building, with photography equipment scattered throughout; on its cream walls hung a mixture of minimalist art pieces and photos of inner-city architecture. The windows were wide and towering, filling the room with natural light and giving a view of the downtown skyline. As Naya looked out, she could see pedestrians walking along, weaving in and out of the cafés and bodegas that lined the main street.

The Girls were sitting cross-legged in a circle in the middle of the space, cracking jokes and quips. Interrupted by her presence, they shuffled apart, making room for her to sit with them.

"Yay, you're finally here. We can get this show on the road," Jasmine said. She pulled a rolled joint out from her handbag beside her and placed a homemade clay ashtray in the middle of the circle. "But first, let's see if we can get our creative juices flowing with a little bit of this."

"Ugh, you're a lifesaver," Evie said. "Yo, can we play some music? It'll add to the *ambiaaaance*."

"Sure. Who wants to DJ?"

Amber raised her hand. "Y'all know I'm all about my playlists. Hand the speaker over."

"Okay, but it's a democracy—we can put in requests," Tori said.

"Don't worry, I got you. They don't call me DJ Ambz for no reason."

"They don't call you DJ Ambz at all."

"I'm working on it. Anyway, what vibe are we going with?"

"Uh, anything with a nice beat, I guess. Nothing too intense," Evie said.

"Awesome. Totally not vague at all. Whatever, I'll just put my phone on shuffle." "I Do" by Cardi B blared through the speaker and Jasmine took the first toke of the joint, bobbing along to the music as she exhaled. When she was done, she offered it to Naya.

"I'm good, thanks."

"Have you ever smoked before?" Jasmine asked, passing the joint across to Evie.

"No, I haven't."

"You gotta start somewhere." She raised her eyebrow, smirking.

"I have to be home soon. I don't wanna turn up high."

"Ah, but that's a part of the thrill. Every time my mom loses her shit when me and Ty come home zooted, it just makes everything ten times funnier." Amber laughed.

"You're mom's a white lady—she's not gonna beat your ass. The rest of us . . . we're risking physical pain," Evie said, blowing out a mist of smoke.

"Yeah, Amber. Check your white-mom privilege." Jasmine giggled.

Amber rolled her eyes. "Anyway, shall we actually start the meeting?"

"Yes. Let's begin." Jasmine pulled out a notebook and pen from her bag and placed them on her lap. "So. I've come up with a name for the zine. *Black Glitter*. If everything goes to plan, a new edition will come out every three months. One zine for each season. So basically, our first edition will come out in September, and it will be the summer edition—we'll be working on it starting now. I told my uncle all about it, and he said he can help me print out multiple copies, and we can promote and distribute them at school when we go back."

"Oh shit. You've really thought this through." Tori raised her eyebrows. "I like the name *Black Glitter* too."

"Right? Ugh, my *mind*. So this zine will basically be a 'for us, by us' kinda thing. A safe space for us, just to put our experiences into words, art, pictures. All that pretty stuff. Something uplifting and fun. I was thinking the five of us could have different roles or specializations. Or at least contribute something unique to it, you know? I'm superheavy on photography, so I wanna focus more on that aspect. You guys got any other ideas?"

"This is so cool! I'm not very artistic but I'll find a way to chip in," Amber said. "Maybe we could cover different topics and themes. Colorism, relationships, hair care, stuff like that."

"Exactly. We can make collages, mood boards, personal essays, advice . . . Share our inspirations and idols, books and films we relate to. Like a collective diary. Just a mash-up of our lives as Black girls in Harlow. And we could expand on it, gather more submissions if other people are interested," Jasmine said.

"Okay. So we'll have a schedule or something, right? Deadlines and shit?" Tori asked.

"Yup. Just so we're on track. I'm gonna make an Instagram account for it, and when we find a date to release, we can work toward it. Is there anything specific y'all wanna work on?"

"I was thinking . . . I could do a relationships column. How to avoid fuckboys," Amber said.

"Okay, but make sure you're not just subliminally waging a war against the Guys with that piece," Tori responded. "I can see it going there."

"Whatever. Naya, you got any ideas?" Amber turned to her.

"Hmm. I was thinking . . . maybe a fashion column?"

"That would be *perfect*. You have such a unique sense of style. I even think you could model. You've got the look."

"I don't like the idea of being gawked at, if I'm honest. I'd model my own designs on myself, but I've got to learn how to design first. When I do, it's over for everyone." Naya smiled.

"Can't wait! Oh, by the way—how's the volunteering thing going? You said you're working at a nursing home, right?"

"Yeah. Today was my training shift; that's why I was a little late. I got Dee to give me a ride into town."

"*Dee?* I didn't know y'all were tight like that," Tori said.

"I mean, we're both working at the nursing home. We drive there together and he drops me off afterward."

"No fuckin' way do you volunteer with *Dee Warrington*. He wouldn't touch an old person with a ten-foot pole if he was paid a million dollars." Evie snorted. "How didn't we already know this? Surely he would have told Tyler."

"Clearly he didn't. Probably too embarrassed. It's just . . . not in his character," Jasmine said.

"Maybe he's turning over a new leaf." Amber shrugged. "You know, getting himself straight. Or could just be trying to win Vanessa back with some philanthropy."

"Now that's what I'd call the long game." Tori laughed. "Still weird how he's kind of just kept it to himself. It's not like it's a huge deal."

"The Bad Boy doesn't wanna lose his street cred." Amber chortled.

"Is he *that* bad?" Naya asked, suddenly discomfited.

"You've seen what he's like at school," Tori responded. "When he actually attends, that is. And *hello*—he cheated on *Vanessa Bailey*, with Karina Fitzgerald of all people. He's trying so hard to be a badass. It's almost like he wants to live up to his older brother's reputation. Dylan Warrington was, like, superpopular in his day—my sister was a freshman the year he graduated. He was this hot blond class clown who loved to start fights and was always getting suspended. No matter how much he acted out, everyone loved him. Dee just isn't the same, even if he tries to be. But hey, I guess he could be turning over a new leaf, like Amber said. Let's see how long *that* lasts."

Naya had a feeling that the Girls didn't really, truly know Dee. They knew him through other people's words—the words in the corridors, the words of Tyler and the Guys. They'd probably never even thought to hold a conversation with him. She knew that Dee *wasn't* a terrible person. She didn't have to judge people—the way the Girls judged Dee, the way the Ampleforth community judged her. People didn't always truly know one another, she thought to herself. People knew the things people did, and the things people said, but never what they thought, what they felt, dreamed, or desired. Three-dimensional beings walked around in two-dimensional suits, trying to find a place in the world to realize themselves and have others see them for who they were. Everyone was a cardboard cutout until you actually tried to find out what was inside of their chest, what was lurking in their prefrontal cortex. Dee wasn't a terrible person. He was just made of cardboard, at least to the Girls.

6

A MAN NAMED

Dee and Naya met Marie Delden in the common room on their first official shift for the Summer Volunteer Program a few days later, interrupting her from an apparent deep, silent brooding. She looked up at them, stretching her lips into a broad, hospitable grin. She stood up and shook Dee's hand.

"Hello! You must be William."

He paused. "No, haha. My name's Dee."

"Oh, right. Sorry, I was told William this morning." She huffed. He wasn't sure whether to believe her or to assume that she was just saving face. He wondered where she would have gotten *William* from. "And you must be . . . I'm sorry. You are?" She smiled at Naya, who introduced herself and went in for a hug.

"I understand you've been hired to keep me company for a few hours."

They both nodded. Naya added, "We're doing it for free."

Marie laughed. "I still remember years ago, when I'd do anything just to bide my time, just like you two. I was much less philanthropic in the process, though. Wish I could have been more giving."

They weren't sure how to reply, and she could tell, so she led them to her residence room.

"This is my humble abode. Do you like it?" She strolled over and stood by the window, which had a stunning view of the garden and the beautiful orange terrain outside. Dee felt a slight pang of jealousy; though her remembrances had wilted away and eroded, she would never lose sight of the landscape she had the blessing of waking up to every morning. And she probably came to the experience as if it were a new one every time.

The room was decorated simply. It had framed photos that looked like they'd probably always been there, even before she'd moved in; an ancient-looking rug in the center of the floor; a wooden desk with miscellaneous items strewn across it (a pen and sheets of paper, a necklace, a jewelry box from which the necklace must have escaped, an old magazine); a wardrobe; and a small bookshelf, which only held around seven hardcovers, all aged. Her bed was neatly made, the pair guessed by someone else who worked there full time. There was nothing in the room which suggested that Marie needed extra physical assistance, and her gait and posture seemed yet to be affected by her condition. Naya wondered how long it had been since she was diagnosed, because she really didn't seem that out of it—though she realized she had no firsthand experience with anyone dealing with mental decline; her grandmother had still been sharp and witty all the way up to her unfortunate departure at age eighty-seven.

"Have you read any of those books?" Naya pointed to the bookshelf.

Marie looked over. "I've read them all, time and time again. They were my favorites back when I was younger. I lost them for such a long time; I'm glad they were returned to me."

"Where were you living before you moved to Harlow?" Dee asked. Naya wanted to tell him, That's a stupid question—you're not going to get anything out of her, silly.

Marie looked vacant for a few seconds before responding, "I simply can't remember. My head is going, child. I don't remember much."

"Did you have a husband?"

She smiled sadly. "Yes. Charles. Married in 1966. I recently heard he passed. Isn't that awful?"

"Uh. Yeah. Did you remarry? Why is your name different?" Naya felt awkward with his blunt, straight-to-the-point questions.

"Different to what?" She went and sat at her desk.

"You were called Violet Winslow before."

"Oh, right. Yes, I was."

"Why did you change it? Why did you run away from your family?"

"I don't know what you're talking about. I never ran away from anybody. These questions are nonsense." She was getting irritated. Naya looked over at Dee, hoping he'd get the message. There was nothing he could get out of Marie, just like with the others who had tried. "William, please get me an iced tea from the café. Add a little syrup. Just a pinch."

"Dee."

"Excuse me?"

"My name's not William, it's—"

"Well, then why did they tell me William this morning?"

Naya walked with Dee to the mini-café over at the other side of the home. Sitting inside were two old men playing cards and a lady singing to herself. Most of the residents were outside, smoking or soaking up the sun.

"You need to work on your communication skills, dude," Naya said as they found an empty table.

"What do you mean?"

"This isn't a police interview. Just ask nice, open questions. Let her ramble. Don't ask stuff she obviously can't answer. She probably remembers the things that mean the most to her. Slowly but surely, she might reveal little truths."

"Well, we won't know what she can't answer until we ask," Dee responded.

"You're being a smart-ass."

"You're the one that came up with the guessing game idea. I need something to work with."

"I know, but this method isn't going to open her up." Naya took her phone from her pocket. "I did some research last night, and I found this thread on Reddit, where people were discussing her disappearance. Have you seen it?"

"No, I haven't," Dee said.

"Check this out." She pulled up the tab on her browser, leaning forward on the table and turning her phone so they could both read the comments. She had found plenty of news articles online, but they all revealed just as little information as Gita had. There was a giant gap in time that just couldn't be accounted for, and it was a daunting yet fascinating mystery.

WARONA JOLOMBA

Timkinz: it's a bit suspicious that she's able to identify an old photo of herself if she has dementia . . .

Greendog76: It's really not. It's a common phenom-
enon. Their memory is not completely erased. It's
patchy and they're prone to confabulate memories,
but they may be able to identify old photos, especially if that photo is of them. It's quite plausible

DanDan669: Yes, my great-aunt was like that. Her
memories were not accurate but they weren't far off.
She'd had an affair with a middling musician in LA
in the '80s that she was convinced was Prince but
it wasn't lol

FlyingInsect: I wonder if someone in the supermarket
helped her to sneak away or something, and she
went off to start a new life

Jadiepie: There's just no way she could have vanished into thin air without any help. Honestly I think
the husband was in on it. Maybe he was the one
who helped her escape, but he had to cover his own
back if people started asking questions, so he filed a
missing person report? Who knows?

BlancaSilva: I doubt that—her daughter said in the
press that the father spent years trying to look for
her . . . if he was just doing it as smoke and mirrors, I
doubt he'd put the act on for that long. I think she ran
away and someone else helped

whirlpoolyoga: not sure why the cops are even
concerned, she was found alive and well and she
hadn't committed life insurance fraud or anything . . .
the SSN brought the cops back to her, after all. She

probably wasn't even trying to disappear, just slipped
under the radar
charllieee898: yeah, but once they traced the SSN,
they had to be sure there wasn't any fraud or foul
play so they could officially close the case

"Interesting," Dee said after they'd read through the thread. "I guess everyone's just as stumped as we are. I was just hoping we'd be able to find out more, you know—'cause we're actually *with* her. Straight from the horse's mouth kinda thing."

"If the feds don't have an answer, it's unlikely we'll get one. All I'm saying is, let her speak. No more narrow questions," Naya said, putting her phone back in her pocket. "I'm gonna get Violet's iced tea from the counter. I also kinda want some coffee. Do you want a drink too?"

"Yeah, sure. Thanks. A coffee too. Just keep it black, no sugar," Dee said.

As Naya got up and walked over to the barista, he further contemplated reasons for Marie's vanishing. It was likely that she'd been running away from an abusive husband, but that likelihood was thwarted by the fact that she had left her daughter in his custody. He thought back to the times his mother would swiftly pack up their things after an explosive altercation with his father; they'd spend a few days at a motel out of town, his mother telling him that they were going to find a safer place for them to live, until his father would eventually succeed in his manipulative campaign for their return. Dylan was in his teens at the time, and he was barely ever home whenever they'd make a brief escape; Dee's mother would be riddled with guilt when she came back, noticing that in her absence, Dylan had taken the brunt of his father's aggression. She wasn't his biological mother, who had been out of the picture since before Dee was born, but she still treated him as her son, despite their age difference being closer to that of siblings than parent and child. She would have never left Dee behind, and given the chance, she would have also brought Dylan along with her. With this in mind, Dee found it improbable that Marie would abandon her own child.

"Here's your bitter beverage," Naya said as she returned to the table. Holding the three drinks carefully between her hands, she slowly placed them on the table and sat down, sliding Dee's drink closer to him before sipping on her own.

"Thanks. It's *way* better bitter. All that extra shit's so gross." He frowned, watching her stir the white froth in her cup. "What should we do after our break?"

"I think we should offer to read to her. That'd be nice."

"We can't both do that."

"Said who? We can take turns. Dibs on you going first," she said before sipping her coffee and wiping away her milk mustache.

"You can't dibs someone else."

"I just did."

When they were done with their drinks, Dee grabbed Marie's iced tea, making sure the lid was securely fitted, and they walked back to her room, only to arrive to find her gone. "She's probably outside," Dee said. "I'll go and give this to her. Just stay and look for something to read, I don't know." He left the room.

From among the books on the bookshelf, Naya found a tattered notebook. She looked at the front cover: a hand holding three red roses. It was titled *The Anatomy of a Worried Heart*. The author was called V.M. Winslow. It was Marie's own book, full of poetry. Naya sat on the chair and flicked through the pages,

intrigued and fascinated. Dee came back shortly after, still holding the tea. "She said she didn't want anything to drink."

"Oh God."

"And she called me William again."

"I guess that's your new name." She laughed. Dee shook his
head, trying to hold in a creeping smile.

"What are you reading?"

"She wrote a poetry book, probably a superlong time ago."

"That's cool." He came over, peering at the pages over her
shoulder. 'To Drown a Fish.' That's an interesting name for a
poem."

"Yeah, I briefly skimmed through that one. The main themes
behind some of these seem to be, like, trauma or heartbreak or
something. Maybe she didn't get along with her husband."

"As in, he was a real asshole?"

"Maybe."

Dee huffed. However awful that guy may have been, he still
would have had nothing on A Man Named Derrick Warrington.

Dylan was born in New Mexico eight and a half years before a
girl named Freya Stone gave birth to Dee. Both of their mothers
had once fallen in love with a man named Derrick Warrington.
When Dylan's mother was sent to prison after a drug bust just
before he turned seven, Derrick relocated to Arizona and spent
the next few months trying to start a new life for him and his
only child. But his drinking days weren't quite behind him, and
whenever he had free time, he'd find himself going from party
to party around the state. He met Freya at a folk festival, and
was mesmerized by her insouciant attitude and rebellious dis-
position. She was a high school dropout taking each day as it
came, crashing at friends' houses, seeking the thrill of nomadic

adventure, drifting further and further away from her family in the Navajo Nation until she cut them off completely. She was enamored with Derrick, despite the growing tumultuousness of their relationship.

When she found out she was pregnant, her carefree life came to a precipitous halt, though her love for Derrick grew stronger. He promised to be there for her when she realized she had nowhere else to turn. She gave him his second son in a hospital in Tucson a few weeks after her seventeenth birthday, and six weeks before Derrick's twenty-sixth. The couple moved to Harlow with Dylan, where they settled. They were determined to start fresh as a functional family; Derrick would get a job and provide for his two sons, and Freya would return to high school and move on to college. She was amazing at chemistry; she could get into the fragrance industry one day, make it as the chair of a company. That was how it was supposed to end up—everything was supposed to be virtuous in the end. But of course, that only happened in fairy tales. Dee's life was anything but. It was a saga of tragedies.

7

ALIENS

On the second day of the program, Dee and Naya were assigned to help sort the books in the nursing home library, and it was a task that would take them both longer than they initially assumed. Naya would stop and peek at almost every title, mentally adding it to her to-read list, or asking Dee if he'd read it before. Most of his answers would be something along the lines of *No, I don't really read*, and she would scowl in disapproval. It was a fairly quiet afternoon, with initially little to no conversation bouncing between the two. Though Dee didn't mind the silence, Naya despised it. She needed to find something to say.

"Why is your hair so long?" she asked him. She was pretty sure it was a dumb question, but one worth asking in the moment, to murder the noiselessness.

He looked up from where he sat cross-legged, with books splayed in front of him. He hadn't tied his hair this time; it hung long and wavy over his shoulders, down to his abdomen. He spent a few seconds trying to figure out whether he should give a blunt nonanswer or the real reason why. He figured the real reason wouldn't kill him.

"It's a cultural thing. A custom. I'm not supposed to cut it."

"Oh. You're Indigenous, right?"

"Yup."

"That's pretty cool. Is it, like, mandatory? Your hair length?"

"Not necessarily. Not every tribe does it, and not every member of the same tribe does. All my family do, though."

"Oh, wow. Honestly, I thought you were a heavy metal fan or something." She bounced a small book between her hands.

"Nah." He shook his head. "Respect to heavy metal, but that's not my vibe. Yeah, I don't know, I think I wanna feel a part of something special, you know? I don't live with my maternal family. I barely ever see them. My mom reconnected with them a few years ago, but it was kinda strained at times. Just a lot of complicated family stuff, I guess."

"Tell me about it." Naya sighed. "Do you think you'll ever cut your hair?"

"I don't know. Maybe. I don't think my mom would be too stoked about it if she knew, though. She'd kick my ass and ask me where my integrity is."

"Amber told me about your mother. I'm so sorry to hear that," Naya said to him.

He looked to the floor. "Yeah, it sucks. It was so sudden. I still haven't really taken it in," he lied. It was all he ever thought about. "But the world doesn't stop turning for nobody. So I've got to keep it moving."

"No! Just take your time. You don't have to rush yourself out of grief. I mean, I'm not the best person to give out advice. I haven't lost anyone significant in my life, except my grandma, and she was *suuuper*old. But I don't think there's a time frame for any of this. It's different for different people."

"I spent weeks acting out after she died. I mean, I was an asshole before, but I didn't care about *anything* afterward. I fought with my ex all the time. I took drugs I'd never usually take. Almost got kicked out of school. It didn't help that my mom made my half brother my legal guardian in her will; we weren't really that close before she died. It feels like I'm living with a stranger sometimes."

"That's gotta be weird. But hey, at least we'll be seniors soon. Then you're heading off to college next year, right? You'll be free to do new things, go to new places. That'll be fun."

"I don't really think about college. I don't know what I want to do. Math is my favorite subject, so I can go from there, I guess."

"I noticed in our finals the other week. You finished the test before everyone else," she said.

"You noticed?"

"It's hard not to notice someone finishing a test before you when you're freaking out on the second question. I hate numbers." She laughed. "I'm not a logical thinker. I'm more of a *visual* person. Hence all these colors," she said, pointing to her outfit.

"It's cool. I dig it."

"Thanks! When I was a kid, I found out that there's this shrimp called the mantis shrimp. It has sixteen color receptors in its eyes. Humans only have *three*. I was blown away trying to envision what they can see that we can't. Then I found out that they can't actually necessarily see more colors than us—they just have better color recognition, or something like that. Anyway, it got me thinking. There are so many different ways of seeing things. *Everything* we see is just through different shades of violet, blue, green, yellow, orange, and red. How unreal is that? And . . . my eyesight isn't the greatest. I'm slowly going blind, which sucks. So . . . I appreciate color."

"Wait. Are you serious? You're going blind?" His face dropped.

"Yeah. My eyesight is already pretty bad. But on top of that, I was diagnosed with Stargardt disease a few months ago. It went unnoticed for a while because my bad eyesight was a given. This just means I'll probably be legally blind by the time I'm, like, twenty-five. So I live in color, I wear it, I make sure it's all I ever see. I describe in color too. Whatever someone radiates, I make sure I can at least see that. I think you're purple."

"Oh. Fuck. *Fuck.*"

"You don't like purple?"

"No, I don't mean that. I'm just . . . you're going *blind*? Does anybody know this?"

She hesitated. "No. I haven't even told Amber or Tori. I found out just before I left Texas. It's not really something I want to announce. I think you're the first person I've told, actually. And the Girls . . . they're awesome, I enjoy their company, but I just don't feel like offloading my fears onto them. We're trying to get the zine together, we need positive energy. It'll ruin the vibe."

"I get that. Shit. That's terrifying. You're a champ for taking something positive out of it."

She shrugged. "I don't really have much choice."

Once the book sorting was done, they had an hour left in their shift. They decided to spend it in the garden, reading some of Marie's old poems to her. Naya didn't know how to react to Marie, who kept telling her that she had pretty blue eyes, just like her baby daughter. She would say that she wasn't sure where her Charlotte was now, and she hoped she could meet her again before she died. She didn't know that she already had. Marie also had no knowledge that the poetry book was hers, even when she was presented with it.

"Wow! This looks nice. Who wrote it?" The three sat on deck chairs, with Dee and Naya facing Marie. They looked at each other, not sure whether it was worth reminding her that *she* wrote it, once upon a time.

"This writer, she's not well known. But you're clearly a fan of her work. This was on your shelf," Naya said. "Shall we read something of hers?"

"Sure, go ahead. That would be lovely."

Dee picked out a poem at random. It was titled "Imago Dei." "Should I read it?" He looked at Naya. She nodded. Though she loved reading, she hated doing it aloud. It was harder for her to gather the printed letters into her retina, and she knew her words would spill out jagged and incongruent as she waited for her vision to catch up with the page. Dee paused, feeling awkward. *But fuck it*, he thought. *This one's for Marie.*

"It's almost as if God electrocuted me.
He zapped me with a million watts
of passion and fear,

oceans of heavy tears,
mountains of heavy feelings.
It's almost as if God recreated the Big Bang
and stuffed it into my rib cage.

I explode.
He fed me
with bottled constellations.
That is the reason I shimmer.

That is why my soul
is dark, painful silence.
That's why I'm breathing.
That's why I sometimes wish
I wasn't.

God made me so that my thoughts
would scatter like the redshift,
all the space between
would fill up in my chest.

God made me in His image,
but it hurts to have infinity
thrust into a finite body.
It hurts to feel sometimes.
It hurts to feel
because feeling means hurting.

I understand why Adam and Eve
were punished.
God hurt.
God made me take a sip of the pain.
The pain of feeling, the blessing of feeling.
No, the curse.
The curse."

"That was amazing!" Marie gushed. "Who did you say wrote this?"

Dee hesitated. Naya swooped in. "You wrote it, Marie. A long time ago. It says in 1964, back when you were twenty. Do you not remember any of this at all? It's wonderful."

Marie frowned. "No, not really. Please, can I see the book?" Naya gave it to her. Marie stared hard at the front cover before flipping through the pages. She frowned again. "It's a terrible thing, not to know your past. I feel like this must have been in another life, like I reincarnated after all of this."

What Naya found heartbreaking was Marie's strong ability to recall most things surrounding her first marriage and her child, and nothing else outside of that. She did not mention anything comprehensive about her childhood, and nothing of her life after her disappearance. It was like her memory had been purposely erased, like its decimation had been planned by something bigger than her. Things she would say didn't seem to add up, like how she said she always read the books on her shelf, yet she didn't even know her own. Every time she mentioned Charlotte, or her husband, Naya's heartstrings tightened. It was a strange thing to witness—a woman who was clearly bright and learned, holding onto memories like sand in her open palms.

"First theory: aliens," Naya said to Dee as he drove them home afterward.

"You serious?"

"No, I'm not serious. Not all the theories have to be plausible. After all, we'll never know. It's like when Amelia Earhart disappeared. *Anything* was possible."

"Yeah, but Marie's still here."

"You think people have been abducted by aliens never to return? They almost always return. They're just different afterward. Like Marie."

"Return from where? Aliens aren't real!" Dee was grinning at how ridiculous this conversation was.

"It's just a theory!"

"Jesus. Okay. Well, then you better elaborate."

"One of her last poems alluded to the universe. I think it's called 'The Birth and Death of Andromeda.' Maybe her poetry book was a prediction of the future, of things to come. So she can't recall anything now, but she saw everything coming. And she just wrote it in riddles. Maybe she knew she was going to be abducted that day she went to the grocery store and never came back. Obviously, aliens erase your memory and stuff. They poke and prod at you, make you act different. They dropped her off in another state and she had no choice but to start her life again."

"I'm pretty sure if I had been abducted by aliens, I'd want to go home after. See my family, make sure I'm still sane."

"You don't know what you'd do if you were abducted by aliens."

"Yeah, I do. I'd tell my mom about it, and she'd be the only person who believed me, and she'd probably crack some weak joke about it."

"Well, I guess if we're talking hypotheticals, I'd probably hope that they'd cured my eyesight. No, given me *super*eyesight. So I'd have, like, X-ray vision and I could see things at microscopic levels. I could read people's texts from far away, or look into someone's wallet and get their credit card deets. Nobody would mess around with me."

"Truth is, we'd probably just become vegetables." Dee chuckled.

"So we're good with the aliens theory, right?"

"I think we need to build on it. Add levels and layers. What kind of aliens? From where? Why? These things matter."

"So you're really getting into this, huh?"

"I'm selectively passionate."

"Haha. Well, the aliens would have to have come through a wormhole, you know, like in *Interstellar*. A species way more intelligent than us feeble beings. Marie wouldn't have been the first person they abducted. In fact, over centuries, they've taken millions of people. Some returned, some didn't. People are still being taken now. Sometimes only for hours, sometimes days, or years. Maybe Marie was up there for two decades. Maybe only a month. Either way, she made it back, and they messed her brain up so bad that her Alzheimer's is some sort of way of covering it up."

"That's kinda wild."

"Right? I should become a storyteller. A *novelist*. I'm gonna work on my sci-fi saga the second I get home."

"You've got to put me in your acknowledgments."

"We'll cross that bridge when we get to it."

8

BLANK SLATE

A couple of days later, Dee and Naya went on their first off-work excursion to eat a late lunch at Benno's Diner after Salvation Hill. She ordered pancakes and bacon with a pineapple smoothie, and he went with a double cheeseburger, fries, and a banana milk shake. They were speaking about anything and everything, from questioning how Salvation Hill got its name when there was no hill in sight, to Dee's hatred for pineapples and pineapple-flavored foodstuffs.

"Your taste buds are broken," Naya said. "This right here—this is *ambrosia*." She took a long sip from her drink.

"It's fucking disgusting, is what it is."

"*You're* disgusting."

"Come on, gimme a break. I showered this morning."

"Your medal will be delivered in three to five business days."

"Damn. Remind me to never insult tropical fruits again." He laughed.

"No, no, go ahead. Just means there's more for me. Always got to look on the bright side." They sat and ate in silence for a few moments, and Naya watched the pedestrians as they walked past the diner's window. But there was only so much silence she could handle. "Is Dee your real name? 'Cause it's usually a girl's name. Not that it matters; names are just sounds that come out of our mouths."

"Damn. When you put it that way, you're onto something. And yeah, it's my real name. Well, kind of. It's . . . a much shorter version. But nobody's ever called me my real name, and nobody ever will."

"What's it short for? *Dupercalifragilisticexpialidocious*?"

"Haha. No, something much less impressive. Kind of embarrassing, actually. I don't even want to tell you."

"Well, you have to now. You can't leave me on the edge of my seat like this."

"It's so uncool. I can't."

"*Please*. Give me a clue at least."

"Shit. Okay. So my first name's my dad's name. Derrick. And my middle name . . . you know Harry Potter? A character from that."

Naya's jaw dropped, then she cupped her mouth, attempting to suppress laughter. "Oh no. Please don't tell me your full name is Derrick *Dumbledore* Warrington."

Dee laughed, shaking his head. "Thankfully it's not that bad. Think . . . Harry's fat little shit of a cousin."

"Oh my God. Dudley?" Naya gasped.

He nodded awkwardly, looking away. "See. I told you. Lame. In my defense, I was born a year before the films even came out, so there's no correlation. My dad thought he'd give me an awful name, and I just couldn't live with the consequences of that kind of rep. I've been called Dee by everyone for as long as I can remember."

"It's cute, though. I like it."

"I mean . . . I'd probably hate it less if it wasn't my dad who'd picked the name. Even worse, he gave me and my brother the same first name, which is idiotic, to put it simply."

"Do you know if your mother wanted to call you something else?"

"She told me that she really wanted to call me Kai. Sometimes I wish that it was my name. I fucking hate Derrick Dudley. Do I even *look* like a Derrick Dudley to you?"

"You could get used to it." She giggled. "Has anyone ever called you that?"

"Only my dad ever did. And sometimes my brother does, just to piss me off. If anyone else ever tried it, I'd probably knock them out. But like you said. Names are just sounds that come out of our mouths. And I don't think changing my name would ever fix my identity crisis." Dee emptied a bunch of fries into his mouth and swallowed them down with his milk shake.

"Do you feel like you're caught in the middle of your parents?"

Dee shrugged. "I don't feel Indigenous. I don't feel white. It's like I don't exist. Well, I do, but I don't know. My parents never agreed on anything, so I was just kind of floating around, not sure where I stood." Dee remembered his mother taking him to a powwow when he was seven years old. He'd been enamored

by the vivacity of it all: the beauty in the singing and the dancing, and the vibrant colors woven into the traditional regalia. It
was one of the first memories he had of his maternal family—
his mother's older siblings, his cousins, and his grandparents all
together, celebrating the joy of their culture. A few days afterward, he overheard his parents arguing, though he was not privy
to the context. One day, he asked his mother if they could attend
another powwow, and she said, "No, your father isn't interested."
It would be three years before Dee attended another one, two
years into his father's prison sentence. Things were much different that time around; the only family member he remembered
seeing there was his uncle Jared, who was still on speaking terms
with his mother. Looking back, it was clear to see that his father
had had a hand in estranging his mother from the rez, and she
never got the chance to build back the bridges before it was too
late.

"It's such a shame they didn't get along," Naya said. "And I feel
like I can relate to you about not knowing where I belong too. I
stuck out in Texas, and I stick out here. There's no winning. I'm
going to get looks and double takes everywhere I go, and I don't
want that to define me, you know? That's not *Naya*. That's not
me. I think that's half the reason I like wearing colorful shit. If
I'm going to attract attention no matter what, it might as well be
about something I have control over, you know?"

"Yeah. I get that. That makes sense. And it suits you."

"Right? Also, wearing too much color is, like, *quintessentially*
gay, so it's on brand for me."

He stared at her, bemused. "You're gay? I mean . . . it's totally
cool if you are. I just didn't know that."

She dissected her food with a knife and fork, chewing it as

she nodded. "Yes and no. I don't know. I'm bi. At least I think so, anyway. Well, I personally think the term bisexuality assumes a gender binary. I could be wrong. Maybe I'm more pansexual. I don't know. I just don't care if you're a guy or a girl, if you're neither or both. I just love *love*. It's so cliché to say, but I think labels are so stifling. Labels are just like names, really. We have to categorize everything, identify everything in one way or another. It's just so limiting. We're more than that," she said, leaning forward and resting her chin on her hand with her elbow on the table. With her other hand, she stole a couple of fries from Dee's plate and nonchalantly ate them. He looked on silently. "The only exception I'll make is with zodiac signs. They're valid. There's absolutely no changing my mind."

Dee rolled his eyes. "Oh God. You can't be serious." He wasn't remotely surprised that she was interested in star signs because it seemed like most girls were. Vanessa would often share memes pertaining to "totally relatable" Taurus traits, and he'd strain to discern anything rational within the absurdity of it all. He remembered getting into a spirited debate with her on the accuracy of horoscopes; he put forth the argument that it was impossible that everybody born within the same four-week period would be experiencing the same fate at the same time. He'd died on that hill of skepticism, and he'd been there ever since.

"I'm not one to play around with the stars, Dee. When's your birthday?" Naya asked. There was something comforting about the concept of whimsical individuality, to Naya—that the universe was just a machine with moving parts, energy flowing through time and space, inclining people to progress through the world in their own ways. Whether it was real was neither here nor there for her.

"I'm not going to tell you my birthday," Dee said. "I'm going to make you guess. You know me well enough, so go ahead."

"Goddamnit. Okay, let me just think . . ." She closed her eyes for a moment, placing her hand on her temple. "Right. Okay. So I think you're . . . a Scorpio." She tentatively stretched out the last word.

"That has to be a lucky guess."

"Oh my God! I was right! Yes!" She pumped her fist, laughing. "I told you I don't play. It just tracks, I can't explain how. My second guess was Aquarius. Wait, look, I'll show you what I mean." She took out her phone. "I have a zodiac app. Tell me this star sign doesn't align with you."

"This is so stupid."

"No, hear me out. Okay: 'The Scorpio is a mysterious and misunderstood sign. Scorpios have a rock-hard exterior, and it takes a lot to truly get to know them. Once you do, you'll find that they're deeply emotional and intimate at their core.'"

"Bullshit. It's just confirmation bias. You could swap that for any other star sign."

"Ah, but you *couldn't*. I'm telling you, this shit is real. Let's go through some of the negatives, shall we?"

"Something tells me I don't have much of a choice," Dee said.

"'Scorpios are very honest, but also very secretive. Nobody will ever catch them off their guard, and their walls are impenetrable—especially around strangers, or people they have their reservations about. Though this may give them the upper hand in certain situations, it also makes them a pain to communicate with.'"

"Are you done?"

"Haha, sorry. I'm getting too into this. What exact date and time were you born, and where?"

"Eighth of November. Tucson, six in the morning." He paused, smiling. "My mom used to call me Yiska, 'cause I was born at the crack of dawn, and I was such an insomniac."

"What does that mean?"

"'The night has passed.'"

"Aww, that's so cute! My parents call me Yaya sometimes, because that's how I used to pronounce my own name when I was a toddler." She laughed. "Okay . . . so your moon is in Aries, and your rising is *also* in Scorpio. It literally *all* makes sense! The stars paint a strong picture here."

"You're just saying words at this point." Dee shook his head. "You surprise me more every day." He looked out the window, holding back a grin. In seconds, his face turned to stone.

Naya looked over her shoulder to catch the sight that had caught him first. Karina Fitzgerald was standing outside, smoking. Her hair had been dyed purple from the indigo blue it was the last time Dee had seen her. He tensed his jaw and squirmed ever so slightly in his seat.

"You good?" Naya asked. He didn't answer. "Who's that?" she asked, having a pretty strong feeling she already knew. Naya genuinely felt awkward, like she had walked in on something forbidden, something that was none of her business. There was a reason she didn't want to pry into Dee's past, and that was because it didn't matter. It had happened, it was done, and the present was a better focus. She tuned out the Girls' words like she had earplugs. She just wished for a blank slate. She was scared to color him in. She wanted the *now* to speak for itself, not the *then*. But she still found herself thinking, *Who's that? Someone from your past, I know. But I don't know what else to say, because I need to fill up this stunning silence with something that might feed me back some noise. I'll ask you, "Who's that?" So that you can say, "Nobody."*

"Nobody," he mumbled after snapping out of his daze. He looked down at his banana milk shake like it was the opening of an endless wishing well. Naya turned around again and saw Karina looking back at them. Apparently, she had always been bad news. But in that moment, she seemed worse. Like Medusa, like a Freudian nightmare, a fatal vice. But as Naya thought about it more, she wasn't sure who the bad person was here. The sheepish, solemn heartbreaker or the intimidating, unapologetic homewrecker. It didn't matter. *Blank slate.* Just as she had to become one when she moved to Harlow, she allowed everyone to be empty so they could fill themselves up, and she could absorb that. No old versions, no history lessons.

Dee apologized for his morphed demeanor. She told him not to worry, that it was all good. He believed that she didn't care; he felt the hospitality in her response. They carried on slurping their drinks and started working on the second theory for Marie Delden's disappearance.

9

PREMONITION

"You wanna speak to Dad?" Dylan asked Dee one evening. It was their father's birthday, and they were sitting in the living room eating dinner.

Dee stared at him. "Why would you even ask me that?"

"I don't see why I wouldn't."

"He knows about Mom, doesn't he?"

Dylan nodded his head. "He found out when it happened."

"What did he say?"

"He was devastated, Dee. He couldn't stop crying."

"Good. I hope he's suffering. I hope he's rotting in that cell. I'm not talking to him. Fuck that."

Dee's mother had called his father on a regular basis all the way up to her death. It baffled him to extremes, trying to understand why she still cared about him, why she still wanted to reach out to him, why she never cut contact with the man who had ruined their lives.

"You should give him a chance, Dee. Hear him out. He's been in there for *nine* years."

"He's the reason my mother's not here. He may not have killed yours, but he killed mine."

Dylan shook his head, grabbing the beer on the coffee table ahead of him. He emptied its contents into his mouth before throwing it to the side and wiping his lips. "He's still your father."

Dee stared at him. "Am I supposed to be grateful?"

"You're being really fucking difficult right now. You ain't got your mom no more, and now you don't want anything to do with your dad. You're pushing your family away. He's said he's sorry so many fucking times, and he's still paying the price for what he did."

"Awesome. I don't care," Dee retorted. The way his father would apologize still haunted Dee; as a kid, he'd always hear him say sorry to his mother after he hit her. She'd always be stifling a sob at the same time. They were sounds that made his skin crawl.

"People make mistakes. If you don't learn to forgive, you're going to be a bitter fuck for the rest of your life. He wants to do right by everybody, but you won't let him." Dylan's words were loose as he spoke, the beer slowly hitting him.

"You weren't there," Dee hissed. He didn't want to cry. "You were partying in Phoenix or whatever. And *don't* get me started on Mom's death. 'Cause you weren't there either. It was just me."

"That night was an accident! He didn't mean for things to go that far. You know damn well that's the truth."

"Oh, right. Yes, because you were the prime witness. Not me."

"You've got to forgive him, Dee. Your mother did. I did. It's just you now. You're isolating yourself."

"Can you show me this line you've drawn between what's forgivable and what's not? Because I can't see it. Like, were those bruises he'd leave all over your back accidents too?"

"Don't you fuckin' dare."

"Well, were they? Was it just 'discipline'? 'Cause I think there's another word for what he did."

"You think because Dad never hit you, you're special, don't you?" Dylan spat. "You're not fucking special."

"News flash, Dylan: neither are you."

Dee couldn't believe that after everything they had been through, Dylan still wanted to speak to their father. All Dee had ever known of Derrick Warrington was watching his mother or brother get beaten while he would hide in the closet or under the table, and afterward his father would get him an ice cream or candy, as if they were somehow laced with some kind of amnesiac drug. It was clear that things must have been a lot better for Dylan before Dee was born. During those years, he'd grown attached to his father, a bond too strong to break. So at this point, it didn't matter what Derrick did. Dylan would still love him. Dee's father never touched him, but he'd shattered everything and everyone else around him. He'd tortured his immediate family, physically and psychologically. Dee was forever damaged in the process.

"You're not special, Dee. Just because you're a mama's boy doesn't make you special. Just because you look different than me. Nothing changes the fact that you're a Warrington, and he's your father. Get that into your thick skull. Things will be a lot easier for you once you do."

"That man is dead to me. And you're a piece of shit for still talking to him. I hope karma gets you one day." He held his breath, staring his brother dead in his eyes, and kept his tears to himself.

Their fight went on longer until Dylan became too drunk to string a sentence together and gave up on his toxic barrage of insults. Mia came around later that evening, and like most nights that she stayed over, Dee would be kept awake by the sound of loud sex. Sometimes he'd put his earbuds in and listen to music full blast; sometimes he'd leave and make an impromptu visit to one of his friends' places; and other times he'd masturbate to the reverberation of Mia's moans bouncing off the walls and, soon after, fall into a lonely slumber. The latter was the most chosen option since Vanessa had left. This time, instead, he snuck outside to his front porch and had a twenty-minute conversation with his volunteer partner over the phone. Her jokes and commentary kept his blood pressure low, since he was still seething from earlier on. He didn't tell her about anything, though. He kept his brother and his mother and his father and his sadness to himself.

◆

A couple of days passed, and Dee and Naya were sitting in Salvation Hill's mini-café on their lunch break discussing their next theory regarding Marie's disappearance.

"There's a window of opportunity to explore government kidnappings and scientific experiments," Dee said. They had just finished having an engaging conversation with Marie out on the grass, asking her what her favorite hobbies were and letting her diverge into already-told anecdotes about the younger life she still had a cerebral grip on. She continued to address Dee as William.

"MK-Ultra were doing their thing in her time," he went on. "It's kinda plausible."

"MK who?"

"MK-Ultra."

"Sounds like an EDM group."

"Haha, very funny. It was a project of the CIA that started back in the fifties. I did some reading on it a while back. I think it was also called the mind control program. They did all these experiments on human subjects, trying to see if they could manipulate their minds through all these different methods, like with drugs, hypnosis, all that kinda stuff." Dee scrolled on his phone, trying to gather more information online. "It was psychological torture to the extreme, man." His eyebrows furrowed as he kept reading on.

"But what was that all for?" Naya asked.

"Well, this online article says that its purpose was to, like, develop and test drugs to use for mind control against Soviet bloc countries in retaliation for similar experiments they did on US prisoners of war in Korea."

"Well, damn."

"Fuckin' wild."

"Where would Marie fit into this?"

Dee shrugged. "It's just a theory, right? The 'Lady on a Stretcher' poem just reminded me of this kinda stuff. Experiments done without the subjects' consent. Clearly some people were kidnapped. Why couldn't she have been one of them? Marie kept repeating in that poem how she wanted to go home. Maybe she signed up for it. It was disguised as something else, a flyer in the grocery store, but it was really a cruel ruse for an abduction. Makes sense, huh?"

"But if she knew she was going to be kidnapped and used for some experiment, if she got so far as writing it down, why would she let it happen?"

"Well, she probably didn't let it happen if she was tricked. Who knows? Maybe these poems weren't literal. They're figurative—a way she could let out her feelings, express herself. They aren't a telling of true events. But maybe she didn't know that she was predicting her own future, that it would all actually happen."

"It's more plausible than the alien theory, I'll give it that." Naya chuckled. Today, she was decked out in all purple. A scoop-necked crop top covered with a lilac cardigan, lavender mom jeans, purple Vans. She had on the same indigo eyeshadow Dee had first seen her with, all those weeks back. Her eyes were almost jumping out at him, that was how bright they were. It was hard not to look straight at them, even harder to pretend that they weren't stupefying.

"Hell yeah, it's more plausible. I've got the most realistic theory here."

"A bit of a stretch, but I'll let you have it. For now. We're only getting started. I thought this was teamwork, a collaboration. But . . . if you wanna make this a competition, we'll see who comes out winning by the end of the summer."

"I'm game." They shook hands like they were ready to commence a kickoff.

◆

The next day, Dee decided to hang out with his friends at No Man's Land. Only this time, he brought Naya along. It was the first time she'd be diverging from activities with the Girls and crossing into unknown territory. She was slightly nervous, but it had been three weeks since summer started, and three weeks since she had been working alongside Dee. Coworkers always hung out after shift hours—it wasn't *wrong*. That's what she told herself.

Hanging out with them went a lot better than she had originally expected. Ash, Wallis, and Levi were there. Tyler wasn't. The Guys taught her a few tricks on their boards, and she fell at least three times, obtaining a grazed knee on her second attempt. Their jokes were a little more abdomen-clenching, a bit more crude, yet also wholesome. They asked her tons of questions about her appearance. Ash thought she was biracial; Wallis responded, "Of course she isn't, you dumbass. I knew some kid like that in fourth grade back in Tucson. My mama told me what it was when I asked her why that one white kid had two Black parents. It's called albinism, right? Pretty trippy."

"Why'd you keep this program thing a secret for so long, Dee?" Levi asked. He was the only one in the friend group who lived in Smithson, and one of the few Black kids who did. He was a little more reserved and serious than the rest of the boys, and didn't spend that much time at No Man's Land. He was often applying for internships and going to TED Talk–like events, on his way to becoming an entrepreneur by the time he was twenty-one. He was the best dressed of the bunch, and it could be said that he was also the most romantically successful too. He had a new girl hooked to his arm every other week. Before he'd met Tori, Tyler followed closely behind in the tally, then Dee (more so in quality than quantity, regarding Vanessa). Dee could tell in Levi's voice what he might have been getting at. Everyone knew that the most scandalous breakup at South Harlow High since Aubrey Wright and Glenn Tryniski's was Dee and Vanessa's. If news got out that there was a new female companion in his life, platonic or not, it would cause unnecessary talk. It wasn't something he needed.

"It's not the coolest thing in the world, is it?" Dee said, legs dangling into the pool. Naya lay along the edge, arm swaying on the wall below. She didn't say anything.

"It ain't that bad. I applaud you for doin' something like that. That's mad respectful."

"Not in Harlow, it ain't. Most of the people in this place just live up in their ivory towers."

"Whatever. This town is trash," Levi said, though he did live in Smithson, so *his* idea of trash may have been a little bit disparate from other people's.

"Isn't it called the Pretty City?" Naya piped up. The guys looked at her. She sometimes didn't know how to feel when this happened. She'd throw in a question that seemed jarring enough to make everyone turn and face her, whether that be with the Girls or the Guys. She'd feel like a fly on the wall, one that had just made itself known. Dee was the only one who didn't bat an eyelid to the sound of her voice, and she didn't know whether to interpret that as appeasing to her timidity or just revealing his lack of interest in her.

"Yeah, it's a superficial town. Everything's surface level. It's just gossip and fashion. Nobody pays attention to the fucked-up shit, like the poor people or the crimes and all of that. This place is just for show. That's why I commend y'all for actually doing something for the community. When I get rich, I'mma do the same kinda thing, tenfold. Open up more homeless shelters, alleviate poverty, you know the drill," Levi said.

"Bravo, Evans." Ash clapped. "You're the hero we didn't know we needed."

"Haha, suck a dick, Ash."

A few minutes later, Tyler arrived with Tori. They walked up to everyone, hand in hand. Tori almost stopped in her tracks once she saw Naya lounging around with the Guys. She certainly wasn't expecting it.

"What's the deal with you and Dee?" she asked her, after pulling her aside a few minutes later.

"What do you mean?" Naya furrowed her brows.

"I thought you'd spend your free time with us, not the Guys. I just wasn't expecting it, that's all."

"Not sure what the issue is. Dee's my volunteer partner. We hang out sometimes."

"Right, I get that, but . . . I don't know, I just thought you'd want to spend *more* time with *us*."

"I *do* want to spend more time with y'all. I want a social life, period. But as it stands, you're always going to parties or doing things that I just can't do. Every time I muster up the courage to ask my parents to hang out past curfew, I'm shut down. I feel like shit always being the first one to leave. With volunteering, I don't have that problem. And Dee's a cool kid. I enjoy hanging out with him."

"Oh, Naya." Tori shook her head. "I didn't know you felt that way. We're still getting the zine thing going, so we're going to spend more time doing things during the day, I promise. You're a supercool chick. Like, awesome. We need your energy in our group. We were literally asking where you were earlier today."

"Thanks. But it's fine. I don't really think there's much I can contribute to the zine anyway."

Tori frowned. "Since when? Why not? What about the fashion stuff?"

"Tori, I don't know anything about fashion. I thrift half my clothes and I know I'm not chic or anything. I wear Birkenstocks and I make earrings out of paper clips."

"It doesn't matter what you wear, it's how you wear it. Just contribute, it's all cool. You'll end up breaking your leg here or something. Leave the Tony Hawk wannabes." Tori crossed her arms.

"I'm allowed other friends besides you guys."

"Yeah, of course! I . . . I just don't want you to fall into anything, you know? Even *I* don't hang out with the Guys on a regular basis. They're crude and gross and annoying. And Dee . . . well, you know what we think of him. Us girls, we stick together. We're a unit. *Black Glitter* is not just something to pass the time. It's something to unite us. Cool, artsy, Black girl magic. That's what we are. There's an invisible chasm between us and the Guys, and we gotta keep it that way."

Naya narrowed her eyes. "I have nothing to contribute to it. The relationship column is *suuuper*hetero, for one. You talk about fuckboy this, fuckboy that, like it's only boys that girls are interested in."

"Well, why didn't you say something when we were brainstorming ideas?"

"I don't know. I didn't want to seem like I was splitting hairs. And I'm not trying to make this whole thing about me. Anyway, I'm still going to hang out with Dee and the Guys, and I hope you're okay with that."

"All right, but all I'm saying is that . . . Dee's temperamental. Things could get a bit messy, and I just want you to watch out for yourself."

"Dee doesn't pretend to understand me. He doesn't assume

anything about me, and he doesn't judge me. Maybe you should try to do the same for him?"

"God, Nai. I'm just trying to look out for you, that's all."

"Thanks, but I can look out for myself."

The girls walked back to the group, diverging as Tori joined a conversation with Tyler and Levi, and Naya sat and watched Dee and Ash skating. Naya kept Tori's words to herself. They were harsh, ominous at worst. This was the blank slate painting itself, the past coming into play. The question became whether the past was more important than the present, than the future. Whether the past was a warning, a premonition, a prophetic memorandum. Naya was to figure this out on her own.

◆

"The Girls don't like you that much. You know that, right?" Naya said to Dee as they sat in the garden at Salvation Hill a few days later, eating their lunches. One of the residents was getting into a heated altercation with the staff near the gazebo, though the pair couldn't hear the subject matter from their distance.

"I only know them because of Tyler. I don't give a fuck what they think about me," Dee responded after an exasperated sigh. Though the Guys didn't really mind Naya, the Girls minded him, and she thought that the reasoning behind their distaste didn't hold that true. To her, he was the opposite of how they said he was.

"I don't know. I mean, they spend time talking shit about *everyone*. But . . . I don't know how to act when they say things about you." *Because I don't hate you like I should*, she wanted to say. *I don't mind you at all.*

"What do they say?" Dee asked, but Naya kept quiet. "Seriously. What do they say about me?"

"They mainly talk about your ex, stuff like that."

Dee sighed. "Jesus. That was literally two months ago. Don't they have anything more recent to talk about?"

"Well, Evie's gotten pretty close to Vanessa since she joined jazz band, and apparently they're always talking about you. Evie relays the information to Tori, Jas, and Amber."

"Vanessa's always talking about me?" His face softened. But he didn't look hopeful; he looked sad, like the past eight weeks he'd spent trying to shake the thought of her had almost worked, but not quite.

"Yeah. I gather. But she's seeing someone. Evie mentioned it the other day. Some . . . guy named Pearce."

Dee didn't say anything. He just poked and prodded at his sandwich like it was a foreign specimen. Naya suddenly felt bad, like she had just pulled out all the stitches in his wounds. She told herself that this stuff didn't matter, but it did, because it still bothered him, and for as long as he was still bothered, it mattered. She knew she couldn't do much to help, being suspended in the middle of him and her friends, but she wanted to reassure him that she was someone he could trust, even when she gave the time of day to people who he couldn't count on in the same way.

"You know, I never cheated on her." Dee scratched his neck. "I just know I didn't. I couldn't prove otherwise, though. That was the problem. I couldn't prove anything, so I was screwed the second the news came out." He shrugged. Not once did he look up at Naya. "Now she's dating *Pearce Wilson*, top-tier douchebag. Fuck. It's funny how some things happen, right?"

"I don't know if it's that serious." Naya tried diluting the tension in the air. "I think it was probably one date. I wouldn't worry too much."

"Do I look worried to you?" he snapped. He didn't—he looked restless, though. Like something was hounding him underneath his skull, tugging at the base of his ribs. She had turned a bad switch on, and she knew it.

"I'm sorry. I shouldn't have brought it up," she said quietly. The one way to tell how stressed Dee was was to watch him throw a knee-jerk rebuttal at the proclamation of his shifted mood.

Dee could never truly admit to being tormented by anything. He didn't need the scrutiny that came along with it—though it appeared now that there was more scrutiny from his efforts to hide his pain. His feelings were leaking through, and Dee was afraid that the truth would, also.

◆

Lady on a Stretcher
by V.M. Winslow

The lady lies on a cold iron stretcher:
She can't move.
Her wrists are tied to the sides,
her ankles anchored down.

She keeps her eyes closed
but water still seeps out, like a broken faucet,
a leaking pipe,
a chest full of turmoil and unrest,
coughing and spluttering, a guttural cry

unleashes from her sandpaper throat.
She wants to go home.

She is naked, no clothes, no nothing.
She wants to go home.

The lady on the stretcher stares up
to a strong light,
one that envelopes her in incandescence,
exposes her to those
who she wishes to hide from.

She lies in a room.
Men with suits write notes on clipboards,
speak in hushed tones
into each other's ears, never to her.
She wants to go home.

They'll cut out her brain,
pump her veins with something
that will eventually cease her humanity,
her livelihood, her ability to feel something.
She wants to go home.

The lady on the stretcher cannot move,
she is an experiment,
she does not know what the hypothesis is,
what the results will be,
she is purely the process,
the middle part,

the question mark,
the ellipsis,

she wishes to be a full stop,
or an exclamation mark,
she wants to be an answer.
She wants to go home.

10

WHITE DRESS

"What was the name of that one?" Marie asked Dee, drinking an iced tea on a chair out on the grass. An hour had passed since lunch, and Naya was lounging by the water fountain speaking to Lionel, one of the residents. He had just recently been admitted after his daughter moved out of state and couldn't take him with her. He didn't have any mental ailments and was extremely invigorating to speak to. He did, however, use a wheelchair. He had been a paraplegic since a car accident in his forties.

"It's called 'The White Dress.'" Dee closed the poetry book up after reading out the last verse.

"By whom?"

"A writer called Violet Winslow."

"Oh. My former self! Gorgeous. A little somber, though, don't you think, Will?"

Dee smiled. "Yeah. A little. Do you want something happier?"

"No, I'm good for now. I think I can read something on my own. Is *Wuthering Heights* still on my bookshelf?"

"I don't know. I'll check."

"No. Wait. I can read it later. Tell me a story. One of your own, not something you've read."

"I don't have any."

"We all have stories. Every single one of us! I could go on and on about mine, but I don't want to wrangle the spotlight into my hands. Take the stage. Tell me something."

Dee scratched his neck, looking around. He caught sight of Naya, laughing and joking with Lionel. "I really have nothing to say."

"Have you not lived a life before today?"

Dee shrugged. "Yeah, I have. Just nothing interesting."

"There is significance in life. There are stories in our breaths, on the tips of our tongues, always." She paused. "I'll give you the time to find yours."

For Dee, creating a story meant walking back through the past, and that was not something he wanted to do anytime soon. It was onward and upward; he'd wait until he had a better story to tell. Until then, he couldn't think of anything to say that wouldn't hurt if it escaped his throat.

◆

After the shift, Dee decided to do something he hadn't done in a long time: drive down to the desert outside of town. Instead of turning back into Harlow, he took his pickup to the gas station and bought a bunch of snacks, with Naya waiting in the passenger seat. The late afternoon sun was boiling, and she had to wear extra sunscreen and switch from glasses to shades. Their lunchtime conversation had shrunken into silence, leaving a throbbing awkwardness between them ever since. Naya knew better than to try and revive it at the time, and the pair went their separate ways until the end of the day. She wasn't expecting Dee's proposal to visit the desert, and she wondered if it was his way of showing her that he wasn't angry, at least not anymore. He was letting her into a sliver of a world he only ever kept to himself, after all.

"I didn't mean to snap earlier. I was being a douche. Sorry," Dee said a while later as they sat in the back of the pickup, parked on empty desert terrain. He blew out smoke from his cigarette, looking down at his feet.

Naya sat adjacent, knees tucked under her chin, looking out to where the fiery terrain met the cerulean sky. "It's cool. No worries."

"*Yeah*, worries. I'm better than that, I promise. I need to work on my attitude. My brother's antics rub off on me sometimes."

"Why? What's he like?"

"He's . . . something. He reminds me of our dad. Which isn't a good thing."

"For real?"

"Yup. He's just so unpredictable. He's got a drinking problem, but I don't think he really knows, or cares. Sometimes he's a big brother, and other times . . . I don't even know. We'll be cracking jokes, talking about sports, or music, you know. Next thing you know, we're fighting. He just turns into this huge asshole, and you never see it coming."

"God. That doesn't sound ideal. How old is he?"

"Eight years older than me, but he acts like a thirteen-year-old playing Xbox. He's just this classic small-town guy who can't see outside his bubble of small-town friends."

Naya sighed. "On the bright side, at least he's young. That gives you a little freedom, right? My parents are in their late fifties. They're so damn stiff-necked all the time. I still have a curfew, I have to tell them every single place I go. Back in my home-town, I'd have to go to church twice a week. Every summer I'd be sent off to work as a camp ambassador for eight weeks. It was fun hanging out with the kids, but everything else was *such* a drag. It might have all been a little more bearable if I had a sibling to suffer through it with."

"Trust me, having a sibling to go through shit with doesn't make that shit any better to handle."

"I guess you're right. I don't know where I was going with that point. It's just . . . I leave the house and I put on a face and I can't really vent to anyone about how toxic my parents can be. Nobody here is going to get it." She shrugged. Harlow wasn't as much of a hive mind as Ampleforth, but it came with its limitations; Naya had been able to relate to some of the kids in her previous com-munity who'd been raised with dogmatic beliefs, and they'd been able to release their pent-up frustrations together. Naya couldn't do the same thing in Harlow, and she didn't want to risk throwing her parents under the bus by ranting about them to people who just wouldn't understand.

"Hmm. It seems like everyone's families have their shit together here," Dee responded. "Like, okay, congrats, your par-ents are still together and they have stable jobs. Good for you." He told her about the spring formal last year, when Vanessa held a pre-formal reception at her house, inviting a handful of predominantly Smithson-based classmates and their parents for professional photos on her one-square-acre estate. When he'd gone inside to pee, he'd overheard Rebecca Bowman, Izzy Phillips, and Erica Brooks speculating about his mother behind the bathroom door.

Why'd he bring his sister?

That's his mom, dumbass. She had him when she was young, now she's a single mom. That's gotta suck.

Well, that explains a lot.

And then they'd laughed. To say that the looks on their faces when they opened the door to find him standing there were priceless would have been an understatement. "Nobody knows shit about my mom," he continued. "She broke her back for me. She ran a store by herself. Just because the Smithson kids' parents are on seventy thousand a year each, working for hedge funds, doesn't mean jack."

Naya sighed, looking at him. "I'm sorry. People suck. Nobody actually takes the time to assess things, you know? Everyone thinks they know everything. I don't think I'm Einstein, but I don't think you need to be Einstein to show a little bit of emotional intelligence."

"Right. It's like, don't judge a book by its cover, all that."

"Exactly. Something a lot of people here have trouble doing. But hey, at least I'm not in my hometown anymore."

"Why did you move?" he asked her.

After a pause, Naya said, "My parents would say it's because we needed a change of scenery and a better school for me to attend before college. That's not the truth, though. I just know it isn't."

"Oh. What's the truth, then?"

"We were kind of driven out."

"Shit. Really? How?"

Naya's heart started beating faster at the realization that she had not yet disclosed this to anyone since moving to Harlow. She took a deep breath, deciding that maybe now was the time. "So . . . I had a best friend at church. Since we were, like, twelve years old. Her parents were *suuuper*religious, even more strict than mine. Everybody's so close-knit in Ampleforth, just all up in each other's business. When I realized I had a crush on my best friend, and she realized she liked me, too, her parents found out somehow. I don't know how, but they did, and they made sure everybody else in Ampleforth knew. It came around to my parents, and it was pretty much game over for us." Naya refrained from telling him of Haley's fate—how she was sent off to a treatment center after relapsing from an eating disorder, and she'd never heard from her thereafter. It was a sequence of events she couldn't help but feel responsible for. It was a guilt she had not yet reckoned with, and she wasn't sure if she was ready to.

"Holy fuck. That's brutal. So, what, your parents just dipped?"

"I mean, it wasn't that quick. We just stopped getting invited to events, people at church stopped speaking to us, and Haley's family—that's her name, by the way—they kind of framed it like she was easily influenced, and she didn't really know what she wanted; I just confused her. All because I didn't hide once it all came out. I kept my head held high, and it pissed *a lot* of people off." She looked down at her lime-painted nails, twiddling them. A soft breeze picked up as the sun crept lower in the sky. "I think my parents realized that Ampleforth was just too hostile. It was one thing having everyone think their daughter was weird, but it was a whole other thing to have this other family wage a war on them, throw dirt on their name, all of that. Just because I admitted I liked a girl."

"Whoa. That's insanity. It's like something from a book. Shit, Naya, that's rough. Were your parents upset with you? When you came out?" Dee asked.

"Um . . . they've avoided it. When I told them I thought I might be bi, they shrugged it off, told me that I'd eventually find the boy I want to marry. Just because they met when they were kids and got married straight out of high school doesn't mean that's normal, that that's how you're supposed to live life. They only see Haley as my friend, to this day. It hurts. They were probably so embarrassed by me. So much so that we had to leave state, just to save face."

"Fuck that. They weren't embarrassed. Sounds like they were trying to protect you, I don't know. They just seem stuck in their ways. You know, like my brother. They just don't know how to act." He thought about how lost he had felt in his world lately, and how he sometimes wished for peace of mind—a clean home without an overflowing trash can or disheveled front lawn would be a start. He looked at Naya and realized that she was paralyzed by that too. She was aberrant and zany, didn't connect strongly with the Girls, and was constantly under surveillance by her parents. She was a prisoner to the norm, to the regular, and she tried so hard not to be. He yearned for something normal; she yearned for the opposite.

"Oh well. Shall we change the topic? Something less of a downer?" Naya asked.

"Good idea. That reminds me, actually—I read a poem to Marie today called 'The White Dress.' It's a bit of a stretch, but I feel like it could help us create the third theory."

"Oh really? Hit me."

"It's probably the most simple. She wanted to get away and start fresh. She was frustrated with her life and the person she was, so she decided to start again under a new name, in a new place."

"Well, that was boring."

"Oh, sorry. Didn't realize we could only run with *X-Files* or CIA shit."

"Shut up." She punched him lightly on the shoulder. "It's a plausible theory. Just boring. Come on, you know it is."

"It is the most plausible."

"But everything she remembers and seems to treasure is everything that happened before she went missing."

"Yet she prefers to be called Marie, and not Violet."

"So?"

"She remembers nothing of her new life but her new name. It all ties down to her identity. She's aware of her past self, but she holds onto her present self. I don't mean the last forty years, but more so her *current* self. She remembers the person she chose to be, and she is that person. She's Marie, with Violet's memories. The transition between the two selves doesn't matter."

"You're so much more profound than you let on, Dee. You know that?"

"I *told* you I was selectively passionate."

◆

White Dress
by V.M. Winslow

I iron out all the kinks and the crumples

in my pretty white dress,
over and over again.

But whenever I wear it,
the moment I move,
the moment I breathe,
I see the fabric
fold and crease and squeeze itself around my skin,
like it is my skin,
and I can't breathe.

So I take off the white dress,
I hang out the sheer cotton,
I let it blow
out in the breeze.

I wash it a million times,
I'll get the iron out again,
I'll straighten out the crooked hem,
stretch out the material
so it fits a little looser,
so it doesn't strangle me alive.

See, I love this white dress,
but it keeps getting stained.
It never fits quite right,
I need to keep washing it,
starting it anew,
straightening it out,
stretching it as far as it can go.

Sometimes I try to wear it differently,
roll the sleeves up,
leave a button undone.
But when I look in the mirror,
it is still me wearing it.

Still Violet, I'm still Violet,
I'm still Violet,
I'm still Violet.

11

JUDGMENT DAY

When Naya's parents decided to move to Harlow, they wanted to find a community bigger than Ampleforth, something that seemed like less of a unified consciousness, for the sake of their daughter, and for the sake of their God. They wanted an extension of their previous world, something with larger walls and open arms, wider than the doors that their former fellow churchgoers had swung closed in their faces. They found Harlow's Evangelical Community Center, situated north of Smithson, bustling with suburban families who could afford to contribute a considerable chunk of their wages to the church's collection plate. The HECC (an ironic nickname, considering it's also a euphemism for the place where sinners would reside at the end of time) was a big flashy building, newly renovated and modernized for the twenty-first century.

It boasted youth pastors straight out of college and PhD students in theology teaching Bible study classes midweek, plus choirs for high school students doing biblical covers of *Billboard* Hot 100s—sometimes acoustic, sometimes with a fully fledged band. On special occasions, the HECC would throw concerts and invite musicians from outside the community to participate. One of Vanessa's first performances in her jazz band had been at the HECC in eighth grade, when she'd had to perform a blues rendition of "Amazing Grace" for a Christmas gig. This church definitely had a warmer feel to it than Naya's previous one, and she was more hopeful—she hadn't dreaded stepping through its front doors. But at the end of the day, churches were still churches, and even if the music sounded better and the preachers were cooler, every church had a ceiling, an unsurpassable limit. When Naya left her first church service at the HECC in the throes of a panic attack, her parents understood that it was probably still too soon. They coaxed and wheedled when they could, but until the memories of Ampleforth were singed from the neural connections in her brain, there was no turning back.

◊

During their desert stop, Naya had invited Dee over for dinner at her house, citing her mother's pristine cooking as an incentive. She lived on the other side of New Eden, in the direction of central Harlow, which meant Dee had to take a bit of a detour into town in order to pick her up for volunteering, only to drive back out again. It would have made more sense for her to walk down to his place so they could go on from there, but he had insisted from day one that she needn't bother. There was no strain in the act. In reality, he didn't want Naya to have anything to do with his world, or at least his home. Yet here he was the following evening, entering hers.

When he knocked on Naya's front door, he was hit with a floral scent in the air. Her house's layout was similar to his, being in the same neighborhood, but the contrast was disorienting; it was like he was stepping into a pastel-colored dream. Naya's mother opened the door for Dee, and as he entered her front hall, he saw that Naya was standing at the bottom of the stairs, beaming. He introduced himself to her mother, straightening his posture and smiling, then glanced down at his outfit: an unbuttoned blue flannel shirt over a white T-shirt. He had thought long and hard about what to wear, whether to go formal and do up all the buttons, or whether not to wear the shirt over the T-shirt at all. He had paced around his room, trying on different pants until he'd convinced himself he was caring too much.

"How're you doing, Dee?" Naya's mother smiled. "We've heard a *lot* about you."

"I'm good. Nice to meet you, Mrs. Stephens."

"No, no. None of that here. It's Rachel. This is my husband, Terrell," she said, leading Dee into the living room. They had a dining table situated where Dee's mother's coffee table would be. Naya's father approached Dee, introducing himself, then shaking his hand. Naya trailed behind them, catching up with Dee and standing beside him. The smell of dinner suffused the air—something zesty and piquant. At every angle, Dee's eyes were met with a framed family photo or some sort of religious décor. Above the central mantelpiece was a framed quote: "If not God, then who?" *Why anyone at all?* Dee thought.

"So how is this volunteering program going for y'all?" Naya's mother asked, hovering around the table, dishing out a selection of Southern specialties: mac and cheese with collard greens, sweet potatoes, fried chicken and grits . . . It was enough to keep one satiated for the remainder of the summer. Since Dylan had moved in, takeout food had become the default at Dee's house. He'd often wake up feeling the fried chicken or pizza grease in his bones, yet somehow his stomach would still always be hollow. The sight of the meal in front of him made him dizzy with hunger.

"It's going great, Mom," Naya answered, realizing Dee was mentally preoccupied, watching the steam rising from the food like it was a magic trick. "We're having so much fun with the residents there."

"Uh, yeah. It's awesome." Dee looked up, swallowing. "There's this old lady there. She's supermysterious. We're trying to figure out stuff about her life, 'cause she has dementia and all."

"So I've heard," Naya's mother responded, sitting down next to her father. "She sounds like a wonder. What do you think, Terrell? Is this Marie lady full of secrets?" Dee could tell straightaway that in this house, Naya's mother was the talker, just like his mother. He thought back to the first time he'd invited Vanessa over to his house, how nervous he'd been because of his mother's tendency to overshare. She'd only ever do it to fill up space in the silence, cracking crude jokes or breaking the ice by unveiling Dee's endearing interior.

"Well, only God knows what happened to that lady, bless her. I think it's definitely a fun way to spend your time," her father said. "Even if you're just making one community member's day a whole lot better, it goes a long way."

"It does. It really does. One moment. Shall we say grace?" her mother said. Before he could even register the moment, Naya grabbed Dee's right hand and held it over the table. He looked at her mother, who held her right hand palm-up, and was unsure if he had to hold her hand for the four of them to create some sort of hand-holding circle. But her mother was already reciting poetic verse, praying without effort and with passion. Everyone's eyes were crammed shut, except for Dee's. *Imagine if God appeared when people had their eyes closed*, he thought to himself. *Then he disappeared when they opened them again. What if he only existed when you blinked? Maybe that's where we've gone wrong.* Though the thought tickled him, as he peeped at Naya's facial expression—closed eyelids and straight, stoic posture—he sobered himself. She was wearing a pastel-pink tank top, one that seemed to blend into her skin. The marvelous glass chandelier suspended above them sent shards of sharp light through the crystal prisms in all different directions, one of which landed on her collarbone. His eyes bounced around the space between her lips and her chest, but nowhere lower or higher. The piece of light was the only thing he could focus on, even once the prayer was over. It took the sudden animation of everyone at the table to snap him back to the now.

"Is this your first time volunteering?" Naya's mother asked once they were digging into their meals, passing around the salt, pepper, and gravy.

"Yeah, it's my first, actually. I think I messed up some of my finals, so I need some redemption."

"Well, that's great. Do you have any plans after high school? I know it's time to start thinking about that kind of stuff, isn't it?"

"I don't know." He shrugged, biting into a forkful of food. "I enjoy math. I'm thinking of computer science. Then I can just hustle my way to Silicon Valley or something," he semi-joked. Tech was one of the few industries he appreciated for its lack of white collars; it didn't require people to dress up in suits just to make calls and negotiate deals. He could head into work in a T-shirt and jeans, and it would have no bearing on his chances of becoming a millionaire. He didn't know if being a millionaire was what he wanted, either, but he hadn't completely rejected the idea. Being the kid who could have added up all of his suspensions into his own seasonal vacation, his dreams weren't quite at the echelon of the likes of Elon Musk, but he at least wanted the option of making it big. So computer science was a good enough place to start.

"Comp-sci? That's pretty cool," Naya responded. "All I can think of are hackers, though. You know the ones? With the cool shades who go, 'I'm in!' after typing some code into a computer?" She giggled.

"Something like that." Dee smirked. "I've got to learn how to code first. It's baby steps."

"Baby steps to technological dominion. Robots are gonna take over eventually."

"Only if you teach them how," Dee said.

Naya's mother spoke. "Naya has such a creative imagination. Always envisioning these apocalyptic scenarios."

"It's true," her father added. "You used to be so convinced you knew when Judgment Day was. Like the ancient Mayans. Hiding under tables before the earthquakes began." He chuckled, shaking his head.

Naya blushed. "*Stop*. I grew out of that. After all, nobody knows when Judgment Day is."

"You gotta live like every day is the last day on earth," her father responded. "Then there's no need to predict anything."

"Great. Are there any more grits left?" Naya asked.

"There's some more in the kitchen, Yaya," her mother responded. "Dee. Are you religious, at all?" Before Naya could stand up to go and fetch seconds, she froze, cringing. *Here we go*.

"Uh . . . not really." Dee didn't know if it was a trick question, but he wasn't going to lie to God-fearing individuals. Well, he wasn't going to lie to Naya's parents.

"You'd be surprised," Naya's mother said. "God works in a multitude of ways. He's probably touched you without your noticing."

He can keep his hands to himself, Dee thought, before saying, "My family never really practiced religion. Nothing that I can remember, anyway. My mother was more of the spiritual type."

"I see. Well, spiritualism is often a stepping stone to understanding the Divine." As Naya's mother spoke, her father nodded in concurrence, chewing his food silently as his eyes flitted between his wife and his daughter's guest.

"Is the Divine a hairy white guy?" Dee pointed to a framed photo of Jesus, in an attempt at a joke. Naya's parents started laughing, and Naya followed suit, trying to conceal the pained embarrassment bubbling its way through her.

"Don't worry. We know that there's been a Western influence. But his physical image has always been the least of our concerns. He exists everywhere at once. There is no image of God. Just an image of his likeness, which we should all strive toward." Naya's mother smiled. Naya wanted to scream, but she held her voice back like it was a hay fever sneeze in the spring.

"I just don't believe in God," Dee responded truthfully. "I don't mean to offend you. I just don't. No matter how hard I try. And to be honest, the thought of an afterlife seems exhausting to me. I can barely prepare myself for next week, let alone heaven or hell."

"The wonders of living in a pluralistic world!" Naya chimed in sharply. "We don't all live our lives in the same way. Some people are Christian, some people aren't. Some are Muslim or Buddhist. Some people believe in marriage, some don't. Some people are straight, some are gay. It's interesting how free will works, isn't it? People can all come to their own decisions on what they value."

"We know, Naya. We get that," her mother said tersely, but with enough softness in her voice to butter the friction.

"Oh, you do? Cool! I'm glad we're all on the same page." Naya stood up, immediately clearing the empty plates. Dee's shirt suddenly felt too warm, and he wanted to take it off. Instead, he rolled up the sleeves and followed Naya into the kitchen. She started rinsing the plates in a hasty fashion, and Dee could tell that she was on edge.

"Do you need any help?"

"No, I'm fine. I'm just gonna throw them into the dishwasher anyway."

"Y'all got a dishwasher? Dang. Living in the lap of luxury." He grinned, leaning over the kitchen counter behind her. When she didn't respond, he stripped his smile away. The sound of dishes, forks, and knives clanking and sliding across the marble worktop conjured up metal clashing in a sword fight. Dee stood silently, toying with the ends of his hair, until she finally slammed the dishwasher closed. She had beads of perspiration on her forehead, and she wiped them away with the back of her hand. In the sudden, real silence that ensued, the pair could hear a muffled disagreement coming from the living room where her parents still were.

"I need to pee," Dee said.

"It's your lucky day. Follow me," Naya responded. She led him to the hallway upstairs before turning in to her own room. All she could think of was her mother's incessant attempts at conversion. How her father always seemed to go along with it, even if he probably thought it was excessive. After her panic attack leaving the HECC, she'd overheard her parents diverging from one another—her mother treating church like the cure to her anxiety, and her father treating it like the trigger it really was. It was he who'd initially suggested they move out of Ampleforth, and it was her mother who'd only agreed on the condition that they find a new church community to settle into. That was their compromise, yet somehow it still left Naya out. Salvation Hill was the chess move that Naya had agreed to in order to appease her household, but the game would never be over until her mother had the last word. Until her mother could convince her that everything she said or did came from a place of love, as her husband stuck by her loyally. They were an army of two with a clear commander in chief. Naya could not breathe around them.

"Are you good?"

"Shit. You scared me." Naya jumped, looking up at Dee from her bed. He was standing at her bedroom door, silhouetted against the hallway light.

"It's dark in here. If you're tired, just say so. I can go home."

"No. No. It's fine. I'm just . . . trying to calm down. Did my parents freak you out? I feel like they did. I really was hoping they'd cut the Jesus stuff out for once."

"No, they didn't. I think I was kinda rude to them, actually. Sorry about that. That food was so fucking *good*, by the way."

Naya almost smiled. "I didn't really want to do the volunteer program, you know. I just accepted that I was not gonna have a life all summer, like my other summers. I signed up because I accepted defeat. How shitty is that?"

"It's not shitty. It doesn't matter why you're doing it. I'm doing it because I'm a jackass who is pretty close to throwing my future into the trash. It's whatever, though. We're in it now. We've been doing it for a month. We have six weeks to go. Let's keep having fun with it."

"How can I have fun when I'm doing this all to keep people off my back?" she said, quickly wiping away tears.

Dee entered the room and closed the door behind him. "It's okay. You don't have to cry." He stood awkwardly, scratching the back of his neck. "It's still fun, though, right? Coming up with theories."

"It's stupid," she whimpered. "There's no point. We'll never find out the truth."

"It was *your* idea. Something to make time fly, remember? It doesn't matter if we'll never know the truth. We're not detectives."

"Whatever," she mumbled. "The highlight of my summer is reading poems to an old lady. Nothing's going to change that."

Dee hesitated for a moment before walking to Naya's bed and sitting next to her. He then wrapped an arm around her shoulder consolingly. They sat in silence for a minute before Naya rose. She took his hand and pulled him up with her, embracing him where they stood. When she let him go, he had a diffident smile on his face. His eyes bounced from hers to the floor. "Is there any food left? I wanna take some home with me."

"My mom always makes more than she needs to. I'll throw it in a container for you."

"Thanks. You're a lifesaver, Naya. Seriously, you are."

"You're welcome."

"I'm really glad I stayed in the office that day."

"I'm glad you did too."

♦

Dee arrived home to an empty house, finding beer bottles strewn across the living room floor. He sighed, walking into the kitchen to put Naya's food in the fridge. Then he paced around the room, suddenly feeling antsy. The silence was sometimes hard to bear. The contrast between this new quiet and the old reality— when the muffled sounds of *Tango in the Night*, *Back to Black*, *Matters of the Heart*, *Stranger in the Alps*, and all the other albums his mother loved would emanate from her room in the warm evenings—created a void that left the house feeling like an isolation tank. But there was no solace in the quietude, in the gentle hum of the air conditioning, or the heightened sounds of the outside world. There was only the reminder that he was truly alone.

He picked up a half-smoked joint from the coffee table in the living room and switched the television on. He went to the DVD rack, where one film stood out to him. When he was thirteen, his mother had borrowed *Her* from a friend and never got around to returning it. He'd walked in on her watching it one night on her thirtieth birthday, bawling her eyes out. She was never much of a crier, but she had unleashed an uncontrollable torrent of tears that night, all the while assuring him that she was okay, that she just loved the film so much it made her heart hurt. It made her feel lonely, but she knew deep down she would never truly be alone, as long as she had him. Dee had never felt compelled to watch the film himself, finding the premise ridiculous and the pacing sluggish. But four years later, he decided to give it a try. And like a cycle repeating, Dee found himself crying toward the end. He was hopelessly in pain, hearing his mother's voice in Samantha's. Wishing everything was different, wishing he had experienced the film with her when she was still alive. The isolation Theodore felt resonated with him; that idea of existing in a vast universe full of billions of conscious beings, but still feeling so stuck within oneself, so alone, hit him like a ton of bricks.

Later that evening, Dee lay in bed and put his earbuds in, trying to drown out the raucous noise coming from downstairs. "Solid Wall of Sound" by A Tribe Called Quest melted into his consciousness as he floated into a hypnagogic state. When his phone suddenly vibrated, he opened his eyes to find a text from Naya that instantly brought a smile to his face.

Thanks for today! You were a great guest. You're great at hugging too. We should do it more often. <3

12

A SCALE OF ONE TO TEN

The following day, Dee sat on Naya's living room floor wearing jogger shorts. His T-shirt was in a heap on the coffee table. Naya sat on the couch, weaving his hair into a French braid. He'd never been an adept hairstylist, and without any help, he wouldn't do much except tie it up or keep it down. His mother had been the best French braider, and almost every time she did his hair, she would burst into a story of how her father had her mother would care for his hair before ceremonies, tying it into a traditional bun, a *tsiiyééł*, after neatening it with a traditional brush, a *be'ezo*. She told him that every so often as a teen, she'd wash her and her sisters' hair with freshly harvested yucca root, keeping it soft and glossy. Once she'd opened her soap store, she'd take frequent trips back to the rez to collect root for shampoos to sell. Her shampoos became one of the most sought-after products in Harlow once people in the rez communities caught wind of them.

Naya's mother had taught her how to braid, telling her that it was important to look presentable at all times. She initially found it a drag, a confusing craft that took too much patience. But like learning to knit or sew, she eventually got the hang of it. She could give herself cornrows or box braids, style her hair in a plethora of ways, wake up feeling like a new person every day. She enjoyed the creation, the art, the beauty that hair held. It took a bit of convincing before Dee allowed her to be his ad hoc stylist on a day so hot he'd do anything to keep his hair from touching his skin.

"I should do this more often, don't you think?" Naya said. A rerun of *Everybody Hates Chris* was playing on the television, drowned out by the sound of the ceiling fan on full blast.

"It's cool. I don't need to be your hair model."

"Well, *I'm* the one doing *you* a favor."

"I'm forever indebted," Dee joked. He'd left the Guys and the Girls at No Man's Land, where they'd been participating in a water-balloon fight. He hadn't been in the mood to be pummeled by haphazard water balloons, instead lounging out of reach of his friends' targeted attacks. When Naya had texted him telling him that she had a free house, he was at her front door within ten minutes. They'd spent the early afternoon lounging in the heat and talking, and as Naya ran her fingers meticulously through his hair, she studied his shoulders, his temples, his back. She realized how odd she felt with him sitting between her legs, both sides of his naked torso touching her bare knees. There was an intimacy that she couldn't quite place, and she wasn't sure whether to savor it or run from it. She was stuck somewhere between comfort and butterflies in her stomach.

We're at NML, where U at? Amber texted her, twenty minutes after his arrival.

Both of them looked down at Naya's phone buzzing on the coffee table. On the television, a young Chris Rock had fainted from heatstroke because he'd finally saved up for a leather jacket and was determined to wear it even on the hottest day New York had seen in some time. It was like the heat was everywhere: in the TV screen, in the room, outside, in between Naya's fingers and Dee's hair. Naya stopped braiding and swiped her phone from the table to respond to Amber's text.

Chillin at home, she responded.

Getting bored. Can we come over? Ur parents home?

Who's we?

The Girls. Duh.

Naya paused, shifting around. Whether her instinct was rooted in selfishness or anxiety, she knew that she didn't want the Girls to crash the moment. She hesitated before responding, *Come over.*

"The Girls are on their way," she told Dee. "I'll finish up your hair real quick."

"You're the popular one now, I see."

"Not quite. I'm just lucky I can host for once without my mom and dad hovering around."

"Fair enough. This show's funny as hell," he said, looking at the television. "Damn. I wish I still had more channels at home."

"You can find it online somewhere, probably. Shall we do a marathon or something? We can start from the beginning. It'll be so fun!"

"We should smoke and watch it. It'll be ten times more fun."

"You know I don't smoke. You don't need drugs."

"I can't believe I'm offering you *free weed* and that's your response."

"White Jesus is watching my every move," Naya said.

"Let me know when he's not looking."

A few minutes later, Amber, Evie, and Jasmine waltzed into Naya's house. Tori, perpetually glued to Tyler's hip, was nowhere to be seen. It was rich, coming from the girl who seemed to side-eye Naya's involvement with any one of the other Guys.

"Well, look who it is! Our humanitarians of the year." Jasmine laughed, sucking on a raspberry-flavored Popsicle. Her lips were tinted pink, and her forehead was dotted with sweat beads. Amber and Evie sat on the couch adjacent to Naya and Dee.

"Cut it out, Jas." Naya stood up after Dee did, unsticking her tank top from her skin.

"Your hair looks nice." Jasmine stared at him, sucking on the Popsicle without breaking eye contact. "Did Nai charge you for her services?"

"Thanks. And . . . no. Just a friendly gesture," he said, grabbing his T-shirt and bundling it between his palms.

"How sweet of her," Jasmine responded, placing herself on the arm of the couch. "If only she offered to help us out the same way. I guess she already has a favorite. We get it, though. You've got a lot to work with."

"Naya, why didn't you tell us you can do hair? We can do a hair shoot for the zine," Amber said.

"I'm not an expert. It's no biggie, trust me."

"Clearly you are," Amber said, turning to Dee. "She's fixed you up supergood."

He stood awkwardly, thinking of an escape plan. This was probably the first time he'd ever been in the Girls' company without the guys. He didn't fool himself into thinking they didn't gossip about him just as much as the next person. The cogs were probably already whirring around in their heads, finding conclusions to leap to. It wasn't just the heat in the air that was suffocating.

"Thanks. I'm going to go home. See you guys later," he said, slinging his shirt over his shoulder and making his way past the Girls to the entrance of the house.

The second he was gone, the girls just looked at Naya. Jasmine started giggling, and Amber raised an eyebrow. Evie looked around the room, whistling.

"That was something to witness," Amber said, breaking the silence first.

"No, it wasn't," Naya said.

"Since when did you guys hang out alone? I thought it was at least with the Guys."

"It's not a huge deal. You make everything seem so scandalous. *Wow*, I have another friend who isn't any of y'all. Shoot me."

"He looked so damn fine just then." Jasmine smirked. "Nice lean body and all. You're lucky as hell."

"Stop being so damn thirsty." Amber grimaced. "I know I've made my mistakes in the past, but we really don't need to go there. Leave Tyler's friends alone."

"Chill out, Amber. We all have free will. Still find him intimidating, Naya?"

"He's my volunteer partner. So obviously not." Naya huffed. The heat had left her flustered, but she'd be lying if she thought that was the sole cause.

"Vanessa's one lucky bitch. Hell, even Karina. Who else? How long do you think the list is?" Jasmine said.

"Y'all are so gross." Naya sighed. Suddenly, she wished to become invisible, or have the seat below her open up and suck her into a lightless void. The butterflies in her stomach usually settled within moments, but now they roamed free, and they were everywhere.

"Are you crushing on him?" Jasmine asked, and Naya said no a little too quickly. "Not even a little, *teeny* crush?"

Naya was a terrible liar. The truth was in the blush on her cheeks. "It's been nice getting to know him. You know, at Salvation Hill and all. He's cute."

The Girls looked at each other, then at Naya. Jasmine squealed. "This is amazing. Please, Naya, when the time comes, you've got to give us your verdict."

"My verdict on what?"

"Don't let her answer that." Amber swooped in. "It's okay. Your secret is safe with me, Nai."

"I don't have a secret."

"Oh. So shall we tell him?" Evie asked.

"God. You're blowing this out of proportion. Get a hold of yourselves. Shall we work on *Black Glitter*? I can style y'all now if you want. Practice for a real shoot later or whatever."

"Aw, she's getting embarrassed," Evie said.

"Do you want to work on the zine or not?" Naya demanded.

"Okay, okay, we won't tell him." Jasmine sighed. "Just to be clear—that's not a promise. I'm not good at keeping secrets. Awful, actually. Sometimes I say shit without realizing. Anyway, let's get to work. Just cornrow me for now. Got a new wig waiting for me at home."

Naya thought Dee was cute, which was right. But somehow

in that moment, it was just as wrong. Now he was going to find out, and she didn't know how to feel about it. She was terrified, yet also intrigued. But she was terrified way more than intrigued. And it was the jittery feeling in the base of her stomach that kept her awake later that night. Then it was the lighting up of her phone at two in the morning with a text from Dee that read: *lol U got a crush on me?*

◆

"What did they tell you?" Naya said in his truck the next morning as they made their way to Salvation Hill. She hadn't responded to the text, but instead her heart had somersaulted into chaotic oblivion, and she'd tried to pretend he had no clue, like the way things were before that moment. But she knew he knew, and she lay restless all through the night.

"The Girls told me you like me." He smiled, keeping his eyes on the road.

"They took whatever I said out of context. And since when did you suddenly believe what the Girls say?"

"I never said I didn't believe them. I just said I didn't care. But this . . . this is interesting."

Naya wanted to vomit. "I told them I think you're cute, which is something I've told you before."

"You've never called me cute."

"Okay. I'm calling you cute. You happy now?"

"So you don't like me?"

"Of course I do!" She looked out of her window, pressing her forehead to the glass, wanting to throw herself from the vehicle at full speed. "You're my friend. Why wouldn't I like you?"

"Okay. So that's it, then. We'll close that chapter."

"Thank you." Naya sighed, turning the radio up to defuse the energy radiating between them. The bass of a rock song she didn't recognize vibrated along the chassis of the truck. She found herself listening hard, trying to follow the melody and forget where she was sitting and who she was sitting with. When Dee suddenly turned down the radio a few moments later, it was like a vacuum had sucked up the sound. Her heart jumped.

"So you *don't* have a crush on me? Just to make things crystal clear."

"No. I don't. I'm running off no sleep. It's too hot and my tired ass isn't in the mood for this."

"Oh, okay. So you were awake when I texted you last night. You just didn't want to respond."

"The world doesn't revolve around you."

"Shit. You're right. What a bummer. On a scale of one to ten, how cute do you think I am?"

"You're killing me right now."

"Seven? Nine?"

"Dee."

"Eleven? Off the scale?" Instead of answering, Naya shot the volume up on the radio again. She rolled down her window, trying to cool off. When Dee turned the radio down again, she sighed.

"Come on, Nai. I wanna know." He laughed. Hurriedly, she took out her phone, searching the time and distance between where they currently were and where they were headed. Then she turned to face him.

"Can you stop the truck? I think I can walk from here."

"What?"

"I'm speaking English, aren't I?"

"Whoa. You're not serious."

"Screw you, Dee." This was the first time he had seen her so irked, in fact. He started to feel bad for teasing her. If the rumor was true, it was unfair to poke fun. She'd done nothing but be nice to him. He pulled over to the side of the road.

"I'm sorry. Don't walk, that's stupid. There's rattlesnakes and shit. And it's hot. *Very* hot. We're only five minutes away."

"I have sunscreen and I'm a fast walker."

"You got antivenom too?"

"I'd rather risk it."

"You're not leaving the truck, Nai."

"You're not telling me what to do," she retorted, whipping the door open and landing on the dusty soil, stomping away indignantly. The second she closed the door behind her, Dee put his truck into the lowest gear and started crawling forward at her pace. This lasted for another minute before Naya stopped walking. "Fuck off and let me walk!"

"Get in, Naya."

"I said no."

"I guess we're both just gonna stay stuck out here, then," Dee responded nonchalantly, leaning back in his seat. They both stayed unmoving, stubborn in their declarations. It was just a question of who would move first, and where they would go. Dee looked at the time, realizing that they were going to be late. He regretted bringing up what the Girls had said, but there was no turning back from that. He was surprised, not only at the revelation, but at her response. He'd assumed she'd burst out laughing, telling him how dramatic the Girls were, but she hadn't. He parked the truck on the side of the road again, a few feet ahead of Naya, and then hopped out. "Let's walk together, then."

"Stop playing."

"I'm not. I don't care if this shit gets stolen."

"So you're willing to risk losing your main source of transport for . . . what?"

"My brother works at a garage. He'll just give me some other piece of shit car, or he'll actually get around to fixing mine. I don't care. Let's go."

Naya stared at him, arms crossed. She could feel her heart galloping. She looked at the ground, kicking sand. By the time she looked back up, Dee was right in front of her, grabbing her arm softly, pulling her along. Like a deflated balloon, she followed him passively. The sun was burning down on everything, lighting everything up, leaving everything exposed. There was nowhere for her to hide. When they reached the truck, she yanked her arm away and jumped back into the passenger seat.

"So you're good to ride, then?" Dee smiled, walking around the front and getting into the driver's seat.

"Shut up and get moving," Naya said.

13

MAYBE DEFINITELY

Tyler and Amber's father, Rory Harper, was a well-known African-American saxophonist from New Orleans who'd relocated to Harlow before the twins were born, setting up a music venue downtown, The Jive, that housed an array of different bands most weekends. Vanessa had been the newbie jazz drummer in the school band back when Dee first started talking to her. He'd met her when she was handing out flyers to her ensemble's first off-campus gig, an event at The Jive; though it was usually an adult venue, they had managed to book the stage for this all-ages show, so high school bands could perform and then the teens in the audience could stick around and watch an array of different old-school adult bands from around town.

Dee almost didn't attend, but he got free entry through knowing the owner, so he thought, *Why not?* And he was infatuated from the second Vanessa stumbled into a ragtime solo when it was her time to shine. She had been drumming ever since she was twelve, but only really got into it once she started freshman year, and she was such a natural. There was solace in her expression, yet partnered with a passion that closed her off from anyone else in the room. But once the song was over and the audience applauded, she looked out into the crowd with enthusiasm and hope that *that one boy* she'd invited had come to see her. Vanessa was just as excited as Dee for them to be in the same room together, for him to witness her as she witnessed him, and he knew he had a crush on her without having to think it through. It was not to say that things weren't difficult at first—mixed signals flashed like faulty traffic lights—but he just knew that he couldn't get Vanessa Bailey out of his head, no matter how hard he fought it. She invaded his psyche, his blood, his bones; she was ubiquitous, omnipresent, within and without. That's how he knew. She was everywhere; she was the universe.

Naya wasn't quite the same. She was a mist in the distance, crawling, moving ever closer, never quite there, but there was this anticipation, this expectation that he'd be cloaked in her presence and wouldn't be able to shake it off, and it was almost always there. It was a slow burn, a maybe. A Maybe. But sometimes the Maybe could hold more power than the Definitely; it hung suspended above him, either to blow away in the wind or fall down on him like rain, and he wasn't sure which. Now that she'd said she liked him, things were getting clearer. Naya was a Maybe, but there was something detrimental about it. He liked her, and he didn't know it. He couldn't hold it down, anchor it to the ground like he could hold down his feelings for his first-ever real love.

The best way he could pay Naya back for making a fool out of her was to invite her on a trip downtown to shop and prepare for the big Fourth of July party that Salvation Hill was holding the next day. It wasn't on one of their usual days, but it meant that they had one regular day of the week off. His plan was to celebrate with Naya, Marie, and the other residents in the daytime, then go to Levi Evans' Independence Day bash later that night and get shit-faced. But he had to look decent for both occasions, so with a little financial help from his brother, he headed out to the Harlow shopping mall with Naya, and they wandered through the stores semi-aimlessly, trying to kill time and keep each other occupied.

In the apex of summer, Central Harlow was bustling with shoppers and tourists, most of whom wanted to break the bank in the glossy designer district. Rows of stores like Prada, Gucci, Saint Laurent, Rolex, De Beers, and Tiffany's formed an invisible barrier between the Harlow residents who could afford them and those who couldn't. Dee never really ventured into town unless he was planning on getting chased down by the security guards enforcing the ban on skating and other wheel-based activities on the grounds of the plaza, adjacent to the designer district.

His favorite chunk of Central was dedicated to the indie strip, where the local shops were situated: the family-owned restaurants, the secondhand thrift shops, the music stores that had existed longer than he had. It was the delicate part of Harlow, disposable in the grander scheme of things. When his mother had got a license to open up her store there six years back, at first the money came raining in quickly. But as each year came and went, and the designer district got bigger, so did the development of branches of hotels and restaurants, ones that you could find anywhere else in America. Soon his mother was in competition with the likes of Lush, The Body Shop, and other notable skincare stores. In the last few years she had been straining to bring in new customers that couldn't see her store hidden cozily from the tourist parts of town, and instead had garnered a flux of fellow Indigenous people driving down from neighboring reservations to cash in on authenticity. Nobody could find a store like Yiska outside of Harlow, and nobody ever would again.

When Dee and Naya walked past the empty store, he looked up and noticed that the rustic sign was gone. A lump built up in his chest and he walked on. They went into a thrift store, where Naya set her sights on a mint-green ditsy floral smock dress with short, ruffled sleeves. She found a bright-blue oversized Hawaiian shirt and placed it in Dee's hands.

"You should wear this at the Fourth of July party."

"What if I don't want to?" he responded.

"Oh yeah. I forgot—you don't want to lose the monochrome. Color is just *too uncool* for you."

"This shit is ugly."

Naya took it from him and quickly unbuttoned it, shaking it in front of him. "Try it on first."

"Sheesh. Fine." They walked to the nearest mirror, where he threw it over his T-shirt and stared at himself. "Disgusting."

"Beautiful." Naya smiled. "You're going to wear it. I'm your stylist now."

He glared at her. "Fine."

"Yay! Let's go pay and check out some CDs across the street."

"I'm so fucking whipped right now," he muttered.

"You've been whipped since you didn't leave Mr. Walters' office that day when you could have."

"You're gonna hold that over my head forever, aren't you?"

"Damn right."

A few minutes later, the pair walked into Moozik, Dee's favorite record store in town. He found the cow print interior and decor cheesy, but he was always sure to find what he wanted at a steal of a price. He beelined to the vinyl section, hoping to find the album he was looking for. After taking a thorough scour, he gave up, going to see if it was with the CDs instead. Naya followed him around, curious to find out what he was dying to buy. When he found it, his eyes lit up. He pulled out a CD with a blue cover showing the silhouettes of two faces turned toward each other in profile. The faces were plain white cross sections, sliced in half to reveal a burst of blues and browns branching out from where their brains and respiratory tracts would be.

"Thank God," he said. "Been looking for this for a while."

"What is it?" She took the CD out of his hands, studying it. "*A Different Kind of Fix*. Interesting."

"It's this British band. They broke up a couple of years ago. I only just discovered them. Superbummed out, but at least I can play their music in the truck."

"That's cute."

"There you go again with that word." He took the CD back from her. "Come on. Show me what you want."

"I don't buy CDs. I don't have a player at home."

"I know, Miss The-Future-Is-Now. I mean for the truck. What's your favorite album?"

"Well, that's a loaded question. I have, like, ten. Per mood."

"We ain't got all day. Pick a favorite. Okay, pick three, at least."

Naya cupped her chin between her thumb and forefinger, miming deep thought. Then she turned around, heading to the

R&B/Soul section. "Gotta be . . . this one." She took out a CD filed under *B*. Then she selected one from *P*, and finally *W*. "Got to be these."

Dee took them from her hands. "*Bad-wism*?"

"*Baduizm*, stupid," she responded, emphasizing the *U*.

"Okay. *Yesterday's Tomorrow*, and . . . how am I supposed to pronounce that?"

"*Ardipithecus*. It's some type of extinct chimpanzee species that we may or may not have evolved from. I don't know, I'm no evolutionary biologist. But this album? Chef's kiss."

"I'll take your word for it."

"Cool. Shall we pay?"

"Yeah, whatever. I've got them, don't worry."

"You sure?"

"No, actually . . . I'm kind of on the fence. I can't decide. That's why I offered to pay."

Naya rolled her eyes, smirking. Then she reached out and placed a hand on his shoulder. "See? You're being cute." And then she touched her fingers to his cheeks, cooing jokingly. Dee stopped smiling, feeling his chest tighten. She was at it again, with one of her too-close yet endearing gestures, like the pinky promise or the hair braiding. She'd already told him to his face that she liked him, so it shouldn't have come as a surprise. This was something asking him, *Why not Definitely?* Naya's heart was stammering in her chest as she tried to figure out whether her playful advances were being reciprocated or not. He was either responding with sarcasm or curtness, and the fact that she couldn't tell which one bothered her. Having a crush was becoming more complicated than it needed to be.

Dee was snapped out of his reverie by the sound of laughter

as someone else walked into the store. He recognized the voice all too well, and it was like he was overwhelmed with vertigo as the world tilted slightly. Karina strutted in, smelling of cigarette smoke, with a phone held to her temple and a huge smile on her face. She didn't notice Dee until he turned around and faced her. Her expression turned dark, and she quickly wrapped up the conversation she was having and stood and stared at him with emptiness.

"Hey, Warrington."

He didn't answer; he just felt his blood simmering ever so slightly. Naya watched, feeling like history was repeating itself. Everything was always on repeat. History was the present. But then, it looked different this time—like a game hunter sizing up a deer; a menace with a rifle eyeing out their trophy. Somehow, Dee was the deer.

"Can we speak outside for a second?" he said, his voice loud after the moment of shrieking silence.

"Sure."

"I'll be back in a moment," he said to Naya before storming out the door with Karina flouncing behind. Naya saw the confrontation that ensued through the shop window but didn't hear any of it. There were times it looked like he was about to kill Karina—take his hands and wring her throat like a wet cloth. But then there were times when it looked like she had stunned him, left him paralyzed, lost for words, on the verge of dissipating. It was a spectacle, something she couldn't quite take her eyes away from. There was more to the story. There was *definitely* more to the story.

"Can we just go home now?" Dee asked afterward in a subdued tone, like if he spoke any louder his voice would crack.

He was paler than paper, clearly distressed. Karina'd never even made it back into the store—she'd just walked off in the other direction, as if her sole purpose was to stir up the ambiance.

"Yeah, let's just buy the CDs and go."

"That girl is a fucking *bitch*." He paced around the sidewalk the second they stepped outside. "There's nothing I can do about it. I can't do shit."

About what? What did she do? What did you do? Those questions ricocheted around Naya's head until it disconcerted her to think about the possible answers.

"Don't worry, it's all good."

"She's trying to hold the fact that we used to screw around when I was in *sophomore year* over me, like it's a brand on my fucking forehead, like I deserved everything, like it's my fault. Does that *really* make it my fault? That I was once a stupid fifteen-year-old kid who fooled around with an older girl from a different school to kill time, to get my kicks, so I didn't have to think about my sick fucking mom all the time? Then I move on and find a *nice* fucking girl, but everything goes to shit once again, because of *her*. She's haunting me . . . she's . . . she's making me pay for it. I deserved it. I deserved what I got. That's what she thinks. *Bitch*."

"It's okay, Dee. None of that matters now."

"I hate feeling like this." His eyes glared with anger, with frustration, with a sadness she hadn't seen from him before. "I just want to go home."

"Let's go, then." She grabbed his arm, walking them both in the direction of his battered vehicle. "It doesn't matter. Whatever happened, it doesn't matter. Do you hear me?"

"Naya—"

"It doesn't *matter*."

The next day, the pair had to wake up earlier than usual so that they could get to Salvation Hill and help to prepare for the garden party before guests and family members arrived. It was going to be a big affair with a barbecue, live performers in the gazebo, and a lot of dancing. Everyone who was able was required to leave their room and celebrate, get in their best outfit and rejoice in the 242 years since the United States of America had broken free from the shackles of Europe.

Dee didn't think there was really much to rejoice in. He found a certain hysterical irony in colonizers fighting for independence in a place that was never theirs to begin with. The Europeans were no longer European, they were *American*, and God fucking bless America. The least Dee could do was party with his ancestors' oppressors. He was also in an odd position, sharing blood with them, since his father was white. So, whatever. There was that saying, after all: if you can't beat them—

"You look pretty," Dee told Naya. She was wearing the green-and-white dress she'd bought. It was complemented by a pearl necklace and earrings, baby-pink eyeshadow, and glossy lips. She was also wearing mascara, which framed her eyes in a way that made them look completely different. Her strawberry-blond hair was up in German-style crown braids. Of course, she had on her Birkenstocks. Freckles that just seemed to appear out of nowhere were splattered across her bare arms.

"You don't look half bad yourself." He had on the Hawaiian shirt and jeans, and had undone the French braids, neatly tying his hair back; his Ray-Bans were perched on his head. Naya was happy to see him trying something different, something exuberant.

It was endearing, watching him loosen up as the days went by. She wondered where he'd be by the end of the summer, or even by senior year. Maybe he was on his way to total transformation, injected with a ray of sunshine, in contrast to the broody junior kid she'd first met. Only time would tell.

As expected, nobody came to visit Marie. She was happy all the same, mingling and chatting with the other residents of the home. The pair had fun conversing with her, reading out the romantic poems she had written, dancing in the noon sun, and indulging in the buffet of food and drinks. A near-retired country singer performed a few old-time hits ("Summer of '69," "Highway to Hell," "Born in the USA," amongst others) on his acoustic-electric as the residents listened, entertained. All the other helpers and workers at Salvation Hill came out to celebrate, and the event was overall a great success. Roy and Gita Crawford gave a speech toward the end of the party, which included a shout-out to their first-ever volunteers: *Dee Warrington and Naya Stephens, junior students at South Harlow High School.*

The sun was glistening, fixed high above the endless vista, everyone was happy, and Dee realized that he hadn't felt this good in quite a long time. These moments were precious— beautiful, ceaseless, but in the same breath, they reminded him that they came and went like water through a tributary, flowing into something bigger, something profound, something even harder to grasp: time itself. Things were always changing. People were forgetting, remembering, letting go, holding on. Dee read romantic poetry to Marie and watched her gush, then not too long after, ask for a romantic piece, as if she hadn't read romance in years. She was a stagnant lake. He watched Naya dance in the summer sun, looking even prettier than she'd looked the day before that, and the day before that, and so on. Things were changing by the second. In the same way Violet was now Marie, Maybe had become Definitely. It had been a smooth transition, so hard to pinpoint where it had begun.

The celebrations went on for longer than originally planned, and everyone started packing up at around five in the afternoon. It had been a long day. Once the deck chairs were folded and the leftover food packed away, Naya and Dee sat down in the garden gazebo. She reapplied her lip gloss, having lost most of it by the time she was done feasting on hot wings. Earlier, Dee had laughed as she'd wiped the sauce off her chest, having missed her dress by a fraction. Now, she rested her head on his shoulder as they spoke about the day they'd just had. The sun wasn't due to set for another few hours, but the sky was painting itself coral right before their eyes.

"You going to Levi's party tonight, then?" Naya asked him.

"Yeah. We're pregaming at my place. The Guys are, anyway. You can join if you want, but you will be the only girl there."

"It's cool. I have curfew. I'll sit it out."

"Fuck curfew. It's time for you to live a little. It's the Fourth of July! A god-awful holiday, but the silver lining is at the bottom of a can of Corona, amirite?"

"Not funny. Anyway, I'm hella tired. We got up early this morning."

"Sleep is for the weak."

Naya laughed. "If you say so. I need my beauty sleep."

Dee looked at her and thought that if this was how she looked when she was tired, she had nothing to worry about. "Fair enough," he responded. "I'll be thinking of you at the party. If I send you drunk texts, I didn't."

"Oh! Now my interest is piqued. I'll be waiting."

"Awesome," Dee said, before noticing the DJ setup to his left, currently unsupervised. His good mood had followed him up to that moment, and it gave him an idea. "Shall we dance?"

"Right now?" Naya asked, bemused.

"Someone left the laptop unlocked. We can search something on Youtube and play it out loud."

"Sure. What are you thinking?"

Dee was already standing at the DJ table by the time she asked. "It's a song from the album I bought yesterday. I think you'll like it."

They danced to "Lights Out, Words Gone," cavorting around the gazebo, disturbing a few of the residents who sauntered out to see what all the noise was about. Some scowled, some laughed, some cheered, and some danced along. Before they knew it, they were parading around with a handful of elderly people in the garden, bopping to the groovy bass line and warm euphony of the vocals in the song. When it was over, people clapped and cheered. Having watched everything from the window, Claire, one of the nursing home assistants, came outside and started leading everyone back in.

"That's a nice thing you did there. Playing music for everyone. They enjoyed it," Claire said, smiling at them. "But we gotta dial it down now. They need more peace and quiet than the rest of us."

"We agree. Sorry," Naya said, grabbing Dee's hand and pulling him into the building. She was one step ahead of him, fingers intertwined with his, and he followed. "Thanks for having us today, Claire. It was an awesome day."

"It sure was! I could tell you were having fun. And I haven't seen Marie this joyful since she first got here. Warmed my heart."

"It warmed ours too. She's an amazing person."

"You two seemed to have bonded pretty well here, haven't you?" Claire said, one hand on her hip. "Would you say that this whole thing is bringing you closer together?"

"Well, we didn't know each other before, so yeah," Dee replied. "Inevitably."

"Well, that's nice to hear! I'm a sucker for a good love story."

"Oh no. It's not like that." His right arm hung slack by his side, and he latched onto his elbow with his left hand, looking down to the ground. Naya stared at him, worried, confused, and amused, all at the same time.

"I read *Pride and Prejudice* by Jane Austen many moons ago. Back when I was really into the classics. I used to underline the sentences and words that stood out the most to me. There was this one that I loved. I might be paraphrasing, it's been a while. But it went something a little like this: 'Had I been in love, I could not have been more wretchedly blind!'" She chuckled. "I'll say no more. See y'all on Friday."

Claire was right. They both knew it, and they knew that everyone saw it, even if to varying degrees. It had got to the point where Marie would watch them from afar before asking them how long they'd been together for, and they'd have to keep reminding her that they weren't together, they were just volunteer partners, just friends, just not-strangers. It had been two days since Naya told Dee she liked him, and he decided he liked her too. When he dropped her off at six that evening, he kissed her good-bye. It took them both by surprise, immobilized them with shock, had their chests and their cheeks burning, but it felt right in that moment. She slid out of the truck, waving, and he smiled back, pulling onto the road on his way home with effervescence brewing somewhere within.

14

A CLOSE-RANGE GUNSHOT

"*Fear and Loathing in Las Vegas* called. They want their wardrobe back," Ash teased upon his entrance into Dee's house. Tyler and Wallis were in the living room with Dee, already three shots into the pregame.

"Eat shit, Ash. I wore it to the nursing home party today," Dee responded.

"Why do I keep forgetting that you're doing that? You're being superquiet about it," Wallis said.

"Do you think if I had a summer job at Benno's I'd have a shitload of stories to tell you? 'Cause it's kind of the same thing. It's just a job."

"What about stories of your colleague? Rumor has it she's tryna smash," Wallis chimed in. "That's what Jasmine said, anyway."

Dee tried not to break his poker face, thinking back to the kiss. "Aren't you a little too old to be playing 'telephone' with the Girls?"

"I mean . . . it's hard not to believe. You get around." Wallis chortled.

"God. You make it seem like I go outta my way or something."

"Well, you tell *us*," Ash said. "If we get to the party and you got Vanessa, Karina, Naya . . . who else? Elle Green . . . am I missing anyone? Anyway, if y'all were all in the same room . . . I mean, you'd definitely be spoiled for choice." He finished off the last dregs of his first beer.

"You're giving me a fucking migraine. Can we change the topic, please?"

"Only if you tell us if what Jasmine said is true," Wallis responded.

"Ah, I forgot. We're all comrades here. My business is your business," Dee retorted.

"Let's cut some slack, guys." Tyler interrupted. "He can enjoy making new friends without y'all taunting him about it."

"How far is the stick up your ass today, Tyler?" Wallis asked.

"Grow up, Wallis. Anyway, Tori's been acting weird with me lately. It's playing on my mind. I don't know what's up with her."

"Damn. She gonna be at the party tonight?"

"She said she would. Didn't seem keen, though."

"You gotta treat 'em mean to keep 'em keen, bruh. Maybe you're just too whipped now, and she doesn't care anymore."

"You're so stupid. She isn't *not* keen, she's just got a hunch about something, and I wanna figure it out. I will later."

"I heard Vanessa's gonna be there tonight," Ash said. "With Pearce Wilson as a plus one. You know. The basketball player who looks like he's been held back in senior year for the past three runs? A fuckin' beast."

"Talk about a switch up." Wallis and Ash snickered. Both Tyler and Dee didn't break a smile. Sometimes the immaturity of their friends wasn't something they could feign tolerance for, even after a couple of drinks. When Vanessa and Dee had broken up, the Guys weren't quick to take it seriously. They'd treated the Karina rumor like it was something Dee should be proud of, a conquest, instead of the misfortune that it actually was. Tyler was the only friend who'd seen through it all, even if he didn't know the details. It was clearly a touchy subject, and he treated it as such.

The rest of the pregame actually became about pregaming: playing cards and downing shots until they were buzzed enough to leave for Levi's bash. His place was within walking distance, so they didn't have to rely on a designated driver to get them all back home afterward. They'd probably end up crashing there anyway. It was already late into the party by the time the group arrived. All four were quite inebriated.

Especially Dee. After spending a half hour socializing with strangers and friends alike, he was bound to bump into Vanessa, and he did. She was sitting on the stairs inside, texting someone on her phone. Probably Pearce, who was currently a no-show. As Dee was en route to the closest vacant bathroom, she happened to be obstructing his path. He swayed at the bottom of the stairs, staring up at her. Throat tightening.

"Ness."

"Hey." She tucked her hair behind her ear. She was wearing a tight crop top and a miniskirt that she suddenly felt self-conscious about, considering the angle she was seated at. "How're you doing? Love the shirt, by the way."

He looked down at himself, then back up at her. "Thanks. I've never been better," he murmured, before trying to stifle a belch. He rubbed his eyes. "I'm kinda drunk. Heh."

"Yeah, I see that."

"How has your summer been? Long time, no talk." He walked idly up each step until he stood at her eye level. It had been around six weeks since they'd spoken outside the school gymnasium.

"It's been okay. Peaceful. I spent some time at the summer house."

"Oh, nice. Jealous. I'm glad you've been having fun."

"Thanks. I heard about your nursing home thing. Sounds wholesome. So sweet of you to do—I'm proud."

"Thank you," he muttered. He had forgotten that he even needed to use the bathroom. He was now desperate for something else—words trying to scrape their way out of the back of his throat. He wanted to ask about Vanessa's new love life, and he did. She frowned in response.

"We've been on a couple of dates. Well, three. He's a nice guy."

"Are you for real?"

She stared at him. "What?"

"Oh come on. Don't act dense."

"Are you talking about the Halloween party last year?"

"Yes, I am. Is this Pearce dude not the *same* guy who came in some dumb costume, 'warrior' paint, and a shitty feather headdress? The same guy demanding everyone call him 'Chief,' running around screaming like a fucking degenerate? You know that got me so mad. We talked about it, remember?"

"Dee, that was almost a year ago. He knows that was wrong of him."

"So you like dating a self-aware racist? Is it like dating a robot with a consciousness? Does it take the sting out of it?"

"I don't want to fight here in the middle of a party." She could already see partygoers paying attention to the exes' heated conversation.

"Not fighting."

"You are, and you're drunk. You should go home."

"You kidding? The party's just getting started."

"Dee, please." She stood up. "Don't embarrass yourself."

"I think the girl screwing one of the biggest fuckin' bozos in senior year takes the cake on embarrassing behavior."

"You're being a prick. What's wrong with you?"

"Oh, I'm fine. Honestly, I'm good. I just see things how they are."

"Yet you still won't admit you cheated on me."

Dee suddenly felt dizzy and held onto the banister next to him. "I'm not going to admit to something that didn't happen."

"You're deluded."

"You weren't at that party. You don't know what happened."

"It doesn't take a genius to figure it out when everyone saw you leaving with her."

"You know what? I don't even give a fuck anymore if you don't believe me. You're clearly doing well for yourself now. You've got a nice Smithson kid on your arm. You two make a *way* better match. Both stupid and rich."

"*Wow*," Vanessa hissed. "I can't believe I dated you for a *whole year*! And I actually loved you. It makes no sense." This felt like a close-range gunshot to his abdomen. It sobered him up, and she saw it straightaway. "You make things so difficult for yourself."

"Well, guess what, Vanessa—I *still* fucking love you, and that's why I'm the bitter ex, the one who lost it all, the one with a chip on his shoulder. I miss you, and I want nothing to do with you, all at the same time, and boy, I can't even tell you how . . . *awful* . . . that feels. I didn't want to lose you to someone like him. I wish the best for you, Ness. I hope nobody ever hurts you like I did ever again. I mean it." He clenched his jaw, tried biting his tongue, but the words tumbled out. "Yeah, I still love you," he whispered. "And I don't know how I do it. I don't know why."

Vanessa had started crying silently as he rambled. She wiped away each tear as it fell.

"Ugh. I need some air," she mumbled, and with that, she pushed past him and stumbled down the stairs. Dee went up to the bathroom to vomit.

Tyler found him some time later, and he wasn't in the best of states. He was tired, on the verge of passing out. His phone had been misplaced too; Tyler had found it in the kitchen and spotted the texts flashing up on his screensaver.

I had fun today, the first one read.

You're so lovely. Soft lips too, said the second.

Cya whenever.

"You made out with *Naya*?" Tyler said to Dee as they sat sprawled on the front lawn of the house.

Dee clumsily lit a cigarette. "No, just a kiss. The fuck. How do you know this?"

"Sorry, my guy. You left your phone on the kitchen counter. She sent something."

"Fuck." All that kept running through his mind were the other possible eyes who may have stumbled upon his phone and seen the messages. Eyes like Vanessa's.

"I mean . . . the texts could be from anyone. You only saw the name as *N*."

"Clearly *N* is for Natalie Portman." Tyler rolled his eyes. "It's nice to see you're moving on."

"I got into a fight with Vanessa. I made her cry. Shit."

"I guess I'll have to take back what I just said."

"I'm just stuck in a limbo, Tyler. Sometimes things make perfect sense, other times they don't."

"It's only natural."

"It's not. My world's folding over, all the fucking time. I don't know how to feel."

"I completely understand."

"I don't know if you do, though."

"Dee . . ."

"Everything is just . . . changing, everywhere," he grumbled, trying to shake off his intoxication.

"Tori's pregnant."

"*What?*"

"Six weeks. She told me an hour ago. She was drinking only chaser, no alcohol. She was acting mad pressed, then just burst into tears in the bathroom, and she told me. Five pregnancy tests. Two cheap ones, three expensive ones. The flashy ones that know how far along, all that shit. All came back positive."

Dee found it hard to decipher his words in his lack of sobriety. "Amber'll make a great mom. She's mature enough. Clever too. You've got a nice family. You'll be a cool uncle."

"*Father*, dude. Father. I said Tori."

"Tori?"

"Tori."

"Tori." Dee sighed.

"I don't know what to do," Tyler said, sotto voce. "I'm . . . stumped. You're the only other person that knows this. I don't even know whether to trust you. You're drunk. But I won't tell anyone about Naya if you keep quiet about this. At least while I try and figure things out."

"I won't tell a soul. You're my best friend."

It was true; he was. They had always been the closest. They always got the news first, they always kept each other's secrets. Dee saw Tyler as more of a brother than he sometimes saw Dylan. He had always felt a part of the Harper family. But now it was growing, and everything was changing, everywhere.

15

THE VERY THOUGHT

"How has she been?" Dee asked Tyler a few days after the party, at No Man's Land.

Tyler lay alongside the skate pool, his palms behind his head, eyes to the sky. "A damn mess. Still hasn't told her parents. I haven't told *mine*. I told Amber last night, though. She said she already knew, that Tori told her a week ago, which was before *me*. I shouldn't be pissed at that; if you're a girl, you're probably gonna tell your girlfriends before you tell anyone else. But I was annoyed, and I argued with Amber for keeping it from me for five days without saying anything, and I argued with Tori, too, so now we're not speaking."

"You really need to fix this. It's a time-sensitive issue."

"I know, man. I'm just . . . scared. We haven't been together that long. I know we've spent nearly every moment of our time around each other, but it hasn't been all Gucci *all the time*. We almost called things off on two separate occasions. Before she got pregnant. Shit, before *I* got her pregnant."

"How did this even happen? I mean, seriously."

"Well, Einstein." Tyler smirked. "I think we all know how these things happen."

"It didn't have to be the case, though."

"So . . . as organized as Tori can appear to everybody, I should have noticed something was wrong when I realized how often she'd forget her volleyball practice shoes at home. Or how she'd forget to get that *one thing* I'd tell her to bring from the 7-Eleven on her way over to my place *every single damn time*, or how terrible she is at remembering names. She has this calendar on her wall covered in all these colorful sticky notes that I'd always make fun of her for. She has a notebook, a planner, a bullet journal. She has all those things because she needs them. She's a fucking goldfish otherwise. She forgot her birth control. That's what she told me. And I was disappointed, both in myself and in her, but I wasn't surprised. She's a goldfish, dude. I fell in love with a *goldfish*."

"Whoa, buddy. You don't want it to get out there that you've been fucking animals." Dee laughed.

"It's funny, 'cause the kid will prolly be a Pisces. A little fish kid. At least that's what I've gathered, judging from the dates. She got pregnant early June. Nine months later, it's gonna be February or March. Now I'm not stupid, I don't believe in any of that shit, but it just occurred to me, and I don't know why, but that really *hit* me."

"You're already giving it an identity," Dee said. "That's why. It's not just Tori, it's something else. Some*one* else."

"That's fucking terrifying, dude. I'm . . . terrified. You and I . . . we both fucked up this year somehow. We both made big fuckin' rookie mistakes with girls. If it makes you feel better to know that."

"You're talking about Karina, right?"

"Well . . . yeah." He looked toward Dee. "Bad mistakes. That's all we've made."

Dee couldn't reply. Yes, he had made many mistakes. He was an awful person. But his mistake was not like Tyler's. It did nothing but consume him from the inside out; no good had come out of it—no silver lining, no light at the end of the tunnel. Just a growing cavity. His best friend's mistake was potentially having a child at eighteen. His own mother had had him young, so he saw nothing inherently awful about that. There was no mistake in life itself. But life birthed errors, it festered ugly chaos and chains of events that the human experience could only classify as *mistakes*. And no, mistakes weren't all bad, clearly. Undesired consequences that arose from misjudgment or wrong decisions didn't always mean the end of the world. *But Tyler, your mistake has nothing on mine*, Dee thought. *I'm scared of myself now. I'm scared of a girl who has no real significance in my life except to taint it. I'm scared of what has happened; you're scared of what may be. It's not the same. You can't tell me it's the same.*

"Whatever decision Tori makes, we'll all be there for her. Even though she hates me."

"She doesn't hate you. She's just a chick. They're hella judgmental. And I love her, so that's what matters. I've never loved anybody more than her."

"That's all you need. Corny, but it's true."

"You right. With your John Lennon ass."

Dee laughed, and then there was a prolonged pause. He felt it right to change the subject. "Speaking of love. I told Vanessa I still loved her at the party."

"I thought you said you fought with her. Doesn't sound like a fight to me."

"We exchanged a few . . . words, in the heat of the moment. Then I went all soft and personal, and she darted. Way to go."

"Damn. Yo, when Pearce arrived, she was all over him, eating his face on the couch and shit. Looked kinda desperate. Whatever you said must have worked."

"But I said I *loved* her."

"Well, do you?"

"Hmm. No. I don't know. I shouldn't."

"Hell no. Plus you've got a new girl now."

"Not exactly."

"Have you kissed Naya since the last time?"

"I might have. We met up yesterday. Made out a little bit. It was . . . nice, I guess."

"Then the fuck do you still 'love' Vanessa for?"

"It's not that simple."

"It could be. Just keep makin' out with your volunteer partner, and you'll be over her in no time."

"That's not *all* it takes."

"Take her out on dates, then."

"Actually, uh . . . I almost forgot to tell you. It's Naya's birthday on Sunday, but she managed to keep quiet about it up until now. I need to do something for her. I know she's into live music, so I was thinking of taking her to see a band at The Jive this weekend. Saturday."

"So you're already on it!"

"I don't know if that's a date. Just a birthday present. Couldn't exactly buy her tickets and make her go alone, could I?"

"It's a date."

"No, but—"

"You're having make-out sessions with a girl who admitted she has a crush on you, and you're taking her out to a show, and you don't want to call it a date."

"Nope."

"Ever heard that quote by Shakespeare? About the rose? Can't remember it. Point being, that shit's just semantics. A spade is a spade, my guy. A date is a date."

◆

The show didn't feature anyone that Naya or Dee knew. It was a small band from somewhere in Nevada, led by a fully tatted singer backed by four decent instrumentalists. They called themselves Melody Spoke, and they were touring in promotion of their sophomore EP, *Terror v. Tranquility*. Dee had checked out a bunch of their songs on Spotify, gauging whether this would be the type of thing Naya would enjoy. *They better be*, he thought, because it was either that or a Green Day tribute band (called Chartreuse Afternoon) on the same weekend. It was a last-minute fix, and it would have to suffice.

"You really, really didn't have to do this," Naya said as they made their way through the Harlow streets en route to the gig in the late afternoon. She had on a Burberry-style checked peplum blouse, dark-blue slacks, and denim wedge espadrilles. "I didn't tell anybody about my birthday. I don't need the attention. It's not even on my Facebook."

"So your friends don't know?" Dee strode beside her, hands in his jeans pockets.

"No, and I'd like to keep it that way. You're lucky I even told you."

"No, *you're* lucky you even told me. Now look where we're heading."

"If this isn't as good as you made it out to be, consider our friendship over. I could have been binging on episodes of *Black-ish* and eating tons of candy until I felt sick and passed out. That's what I call a birthday treat."

"This birthday treat is a million times better. You know why? 'Cause I'm a part of it." He laughed.

"Don't flatter yourself."

They'd first kissed five days ago, and since then, things had been on a steady incline. They were getting closer. With every gesture and word they spoke, there was another level of meaning. The day before, they'd lain on the grass in the Salvation Hill garden, reading after an hour and a half of book sorting. While Naya took out a copy of *Go Set a Watchman*, Dee flicked through a tattered *1984*, only half paying attention. He said that he was never much into reading, and he meant it. But he felt the need to assure the girl he liked that he was willing to give it a try. Really, he was daydreaming as he fingered the aged pages, itching for the day to end so he could kiss Naya in his pickup. Her lips tasted like pink grapes, and her hair smelled like cocoa butter. He'd never paid attention to these things before, but they were scents that controlled him now, smells he couldn't shake off.

They stood in the front row at the show, since there hadn't been a huge lineup before the doors opened. An array of people showed up, most dressed like hipsters and professional art critics.

It was a side of Harlow that Dee hadn't even known existed. He just knew skate parks and trashy neighborhoods, and the music that went along with them: the hip-hop and rock his friends played, or the EDM that blasted from speakers at parties. The summer was granting him new surprises, and he was liking it.

It took a while for the band to arrive; there was a two-hour DJ set that they hadn't been made aware of, and people spilled into the venue slowly and intermittently. Dee thought it a good idea to put his fake ID to use and take a trip to the corner store that he visited the most, to buy a few beers for them to drink during their wait. He and Naya spoke and chugged, joked and drank, and by the time the band got there, the pair was slightly bubbly with intoxication. It wasn't Naya's first drink, but it was one of the few she'd ever consumed, for glaringly obvious reasons. She didn't feel like she was rebelling, even though she knew she was. If her parents could smell a drop of alcohol on her breath, she'd be crossing out all the free days on her calendar to make way for chore on top of chore. But that didn't matter in the moment. The good music and lively atmosphere mattered. The arms of a pretty boy slung over her shoulders as his chin rested atop her head were what mattered.

Melody Spoke performed a neo-soul rendition of Billie Holiday's "The Very Thought of You," which had every couple slow dancing like it was prom. It was a wonderful moment, and Naya couldn't think of a better way to celebrate turning seventeen. *Black-ish* and snacks could wait.

◆

After the show, they walked to Silver Rock Plaza. It was almost midnight, which was way past Naya's curfew. She was still tipsy, losing her balance as she tried to walk along one of the benches, arms outstretched. She felt the vibration of her phone buzzing in her pocket and knew that it was one of her parents.

"Why do you smoke?" she asked Dee as he sat below her by the plaza's fountain, lighting a cigarette.

"I don't know." He shrugged.

"You don't know? . . . Okay."

"Is there any justification I could give you that would make you think, *Actually, yeah, he's got a point*?"

"I mean, I guess not. But I just wanted to know the reason. Was it peer pressure? Stress?"

"I'll save that answer for my first therapy session," he responded. Dee had never initially been fond of smoking, despite always seeing his mother alternating between Backwoods cigarillos and packs of Camels. It was actually Karina who had gotten him hooked, always offering him a roll-up or two whenever they'd met up in the past. There was always an intimacy in their sharing cigarette kisses, always something alluring about it. It made him feel sophisticated. Older. Smoking was something that he'd never managed to cut ties with, even though he had with her.

"I'd be so scared of getting cancer if I was you," Naya said.

"*Everything* gives you cancer. Microwaves, phones, deodorant, processed meat . . . alcohol, pollution, *Keeping Up with the Kardashians* . . . I could keep going."

"You're such a smart-ass. You don't have to bump up the chances, you know."

"Gimme a break, Birthday Girl. I'm gonna quit when I'm eighteen anyway."

"So you have four months left."

"Exactly. I'm gonna try and improve myself, little by little. Let me be a lowlife for a little while longer."

"I don't think you're a lowlife. You've never done anything that most kids our age don't do. You're a good person. You don't need to improve yourself." She stood on the bench, towering over him. The water from the fountain glistened in the moonlight, and the giant metallic rock sculpture in the middle of the plaza cast out light like a diamond.

"I really do, though. I need a rebirth."

"No, you don't. I like to keep shit simple, you know? It's like . . . you're born, and then you die, and everything that happens between means everything, and it means nothing at all. Living is just being, until you can't be anymore. You can be anything at all times. You can be terrible, you can be amazing, it doesn't matter, just *be*. Don't try to think hard about it. That's what I'm always telling myself." She stepped down to sit beside him.

"Nice philosophy. It's like optimistic nihilism." He turned to her, holding her closer and planting a kiss on her forehead. "I'm sorry I smell like cancer and booze right now. I need to shower."

"I don't mind. It's eleven forty-seven. I've got to get home."

"Oh shit. Yeah. Let's head back."

They stopped at the end of Naya's street so he didn't have to walk her all the way to the front of her house. Her drunkenness had been wearing off with every step she got closer to home, and a new fear flooded her chest. They kissed on the corner of the street before telling each other good-bye. She thanked him for the amazing birthday present and strode off as Dee watched. Everything was always changing, everywhere, and this was one of those moments.

16

FOR YOU

Naya's parents were still awake when she entered the house as quietly as she could. Her mother was in the living room, sipping on red wine. Her father was reading something on his laptop.

"I'm sorry I'm late," Naya began. "The show ran late. Some technical issues." She stood at the other side of the room, afraid that they'd smell her even after she'd cloaked herself in perfume. Not that it made a difference.

"You've been drinking, haven't you?" her mother asked accusingly.

Naya was so close to bursting into laughter and tears at the same time as she stared at the drink her mother was holding. *The hypocrisy*, she thought. "We had a few drinks after the show.

Jasmine and Amber and me. Nothing wild." She didn't think telling her parents she was actually on a date was going to placate their concern regarding her whereabouts.

"Ah. So *here's* where the slope begins to get slippery." Her mother raised an eyebrow, shaking her head.

"You're kidding me, right? I've been in Harlow for, like, nearly four months and the *one time* I break curfew you lose your minds."

"Naya," her father interjected. "You've got to understand our concern. You're entering into your *final year* of high school. We don't need you losing your way."

"Are you telling me that every single kid who is graduating with me next year is going to fail miserably, and I'll be the only one on top because I avoided having a social life? 'Cause that's just not true. And it's also messed up."

"Naya. We had a birthday dinner set up for you this evening, at a restaurant in town. We thought you'd be back home a lot sooner. Did you not see any of our texts? Were you *that* busy that you couldn't answer any of them?" her mother responded, perturbed.

Naya's heart sank. She'd had no idea that they had planned something for her birthday. But then she felt the anger rise up again. She wasn't going to be guilt-tripped this time around. "You literally could have told me that," she said, voice wobbling. Whenever she was frustrated, her feelings always turned to waterworks. She hated it. "How was I supposed to know? My birthday's tomorrow, not today. And you could have told me that I was having a birthday dinner. Given me a place and a time. I would have turned up. Instead, you just nagged at me to get home, while I was enjoying myself elsewhere for once."

"Clearly, this was just a bit of miscommunication," her father said, straining to defuse the tension in the air. "An unfortunate one, at that."

"No, it wasn't." Naya hit back. "I get good grades. I've never gotten in trouble at school. I'm not directionless; I know what I want to study at college. I'm *volunteering* at a nursing home, for crying out loud. But it's not good enough for you. I do *one* thing differently, and I'm on a slippery slope."

"Naya Grace, quit the dramatics." Her mother stood up. "You're more than enough for us. You're our *only* child. We fought tooth and nail to bring you into this world. We don't take that for granted at all. We just want you to be the best person you can be. You don't need all of these other distractions. You're going to get there eventually, but you need to stay on track."

"You think putting pressure on me is going to work? Or dismissing anything about me that you don't understand? Like how Haley wasn't just a friend, Mom. I wasn't just 'figuring myself out.' You met Dad when you were younger than I was when I met Haley. But I guess you'd figured yourselves out by then, and you've never changed."

"I think we've said enough," Naya's father said, standing up and looking at her mother. "We've made our point clear."

"If you're going to ground me, just do it." She wiped her tears away.

"It's your birthday, Naya. We're not going to ground you," her mother said. "But we won't condone you breaking our rules again. We have them in place for a *reason*. At the end of the day, we're Black. We have to work twice as hard in this world to get our dues—for people to take us seriously. Keep that in mind at *all* times."

"Sure," Naya muttered.

"And remember—if you ever want to start coming to church again, the door's wide open for you." Her mother turned toward the kitchen. Her father followed, and Naya spun around, storming up the stairs.

This was one of the moments that being alive, knowing life, knowing death, knowing everything, felt heavier than lead. Her parents always told her how she was so unique, a one-in-a-million child, not just because she looked different but because it took them years to conceive her. They were told that the chances of having children were next to none, and then Naya came to them and changed their whole world. But their world was small. It didn't expand; it didn't accommodate her. She wondered: what was the point of their fighting to bring a life into the world if they couldn't find a compromise for their towering expectations of her?

Naya went to the bathroom to wash the makeup and tears from her face. Checking the door was locked all the way, she stripped down to her underwear. She looked in the mirror for a long, long time, studying her small, flat chest and her alabaster skin. She poked and prodded at her stomach, her hips, her thighs. Then she picked up her phone, taking a deep breath, straightening out her posture. She sat on the counter near the sink and turned to face the mirror. *Happy Birthday to me*, she thought to herself as she opened her camera. *But this one's for you.*

◆

"Ever thought of cleaning this shithole up every once in a while?" Dee asked, walking into his house after dropping Naya off. Dylan was propped up on the couch watching *The Martian*. The room was in disarray again, as if in a constant state of pregame drinking and partying that was never cleared up. The morning after the Fourth of July party a few days before, the last thing he'd wanted was to do housework, but Dee had cleared away all the bottles and scrubbed everything clean. The heat, coupled with his raging hangover, had had him doubled over the same bucket he'd just used to mop the floor, but nothing made him feel worse than the thought of treating his mother's house like a trashy mobile home. His brother, on the other hand, never seemed to mind.

"Damn. Imagine being stranded on Mars. Such a fuckin' bummer. I'm making vodka with the potatoes and then waiting to die," Dylan said, taking a swig from a bottle.

"That figures. There's so much shit around here. Why do you live like this?" Dee walked into the kitchen to grab a trash bag, throwing in the empty cans along his pathway back to the living room. He dropped the bag on the floor right in front of his brother's feet, then sat himself on the couch adjacent. "You do the rest."

"Calm down. I'll fucking clean it up. Gimme a minute, let me finish the movie."

"You're going to finish the dumb movie and then pass out, wake up in the morning, and go to fix cars for a few hours—mine not included—then pick up a six-pack on the way home and start this shit all over again."

"You know me all too well." Dylan laughed. There was something about his voice that made Dee want to leave a dent in his head. It was like he couldn't understand his anger, like Dee was the one bothering Dylan, not the other way around. He almost understood—there had been a time when his mother would do the same thing to him, get at him about not cleaning up after himself. As angry as she got, Dee had always felt that she was overreacting, like mothers did. Deep down, though, all was already forgiven because he could glide through life knowing there'd be someone to do his laundry, to pay the bills, to be an adult while he was still a kid. That wasn't the case anymore. He stared at his brother for a long time, trying to regulate his anger, just as present as he was, taking up space, filling up all corners of the room.

"You've got a problem. All you do is drink and do coke. Inviting your redneck friends over, letting them talk shit about me. Don't think I never hear it, 'cause I do."

"The fuck are you talking about?" Dylan paused the film, sitting forward on the couch.

"You never defend me. You laugh along with their dogshit jokes. They're never funny, by the way."

"You're gonna have to elaborate, buddy."

"Oh yeah. There's a chance you don't remember. You know, being a blacked-out mess and all."

"Whatever my friends said, they probably didn't mean it. A joke is a joke. Don't take it to heart. Not everything has to be so fucking politically correct."

"Not everything has to be a joke either."

"Christ! Fuck, calm down. I'll tell them to cut it out. They won't mention you again. Is that cool?"

"Look. I just don't want you to let them insult me. If you don't say anything, you're just as shitty as they are."

"I'm not taking sides here." Dylan held his hands up. "I'm just trying to have a good time. You need to loosen up."

"You need to sober up."

"Until you're paying the goddamn rent here, I don't think you're going to tell me how to live my life."

"Okay. Stay a drunk mess. I'm sure some of the life insurance money was put aside for twenty cans of Bud Light and a gram of blow a day."

"Don't start with me. You reek of alcohol and cigarettes right now. You've got the fucking nerve," Dylan spluttered.

"So it's the blind leading the blind here." Dee shrugged. "I'm going to sleep." He stood up abruptly.

"Hold up. Don't go nowhere. You've got to kick the attitude. You don't need this big-ass chip on your shoulder *all the time*."

"That's the problem. You don't really know me at all."

"Let's see how much Freya's family knows you, shall we? Way, *way* better than I do. Hence why you're still here and not with them right now."

"Clean your shit up, Dylan. Goodnight."

"If she'd wanted one of your aunts or uncles to take over after her, she would have written them into the will. But she didn't, Dee. She knows Harlow is a better place for you."

"That's just not true at all. You don't know why my mom did what she did. You're just happy you got something out of it."

"Yeah. Wiping your ungrateful ass is what I got out of it." He finished his beer before violently grabbing the trash bag in front of him and throwing the can inside. He pressed Play on the movie and *The Martian* started up again.

Dee went upstairs to shower, spending a longer amount of time than usual under the stream of water. He was thinking back to the date. Naya had been helping him to forget about things. Helping him to forget about Dylan, Vanessa, his mother. He'd never forget about his mother, of course, but her death was haunting him less. Her death four months ago. There was no way he could forget that, but he had to move past it. He just had to move on.

He was still seething from the argument with his brother. Sometimes he hated him so much it paralyzed him, but most of the time, he pitied him, which was probably worse. After he showered, he went to his room and collapsed on the bed, staring at the ceiling. To stop himself from falling into troubled thoughts, he picked up his phone. There were three messages from Naya. The first two were just attachments. He opened them.

"Holy shit," he whispered. Then he started grinning like a Cheshire cat, and his heart was hammering, his skin heating up. She'd sent photos of herself. Bathroom-mirror selfies, where nothing but porcelain, flesh, and underwear were on display. She'd sent a final message underneath the third photo: *Just my way of saying thanks.* He wouldn't have thought she'd had it in her to do something so racy, so revealing. Because now he wanted her more than ever before, in every way. He lay in bed, eyes open, no sign of sleep anytime soon. He was jittery, both with anxiety and exhilaration. It was like all the atoms in his body were high energy, bouncing off each other with no room to move. He was excited about Naya, but he was also afraid. Of all the eyes that watched his every move, of all the friends that talked, and of the crumbling house he lived in. He was afraid; he knew it. But better to be scared of the future than of the past.

17

A GLASS HALF FULL

Naya was cross-legged on Dee's bed, two evenings later. She was taking in her surroundings, studying the color of the walls and the album cover posters papering over them: *The Sun's Tirade*, *Because of the Times*, *Salad Days*, *Combat Rock*, placed strategically above his rack of vinyl. There was a large coffee-colored rug in front of his bed in the center of the room that had two parallel strips of red, white, and black diamond shapes running across the negative space. Naya assumed it was a traditional Navajo pattern of sorts.

Dylan had a friend's bachelor party to attend in Vegas over the weekend, so he'd left for drinks at a bar with the other groomsmen before his evening flight, while Naya and Dee were still in the middle of their volunteering shift. Dee had jumped at the chance to invite her around, and she'd accepted, using Jasmine as a sleepover alibi for her parents. They had seemingly eased off her after their argument on her birthday, and she'd taken the first opportunity she had to spend an evening with Dee. She was curious to find out how he lived when he wasn't with his friends, or with her. She was impressed so far, and admired how he tried hard to keep his life in order.

She picked up a framed photo from his bedside table, knowing immediately who was in the picture. "This is your mom, right?"

"Yup," Dee responded, sitting down at the end of his bed.

"She's so beautiful," Naya said, before realizing that she'd spoken of her in the present tense. "I bet she was the coolest."

"Cool is an understatement. She was ice-cold."

"You look identical. It's remarkable."

"So genetics isn't just a conspiracy theory?" He smiled, taking a long toke from the joint in his hand. He had his bedroom window wide open to disperse the smell and invite the relieving breeze inside.

"Imagine if genetics worked like customized *Sims* or something," Naya said. "You could give birth to literally *anyone*. Zero resemblance. Any race, any gender, any anything. That'd be wild."

"I've literally never imagined that, Nai. You really are creative."

"I don't know. Sometimes that's how I feel about myself, you know? Like a randomized Sim. I look literally nothing like my parents, or my family."

"No, you do. You look like your mom. I see it. Same smile." He passed the joint across to her, and she took it.

"I know. But at first glance . . . I don't think people notice that." She took a tentative drag. Up until this point, she had never smoked anything; she felt it was at least time to experiment, considering it was the one pastime both the Guys and the Girls had in common.

"If you care about what people notice at first glance, you're caring about the wrong thing."

"I guess you're right."

"My mom didn't give a shit what anybody thought about her. Nobody could tell her anything she didn't want to hear."

"I guess that's where our moms differ," Naya said. "Mine cares *too* much. She thinks she owes it to an omniscient supernatural being to be on her best behavior at all times."

"That's gotta suck. I get it, though. Keeping up appearances for a higher power probably gives you purpose in life."

"That's all it is, though. Appearances. A performance. It's like . . . I wonder what my parents would have been like if they weren't raised in Ampleforth. Like, I don't know, what if they'd been raised in Brooklyn, or Miami, or Canada—anywhere but there. I wonder how that would have affected my upbringing."

"I wonder the same thing about my mom too. What it would have been like if she had never left the rez."

"These are things we'll just never know," Naya said. "I guess it doesn't matter anyway. It's where we're going, not where we've been."

Dee stayed quiet for a moment, then he moved to the other side of the bed beside Naya. Leaning back on the headboard, he looked up at the ceiling fan and bit the inside of his lip. "I really fucking miss her," he said.

"I'm sorry, Dee."

"I don't know how to live. I don't know if it matters where I'm going."

"Of course it does, silly."

"Thirty-four," he said. "That's how old she was. She lived twice as long as I have. I always think to myself that's literally *nothing*. By the time she had me, she had reached the halfway point of life."

"It's not fair. It's bullshit. But she's not completely gone. You have her somewhere inside you, I'm sure of that. Until the last person on this earth that has even a teeny-weeny *semblance* of a memory of her is no longer alive, she's still here."

"That's a good point," Dee said. "Your glass is always half full. I like that."

Naya kissed him on the cheek. "I'm always here for you."

"I know," he said. "I know."

They shared the rest of the joint before lying back on the bed. Naya was wearing a stonewashed denim maxi-skirt and her pastel-pink tank top, the same one she'd worn when she invited Dee for dinner with her parents. He thought back to that moment, midprayer, when he'd spent thirty seconds straight just staring at her collarbone. Then he reached out and ran his fingers along it.

"What are you doing?" Naya asked, feeling heavy from the marijuana. Everything was spaced out, not quite real. She could feel everything more strongly too. His touch was like a spark between the sliding wheels of a train and the rail tracks.

"Nothing."

"Yeah, you're touching me."

"I'm sorry." He closed his eyes. "I'll stop."

"I didn't say stop." She took his hands, placed them back where they were. "Ugh. I have the boobs of a twelve-year-old famished boy. You feel those bones right there?" She slid his finger to the ridges under her skin.

"Feels fine to me. I have the same thing. We all have bones, Nai."

"But I'm a girl. You're not supposed to see mine."

"Says who?"

"Says society."

"Society says a lot of shit." He stroked her jaw with his thumb. "You know I think about those photos you sent all the time, right?"

Naya flushed crimson. "Oh God, don't remind me. That was pretty nerve-wracking."

"Don't worry. I enjoyed it."

"I'm glad to have made you that happy."

"You really did. I'm gonna be honest with you." He sat up. "I did things I'm not proud of. You really found my weak spot."

"Oh come on. Nudes are every guy's kryptonite."

"Yeah, but what's important here is that *yours* are *mine*."

"You have a point. I'll take it."

She pulled herself upright, kissing him. They made out for a long, long time, sliding down to lie beside each other before eventually untangling their fingers. Naya's whole body was on fire. Certain places more than others. She didn't want to be the one to initiate anything, so she secretly hoped that he would. But she was also afraid that he might.

"Do you wanna have sex?" he asked quietly. She sat up, staring at the floor as her leg hung off the side of the bed. She didn't say anything. "I mean, it's completely up to you. I wouldn't try anything otherwise. Oh God. That sounded so . . . desperate. Forget I said any of that."

"I've thought about it a couple of times."

"You have?"

She paused. "Maybe."

"Well, I'm relieved. And flattered."

"Why would it be a big deal to you anyway? You've slept with girls before."

"Doesn't matter."

"Kinda does. For me, anyway."

"Why?"

"I don't wanna have to spell out the obvious here."

Dee screwed up his face, perplexed. Then the realization hit him. "Oh."

"Yup."

He frowned. "What about the girl? Haley."

"I'm down for changing definitions of the word *virgin* to exempt anyone who's gone to second base, even with someone of the same gender, but unfortunately that's irrelevant. Good old misogynistic heteronormative bullshit. Hah."

"Hetero-*what*?"

"Look, I'm a virgin. I've never had sex before." She looked at him, going quiet. "Even if I think about wanting it, I'm still kinda nervous."

He lay his head on the pillow. "That's fair. We don't have to do anything. I guess I'm just rushing things because . . . it took me a while to realize I liked you, and I don't want that realization to end. I just want to realize it over and over again."

"Don't worry. We still have time." She lay next to him, draping an arm over his rib cage. "Hey, Dee. I think I know the exact moment I started liking you."

"When was it?"

"When you didn't leave the office that day."

"You *know* I would have been an ass if I'd walked out."

"Yeah, but I didn't know you then. I would have been pissed for a couple of days, then I probably would have gotten over it.

I'd still have ended up hanging out with you because your friends are my friends, so I wouldn't have cared."

"I felt bad." He frowned. "And I thought you were cool."

"Dee Warrington has a moral compass. Who would have thought?"

"Can we kiss some more?"

She smiled, and they locked lips. They were so lost in each other's grip that they almost missed the sound of activity in the belly of the house. There was a crashing thud, partnered with a hollered profanity. Dee's heart sank; Dylan was back. He must have missed his flight. Now here he was, bulldozing his way through the tranquility of the moment.

"It's my brother. Stay there." He hopped off the bed in nano-seconds, leaving the room and rushing down the stairs. Naya sat and listened, trying to make out what was happening. All she could hear was Dylan laughing and Dee responding in an irked tone. She was trying to eavesdrop on the world that he hid from her.

"Dylan, what the fuck?"

"Whose shoes are those?" He snorted, pointing at Naya's silver Birkenstocks.

"My friend's here. Why aren't you in Vegas?"

"I missed my flight. I'm catching a later one tomorrow at noon. You been smoking my weed?"

"Just a little."

"You know this is a very . . . Netflix-and-chill scenario you've got going on here."

"Can't you go to Mia's or something? She lives closer to the air-port. Or . . . or stay with that friend you were supposed to hang with."

"I left a shit-ton of stuff here. Like my passport and ID. Thought I'd call it a day and get an early night."

"I guess all the drugs have fucked up your brain, that's why you forgot everything. Also—it's one thirty in the morning. Not exactly early, is it?"

"Time is relative. Can I say hey to your friend?"

"She's asleep," Dee said in a hushed tone. "You're making noise. Keep quiet or take a hike."

"She doesn't look very asleep to me." Dylan laughed, looking up behind Dee. Naya was standing at the top of the stairs. "Hey, girl."

"Hi."

Dee sighed. He knew it could only get worse from this point.

"You're his friend, huh? Don't think I've ever seen you before. He's certainly never mentioned you."

"It's okay, I'm fine with that." She shrugged. She knew things were complicated between the brothers, but somewhere inside her, there was a pang of disappointment in this discovery. "I'm Naya, by the way."

"Come on down, Naya." Dylan beckoned to her, and she came downstairs. Dee stood with his fists balled, trying hard to contain himself. She could see the expression on his face, thunder etched into stone. "I'd like to think my kid brother's just hiding all his friends away. How'd y'all meet?"

"We work together at Salvation Hill."

"The nursing home?"

"Yup."

"Oh, so you're the partner! Ain't that sweet. You . . . mixed race or something?"

"No, I'm Black."

"Really?"

"One hundred percent."

"Huh." Dylan stared skeptically, scratching his jawline. "You two got a thing going on?"

"No," Dee responded a tad too quickly. "We're just friends. Come on, Naya. Let's finish the film we were watching."

"I thought you said she was sleeping. I may be dumb drunk, but I'm not dumb."

"I don't have to explain myself to you," Dee said, turning around and walking up the stairs. Naya followed.

The air in the room was different now. Dee wasn't in the mood to explain himself to Naya either; he was tired and upset. Things seemed to be bliss for moments on end until something ruined it. This time it was his stupid, racist brother. Dylan's appearance rocked everything.

"You know, I would have left now if I hadn't told my parents I was sleeping over at Jasmine's," Naya said as she stripped down to her underwear. "All of a sudden I don't feel wanted here."

"I told you to stay in the room, didn't I?" Dee retorted. "You didn't listen. When I say these things, I mean them."

"You don't have to protect me from your brother. I don't care that he's an ass."

"Hey, well, I do. This is one of the things that does matter, and I can't let you act like it doesn't."

"I'm sorry." She sucked in her breath. "I just don't want to be hidden away all the time."

"I'm not hiding you from anyone, Naya. I just didn't want you to meet my brother."

He sat on the bed, pulling her toward him, wrapping his arms around her torso, ear resting on her sternum. She stood, clasping her hands around the nape of his neck. "I like how things are right now and I just don't want things to change," he murmured.

But everything was always changing, everywhere.

18

TO DROWN A FISH

If u didnt use condoms last night I'll fuck u up!!!

Don't be havin no weird lookin babies on my watch.

I left cash 4 food on the table

Dee awoke the next morning and rubbed his eyes as he looked at the thread of texts from his brother. Naya was still asleep, snoring softly. Her eyelashes were like snowdrops, and he wanted to run his fingers along them. Instead he sighed, sitting up and thinking of how to respond to Dylan. He knew instantly that he probably didn't like Naya and that he'd be making disparaging remarks about her to his shitty friends. There was nothing weird-looking about Naya at all, not in the slightest. She was different, that was for sure, but that was that. Dylan seemed to

184

have an aversion to difference. All of his friends looked the same, thought the same things, carried the same level of ignorance in their words. Dee turned to look at the framed photo of his mother, envisioning how she would have reacted when she'd met Naya for the first time. How she would have invited her over for dinner at the first chance she got, and teased Dee about his new love interest. Instead, he had an apathetic, detached older sibling who had no interest in his life or his friendships. It was like he was nothing more than a nuisance to Dylan.

I hope all ur shit gets jacked and ur stranded on the strip, Dee texted back. *Thanks for the cash. Im serious tho. Dont come back.*

"Good morning," Naya mumbled, stretching herself in bed as she rose into consciousness.

"Hey," Dee said. "I was watching you sleep."

"Giving Edward Cullen a run for his money." Naya grinned. "I really wanna kiss you right now but I have morning breath."

"I guess if we both have morning breath, it cancels itself out."

"God, you're so clever." She giggled.

Is that freak show gonna move in w you or something lol? Dylan responded a minute later. *Get a hold of urself. U need me.*

Dee frowned, placing his phone on the bedside table facedown. "God, I hate my brother."

"What's he saying?"

"Doesn't matter. Just being his usual self."

"Sorry about that," Naya whispered. "Families suck. Speaking of such, I think I'll have to head home soon. If I'm not back by noon, my parents will probably call the cops." She stood up and left his room, going to brush her teeth. Dee's phone vibrated again, but he didn't check it. Instead he clenched his jaw, suddenly fighting back tears. He didn't want Naya to leave, not yet.

It was a stupid thing to be upset about, considering they lived in the same neighborhood. He just knew that day was going to be one of the bad days, when the cavity in his chest reminded him it was there, and it was still growing.

◆

Once Naya had left, Dee skated to Tyler's house and walked in without knocking. Tori, Amber, and Tyler were sitting in the living room, and they all turned their heads in unison as he appeared.

"Yo, dude," Tyler greeted him. "How's it going?"

"Fine," he lied. "Are you guys good?"

"My parents aren't home. We're just talking about . . . you know."

Tori looked at the floor. She was wearing Tyler's sweater and her hair was tied up in a loose puff. She had no makeup on, and anyone would've known that she was a little bit worse for wear.

"I know Tyler told you," she said to Dee. "It's all . . . pretty messed up."

"You still haven't told anybody else?"

"I'm gonna tell my mom and dad tonight. Tyler's gonna tell his parents soon too."

Dee walked over and sat with them. "Have you made any decisions?"

"I don't want an abortion," she said almost instantly. Amber had an arm around her and was softly rubbing her shoulder in comfort. "I can't do it. My parents are gonna be mad, but I know they'd still be there for me. I'm just devastated because I was gonna go to college on a sports scholarship. I was gonna join the track team. Now I gotta wave all of those things good-bye."

"You don't have to. You're still so young. A child won't ruin everything."

"Everybody's gonna stare at me at school once I can't hide it anymore. They're all gonna talk. I don't know if I can deal with that."

"You can deal with anything. You're Victoria fuckin' Richards," Dee said.

She managed to smile, even in her deep brooding. "You aren't all that bad, you know? I feel like shit for always being mean."

He shrugged. "It's whatever."

"I used to really judge your family." Her voice went quiet. "When I found out that your . . . mom—that she had you so young. I used to think that was why your life was so unstable. Why you weren't so great at school, and why your home life was messed up. But I know now that it was wrong of me." She sniffed, holding back tears. "I was a bitch for that."

"Don't worry about it. There are bigger problems to handle right now."

She nodded, wiping her eyes. "I'm trying to adjust. I'm trying to get used to this."

"You've got this, Tori. Don't sweat it. We're here for you," Dee said consolingly. As much of a hard time as the Girls gave him, he knew deep down it came from a place of misunderstanding. It was just idle gossip, bandwagoning off the school's fixation with the trope of the popular kids and the misfits. His personal life had been under scrutiny ever since he'd started dating Vanessa. He was used to the judgment at that point; he could move past it. At the end of the day, his best friend was going through something he had ample experience with: growing up too fast. If his mother could manage under her circumstances, he was certain Tori would be okay too.

"You're an angel, Dee," Tori said. "A real-life angel."

Tori told him that she knew about Naya, that Tyler had broken his promise and told her. He turned bashful, awkward. *At least now it's just my brother who's the only obstacle*, he thought. That was somehow still awful. He could handle his friends having an issue, but not his family. Not his own flesh and blood. He knew Dylan was troubled and tainted from his upbringing; he'd been raised with hostility, and he carried a soul filled with rancor. It was something that even Freya Stone couldn't fix. Dee was frustrated that the one thing that had been keeping his life bright was gone forever. He missed his mother, and as he left Tyler's place later that day, a feeling of heavy sorrow came over him.

The night had not yet passed, and it was here to stay.

◊

"Hey. You haven't been answering my texts." Naya slid into Dee's car on the morning of volunteering three days later. They hadn't spoken all weekend, since she'd left his house. Really, it was more that Dee hadn't spoken to her.

"I've been busy."

"Doing what, exactly?"

"Does it matter?"

"Wow, okay. Wrong side of the bed this morning?"

Dee kept quiet. Naya could cut the tension in the air with a knife. Trying to ease it, she reached out to touch his neck, but he flinched. It was only the slightest move, though it stung just as hard as a slap to the face. She wondered what she could possibly have done wrong to warrant his reaction. Instead of trying to start a conversation, she turned the radio up as they made their way to

Salvation Hill; Jeff Buckley's "So Real" blared from the speakers. Dee was stuck wallowing in sourness for the remainder of the day, barely uttering a word to anyone, including Marie. He still read a few poems from her book to himself, heart sinking when he came across "To Drown A Fish." It made him think of things he really didn't want to think about, and the thoughts writhed through his brain well into the afternoon.

Naya spent an hour sorting out books and DVDs, wasting more time reading the backs of them than actually working, to make the time go faster. She tried so hard to break the silence in the room where Dee just stood, chewing on the inside of his cheek, staring at nothing in particular.

"Don't you find it annoying how most of us are erased from sociopolitical discourse?" she bemoaned, reading the blurb of a book on racial inequality. "Yeah, they spend time talking about the African-American struggle. They spend time talking about the female struggle. But what about the African-American female struggle? What about . . . the Asian female struggle? The *Indigenous* female struggle? They're not all the same. Can't just talk about women like we all go through the same shit. And look at *me*! My Blackness is challenged every day of my life. Sometimes I used to doubt whether I could even say I lived the real, authentic experience of a Black girl in America. Like, with the Girls and the zine . . . It's like . . . a girl with blond hair and blue eyes can't possibly know the struggle, right?" She was rambling. Dee just shrugged in response. "And don't get me started on their skewed statistics. God, no. Like the gender pay gap? What about the race pay gap? What about the crossover between gender and race? And . . . the way they always act like rape cases are the same through all the races, or even all the genders. Or domestic abuse.

There are things that people just don't talk about. Minorities are way more likely to go missing. End up in dangerous relationships. Hell, even in Indigenous communities—"

"Do you ever stop talking?" Dee blurted.

"What?" Naya blinked, turning to face him.

"Not everything has to be a big fucking political discussion."

"Oh, so because I don't think politics is separate from real life, *I'm* the bad guy?" She turned away, placing her pile of books on the shelf one-by-one.

"I take it you'll be running for Senate at some point, then?" Dee said, picking up another stack of misplaced books from the table. They were on opposite sides of the room with their backs turned toward one another, talking over their shoulders.

"That's not what I said. I just think politics overlooks intersectionality and it's *not* cool. It's not representative."

"Using big words isn't going to change anything."

"You're kind of missing the point."

"Whatever. All this politics, all these stats. They've done nothing for me. I don't care. You have your problems, I have mine. Let's just leave it there."

"Let me know if burying your head in the sand does anything for you," Naya responded.

"Oh give it a rest, Naya. You're giving me a headache."

Naya didn't want to break in front of him, but she was sure she was close to it. Her heart was in her throat, and she felt hot all over. Over the weekend, a switch had been flicked, and things had changed. Dee was becoming the colder, distant boy that she had first heard about, before she'd given him a chance, tried to get to the bottom of him. She saw something in him, and it was like an abyss. She was peeking into the cavity. It was hurting every bone in her body.

Later, at the end of their shift, Naya stood her ground. "I'm not going home with you. Don't even argue about it," she said with her arms crossed as they stood outside the nursing home.

"Okay," Dee responded. "Whatever."

"Asshole." Naya took out her phone, texting Amber, hoping she was free and that she could come and get her from Salvation Hill. "You don't have to be this way. I really like you, and you know it."

"You don't have to like me."

"I wish I didn't," she whispered. "You're not nice."

He paused. "How are you gonna get home?"

"Just get in the truck and leave me alone." She looked down at her phone, seeing a text from Amber. She was on her way, along with Jasmine and Evie.

"I'll see you around, I guess," Dee said, walking up to his vehicle and slamming the door closed once he was inside. He backed up and drove to the gates, his tires spraying red soil as he turned onto the road and sped away.

◆

To Drown a Fish
by V.M. Winslow

You can't drown a fish under water.
You must lure her onto land.
You must show her how beautiful the shore is.
The promises it bears.
You can't drown a fish in the ocean; she's too comfortable here.

You have to drag her out of her element,
choke her with a pure intensity.
You have to constrict her airways,
make her believe you are the only one
who can help her breathe.
To drown a fish, you must love her
with your fingers around her neck.
You must administer mouth-to-mouth
with your hands wrapped around her lungs.

19

STRUCK BY LIGHTNING

Harlow was not a place where rain fell. It was an arid landscape, prone to droughts and sandstorms. But on one July afternoon, the clear blue sky was suddenly blanketed by a bank of menacing cumulonimbus clouds, shooting down thick, heavy raindrops in an unrelenting torrent, moments after the sun had been shining bright. The Guys had quickly dispersed from No Man's Land with their T-shirts over their heads and the smell of petrichor permeating the warm air. Dee walked briskly in the direction of Naya's house instead of his own, landing at her doorstep a few minutes later.

"Got lost in the storm?" Naya asked him once he stood inside her hallway. He was soaked from head to toe, his blue jeans turned black and his white T-shirt sheer against his skin.

"No. I just didn't want to go home. It's a mind-numbing void over there." He looked down.

"You're drenched."

"I am," he said.

"Take your shoes off. Stay there. I'll get you a towel." She turned and ran upstairs, returning a few moments later and throwing one to him. He caught it, patting himself down. "Are your parents home?"

"No. They've made besties with a neighbor who works at the HECC. They're having a late lunch or something, I don't know. Why?"

"No reason." He shrugged, then he paused hesitantly. "Look. I wanted to apologize for the other day. I'd had a terrible weekend. I took it out on you."

Naya sighed, a lump rising in her throat. "It's whatever. We all have bad days. You wanna go upstairs? It's weird just standing in the hallway like this."

"Uh . . . sure." With the towel slung over his shoulder, he followed Naya up to her bedroom. The rain was still plummeting to earth, and the sky was dark. The humidity in the air caused the windows to steam over, and Naya went over to swipe at the condensation with her hand.

"Haven't seen this in a while," she said. The sky split into the heavens, a white light flashing like the snapshot of a Polaroid, followed by an apocalyptic boom. Thunder.

"Kinda crazy," Dee said. "My pants feel ten pounds heavier right now."

"You can borrow my clothes if you want. I've got some baggy sweatpants somewhere in my closet."

"Thanks," he responded as she fished through her belongings

for some old loungewear. Naya was quite tall, but she still knew that anything she owned would probably end above Dee's ankles. It was just a risk he'd have to be willing to take.

"You smell like sweat and rain," Naya said, handing him a baggy dark-green T-shirt with *Looney Tunes* graphics and a pair of sky-blue sweatpants. "You can use my shower first."

"Oh. You sure? Thanks. I'll just use this towel if that's cool."

"Go ahead."

As she waited for him, she thought back to the argument they'd had. It was all she had been thinking about. Even when the Girls had come to her rescue, heading to Jasmine's uncle's studio to work on the zine, her mind had been preoccupied. She was of two minds about everything, but ultimately, when she looked into Dee's eyes, all she saw was someone who was hurting. She wondered if she felt his pain more than she could feel her own.

He returned from her bathroom a while later in her clothes, the towel wrapped around his hair like he was a client at a spa. "I feel like a brand-new person."

"You look like one too." Naya laughed, grabbing a hairdryer from one of her drawers and handing it to him.

"I'm really getting some five-star hospitality here."

"Some may call it Southern," she responded. "How's everything holding up at home?"

He sat at her dressing table, drying his hair. "I don't wanna talk about it." He raised his voice over the loud hum. Naya sat back on her bed, twiddling her thumbs. Another crack of thunder hit outside, making her jump. Dee's hair was still slightly damp when he turned the hairdryer off. He turned to face her. "It sucks. That's all I can say. And I can't go to Tyler's place anymore because of the whole Tori thing. Which is, like, I get it. But I don't want to hang out with Ash, Wallis, or Levi."

"So I'm your fifth choice. That's so sweet," Naya teased.

"You know what I mean."

"No, I know. Just messing around."

"Besides, I can't cuddle with the homies. *That's* what I really want to do right now."

Naya raised her eyebrow. "Well, what are you waiting for?" She patted the pillow next to her. He smiled, striding toward the bed and lying down beside her. They watched the rain on the window for a few minutes.

"You smell much better now," Naya murmured.

"Courtesy of your shower gel." He tucked his left arm under hers, draping his right arm across her chest. He squeezed her softly. Her heart was racing. She turned to face him, and they kissed. Then, just as quickly as he had put her clothes on, he was taking them off. She followed suit. Soon, all items of clothing had been peeled off, unbuttoned, unbuckled, and left in a heap on either side of the bed. She wanted to feel the warmth of his skin on hers, his hair, his chest, his lips, his everything, his everywhere.

"You got any . . . uh, you know . . . ?" Dee asked between kisses. Naya reached over him and opened her bedside drawer. "I guess health class really did come in handy." She beamed, retrieving a condom packet and handing it to him. He lay on his back, opening the packet and putting it on, and she climbed on top, straddling him. She bent down and cupped his face in her hands, kissing him again. It was exhilarating, it was alien, it was home. It was all action, all animation, all laughter, soft sighs, heavy sighs, low groans, soft moans. It all happened so abruptly. It wasn't happening, and then it was. They had both been running away from their own troubles at the speed of light, and now they were running into each other, moving closer and closer until there was no more space left between them.

By the time they were done, the storm had passed and the sun was peeking through the clouds. Neither of them spoke for a while, basking in a mellow placidity. Naya was the first one to move, reaching for her T-shirt on the floor. She slipped her underwear back on and went to open the window. Dee watched her every move.

"What shall we do now?" she asked.

"We could watch something," he responded. "Maybe that show. Chris-something?"

"Yes! Okay, let's do that."

"Nice." He smiled, getting off the bed to dress himself. "Shame we haven't got something to smoke, though."

"I'm sure White Jesus is relieved." Naya smirked. "That's one more sin I don't need to shove in his face on the same day."

"They've already got a space reserved for you in hell, Naya. Just face it. We're done for. The underworld is calling us. That storm—that was God, and he's pissed. Someone probably got struck by lightning, and it's all your fault."

Naya shook her head and rolled her eyes, grabbing her laptop from the table. "Whatever, dummy. Let's watch the show."

◆

Dee strode into No Man's Land as the sun was setting. Three episodes into *Everybody Hates Chris*, he'd got a text from Ash letting him know that the Guys were back at the park now that the rain had cleared. So he'd left Naya's house, not wanting to go home just yet. He told her he needed to leave but really, he didn't. He just needed time to take everything in. Skating through the New Eden neighborhood, watching kids playing ball and people walking their dogs, he had never felt more in the moment. And it was written all over his expression as he approached his friends when he got to No Man's Land. Though his jeans were still slightly damp, they were a better choice than Naya's blue sweatpants. The Guys pointed out the *Looney Tunes* T-shirt as soon as they saw it.

"Where'd you get that?" Ash started. "Never seen you wear that shit before."

"Naya lent it to me."

"Your sharing clothes now? Okay, okay. That's interesting. *Romantic*, if you will," Ash said, followed by a chorus of laughter from Tyler, Wallis, and Levi.

"My clothes were wet. Big deal."

"So you didn't go home like the rest of us?" Wallis asked. "You've been over there for, what, the last couple hours, huh? That's . . . *something*."

"It's nothing." Dee huffed.

"I think you got laid," Ash responded. "Ain't no way you were just hanging out over there."

"Honestly, I thought y'all weren't speaking," Levi said. "I can't keep up no more."

"Well, I went over to apologize. We're good now."

"Ah, so it was make-up sex?" Ash snickered.

Dee paused, looking down. He tried not to smile, but it was like a reflex. His silence was just as good an answer as saying yes.

"Oh shit! So *that's* what's up!" Tyler punched Dee in the arm as the boys all started hollering. "This is wild. You had sex with Naya?"

"How was it?" Ash asked him.

"Uh . . . none of your business."

"I'm happy for you, though. She's a cool kid. Don't screw this one up," Tyler said, nudging him.

"I'll try my best." He looked up at the sky, watching a flock of birds glide across the vista. His head was somewhere up there, floating inside the remaining clouds, and every atom in his body was bouncing around. He felt light and boundless, and happy. Very, very happy.

◊

Though Naya was feeling everything at once, it wasn't all pure bliss. She also felt weird, uncomfortable. Both physically and in her mind. She was already overthinking, wondering if Dee would text her anytime soon, wondering how to act toward him the next morning for their Salvation Hill shift. She felt that maybe she'd been almost too quick to forgive him over their argument, but also knew he had been hounded by sadness, and though he was yet to open up about it, there had to be some temporary distraction from it all. Her own issues had been crawling back into her mind—thoughts she'd told herself were buried deep. She wanted to forget about her parents, about Ampleforth, about Haley, about her worsening eyesight, about everything. She wanted to help him forget about everything too.

Somewhere in the back of her mind, there was something that begged for her to feel awful about what she had just done. Having extramarital sex with a boy in her devout Christian parents' home definitely left a funky feeling in the pit of her stomach. The fear was beginning to creep in.

"I don't know how I feel. I'm kind of nervous," she told Amber over the phone minutes after Dee's departure.

"Of what?"

"The aftermath. I don't want to be a typical girl, but . . . I don't know what it meant. He's still just my friend. We're still just volunteer partners at a nursing home. Just mutual links in a friendship group. That's all. Right? I don't know."

"That's something for you to work out between yourselves," Amber said. "I don't think things should get that complicated if you just talk it through. I'm guessing you patched things up after the other day, right?"

"Well, yeah. He came over to apologize."

"Oh, well, I'm glad you worked through that. I'm so *happy* for you! You know, we all predicted this. Jas, Tori, Evie, and me. Even the Guys did."

"Huh?"

"Okay, so it was just a running joke. You sort of knew that too. But yeah, we all just thought, *Wouldn't it be wild if they actually ended up hooking up?* Like, bonding at an old people's home actually brings them together? And it did! Fuck. I'm so jealous. When school starts, I'm gonna hope I get partnered up with Brandon Lerone in science lab. Maybe the same shit will happen to me, who knows?"

"Sure, I guess?" Naya smiled.

"Ugh. Fuck you, Naya! I'm too jealous. I need to go. I'll talk later, 'kay?"

"Wait—"

The line went dead in an instant. Naya's heart was hammering. She wanted to tell Amber not to tell anyone else just yet, but she knew it was already too late. She felt everything all at once.

Nervous, excited, afraid. She was happy, though. Of that, she was certain.

◊

Dylan and Mia were arguing in the kitchen when Dee came home that evening. The high had worn off by then, but he was in a good mood, at least until he reached his front doorstep. Dee could hear that this fight was more intense than usual, like everything had been kicked up a notch. The couple almost didn't notice him enter the house. He leaned on the kitchen's door frame in silence. Then Mia turned and stared at Dee with a certain kind of trepidation in her eyes.

"Your brother is insane," she hissed at him. "There's something wrong with him."

"Shut up," Dylan said, erupting. It was the drunkest Dee had ever seen him. Mia was also wasted, but her condition paled in comparison to his brother's. "Don't listen to her. She's just a whore." The second Dee's presence had become known, the couple began only referring to each other in the third person, like they weren't in the room together—like he was the arbiter of their disagreement.

"What the fuck is going on?"

"This is the millionth time I've broken up with your brother, but it sure as hell is the last, *lo juro por Dios*. I swear to God."

"She's gonna come running back in a couple days, you watch—"

"He needs help." She strode toward Dee, placing her hands on his shoulders. She was much shorter than both of them, but there was a certain dominating force in her gesture, something that told him that he should listen to her. He then saw the bruises on her wrists, and the hair on the back of his neck prickled. He looked at Dylan, who was so far from sober that the only way he could be introduced back to reality in the near future would be through an IV drip. "You need to watch out for yourself. He's not a good person. I know he's your brother, I know he's here to care for you, but—"

Dylan stormed over, grabbing Mia by the arm and yanking her backward. "What bullshit are you feeding to my kid brother, huh?" he taunted, standing with his face less than an inch away from hers.

"Dylan, what are you doing? Stop it." Dee stepped in between them, staring him down. Mia stood with her arms crossed, breathing heavily behind him. "What did you do to her?"

"Nothing that she didn't deserve," Dylan mumbled. This was something that sent a shockwave through him, because he sounded like A Man Named Derrick, a man who was supposed to be long gone, a shard of the past. But here he was, standing in the kitchen, swaying and jeering, jaw clenched stone tight. "If she thinks she can get away with cheating, she's wrong."

"We are not *together*! What part of that don't you understand?" Mia hollered.

"Why are you here, then?"

"I told you, I'm collecting my shit, and I'm making it clear to you that it's all over. I'm done. This is all over. You understand?"

"You'll be back by next week, I swear on it."

"*Ay, pendejo*! Get the memo, it's over. OVER. Cunt."

Dylan attempted to grab Mia again, but Dee stood between them. "Just drop it, bro. Get your shit together."

"What the fuck do you know about anything? You're just a *kid*.

You're mistaken if you think you can tell *me* what I can and can't do."

"You're causing a scene. I could hear it from outside."

"My house, my rules. Whatever I do goes, whatever I say goes."

"This is my mother's house, actually," Dee said calmly, despite his blood boiling.

"She handed this shit over to me, kid. You saw the will."

"Yeah. Because she trusted you to be a better person. But we all know that was her fatal flaw. Trust. Trusting monsters, seeing the good in evil," he hissed, squaring up to his brother. Mia watched, eyes wide. "You're evil."

"Say that again. Go ahead. Do it."

"You. Are. Evil. I'm ashamed to share blood with you. It bothers me more than anything in the world."

Dylan slacked his shoulders and relaxed, turning around as he let out a long, hearty laugh. There was a split second between his shift in posture and the sudden brute force that came hammering down on Dee. There was a shriek, deranged laughter, and then there was darkness.

20

UNDO

"Hey."

"Hi."

"What's up?" Naya opened the truck door and hopped inside, shuffling around in her seat for a few seconds as a way to distract from her frenzied thoughts. She wasn't sure what to say or what to do, and she wondered if Dee was overthinking everything as much as she was. He sat with a cigarette in his mouth—the first he had smoked in the car with her present. He also had his Ray-Ban shades on, and he stayed looking out the window, as if in deep thought. Naya thought he might forget to drive off and instead just stay there, pondering. Her heart tumbled as she glimpsed the hickeys she'd left on his neck. She placed a hand on his thigh. He stayed unmoving, unmoved. Something was off.

"I'm good."

"You can't smoke here. My parents will see."

He looked to the ground, sighing. Then he stepped out of the truck, moving out of view of Naya's house. He finished his cigarette hastily, crushing the butt and stepping back into the truck. "Sorry," he muttered. He wasn't behaving as usual, and Naya could tell straightaway.

"Why are you wearing shades? It's not even sunny today."

He shrugged. "I'm hungover. I don't look too good," he said.

"You're lying. You never look bad when you're hungover."

"There's a first time for everything."

"Look at me." He did, albeit sheepishly. It was once he was facing fully in her direction that she could see where the issue lay. The Ray-Bans could not cover up the entirety of the bruise under his left eye—it spilled purple onto his cheekbone. "Shit, Dee. What happened?"

"I got drunk and I fucked up my eye."

Naya stayed silent for a second, scrutinizing his body language before tutting. "You're still lying."

"Gimme a break."

"How did you fuck your eye up?"

"I. Was. Drunk. Shit happens." He restarted the engine of the truck and pulled out of the driveway onto the asphalt of the road. "Can we just go to Salvation Hill and drop this?"

Naya knew he was hiding something, but she didn't want to pry when he clearly didn't want to tell the truth. He had gotten into a fight with someone. There were not many enemies he had that she could think of off the top of her head, unless it was Pearce Wilson or someone like that. If that was the case, she'd be annoyed, to say the least, so she swatted that idea out of her mind. But then something hit her like a freight train—something that was so obvious. It was his brother, Dylan. It *must* have been. She'd only met him once, but he did have an intense aura about him. She'd felt a strong bloodred when she met him, something alarming, like a matador to a bull. Like danger. Naya could sense the undercurrent of distaste that Dylan had toward her, assuming it was because she wasn't an ordinary-looking girl, a run-of-the-mill chick; she was eccentric, she was weird, she was Black. He had a problem with her, but that was the least of her worries at that moment. Dee's brother was hurting him, and that left a fraught feeling in the pit of her stomach. She didn't want to jump to any conclusions until she could be 100 percent sure that her assumptions were truth, so she just had to be there for him in the meantime. That was all that mattered.

"Wait, hold on. Lemme do something." Naya reached into her backpack once the truck was parked in the lot of the nursing home. "I carry concealer around when I'm breaking out." She pulled out a tube of ivory-colored cream. It was maybe a shade too light for him, but it would have to suffice for the time being. "Do you want me to apply some under your eye?"

He shrugged, biting the inside of his cheek. "Sure. As long as I don't look like a girl."

"Whoa, dude. Watch out for your masculinity. It's a lil' fragile." She chuckled, turning his face toward her and removing his shades. The shiner was worse than she'd imagined; his eyelid was swollen, leaving his eye only slightly ajar. It was all purple, indigo, hot pink, with the bruise clustering toward the inner corner of the eye, stopping at the bridge of his nose. Naya was furious, having made up her mind about what had happened. She didn't want to dig or ask any more questions, so instead she applied the concealer as softly as she could. He still winced, sucking in his breath as she got closer to his waterline. When she was done, she just stared at him for a long time.

"Do I look like a girl?" He smiled sadly.

"You look pretty." She placed a hand on the side of his face, scrutinizing the cover-up job. "Just keep your shades on. The sun's coming out now, see?" She was right.

"Thank you. I mean it."

"Nothing to thank me for."

"Thank you, Naya." He kissed her softly. Then they exited the vehicle and made their way to the entrance of Salvation Hill.

◆

An hour or so later, the pair were sitting in the nursing home's gazebo at lunch. Naya thought to bring up the Marie-theory game as a way to spark conversation between them; there were fewer words than usual being exchanged, courtesy of Dee's particular quietness that day. "Why haven't we looked at the possibility that Marie was kidnapped and made a part of some weird cult?" she asked him, watching the gardener water some flowers on the other side of the garden.

"Hmm. I suppose. It's kind of similar to the MK-Ultra theory, though. Getting kidnapped and all."

"No, but it isn't. It's totally different. She could have been brainwashed and radicalized, gotten so deep into the cult that it was almost impossible to escape. Maybe the name Marie Delden was given to her by the cult. Why else would she change her name?"

"I think if she had been radicalized in some group, it would have changed her character a lot more. She says and does nothing that alludes to having lived that kind of life. She doesn't mention anybody or anything mystical like that. She doesn't seem too religious. I don't know. It just doesn't hold," Dee said, tapping his foot on the ground.

"Remember, it's not about what she recalls. It's about what may have been the case. If we just go purely by her recollections, we have no answers, no theories. A person's life can't just be everything they remember; other people are involved. Other people knew her. She existed somewhere within this world, and maybe she had networks of relationships with people from all walks of life. Maybe she stuck around with the same circle for forty years. Either way, she wasn't completely alone, right?"

"Not necessarily. As underwhelming as the thought is . . . she could have moved to Harlow the second she disappeared, living alone here all this time."

Naya rolled her eyes. "Still. She would have met people, known people. Why doesn't she have friends? Did she enter into other relationships? Who knows, maybe she did get remarried and had another kid, just divorced and left her family again. This might be her second or third name change."

"Maybe." He was closing himself off again, making it clear that today was not one of the days that he felt like digging into Marie's hypothetical life.

The two sat in silence for a while. Then Dee turned to Naya, draping an arm around her shoulder. Something was clearly troubling him; the past week had not been great. She tried to think of something to say that could lighten his mood.

"You know, I enjoyed yesterday," she said softly. "It was nice."

"I'm glad." He looked at her, their faces inches apart. He still wore his shades, but he was close enough for Naya to see through them. She saw his bruised eye and wanted to kiss it away. "I enjoyed it too."

"Yay."

"How do you feel right now?"

"I feel okay."

"Are you sure? I mean . . . you know."

"Yeah, it was my first time, yada yada. It's cool. It's all human nature. Virginity is a social construct, you know."

"Fair enough. I was just wondering if your parents would freak if they found out."

"Yeah, they would, but I think they already have it in their heads that I've done it. And I'm a kid who's full of sin according to them. I know they love me, but they don't know me. Turns out that those two things aren't the same."

"I just hope you have peace of mind."

"Always."

"I'm glad."

"Same."

"Same."

"Shut up." Naya laughed, turning her face away.

"So are you down to do it again?" he asked quietly, smiling.

"Hold your horses, kiddo. We should slow down a little. We're just friends, after all." She shrugged.

"We're not friends." He frowned sarcastically. "We're just volunteer partners. Don't get it twisted. Once our shift is over, we don't know each other."

"I hate you sometimes." She laughed.

"What about the rest of the time?"

"The opposite, I guess."

"Ditto."

◊

Dylan was standing on the front porch, leaning on Dee's newly fixed car. The hood was a different color from the rest—most likely part of a different vehicle. It had spent months in the garage as his brother found ways to avoid repairing it. After planting a fist on him the night before, it seemed he was finally met with the feeling of real guilt. The moments following the punch were surreal. Dylan had sobered up immediately, realizing that he had knocked Dee unconscious. Mia was screaming, threatening to call the cops, weeping and uttering profanities in Spanish. Dylan begged her not to get law enforcement involved because it would "fuck everything up"—he'd lose custody of Dee.

Once Dee came around half a minute later, he was completely dazed. Even still, he hoped for the same thing, that the cops wouldn't turn up and complicate things. He told himself he could handle his brother, even as he found him becoming more and more dangerous. There was a weakness he could see in Dylan as he begged his ex-girlfriend, nearly on his knees, turning mousy and powerless within seconds, not to call the police. He felt sorry for his brother, oddly. Maybe the pity he had somehow held more weight than the fear. That must have been how his mother felt for all those years. That's how they got to you—they convinced you that somehow they were still vulnerable, and somehow your suffering was on par with theirs. Somehow, they suffered in their wrongdoings just as much as you did. You were the victim, and so were they. It was a constant cycle.

"Hey, kid. Here's your whip." He threw the key at Dee as he walked toward him.

"Thanks."

"Wanna sit and drink? Or maybe not drink, actually. I don't know." He scratched his neck. Something Dee also did in times of awkwardness. A shared trait. "We can smoke some hash. Watch something. Or . . . or you could tell me about your volunteering thing. We can talk about anything, really. It's up to you."

Dee hesitated. "I'm kind of busy tonight. Gonna go see Tyler in an hour. We could do something tomorrow, though."

"Sure. Whenever." Dylan lit up a cigarette, offering him one. He reluctantly accepted. They stood and smoked together. "You know, I truly am sorry, Dee. I don't know what got into me. I need to lay off the alcohol—"

"Forget it. It's over, it's in the past."

"You were right. Your mom did trust me to look after you, and I've failed miserably. I'm fucked up. I'm a shitty person."

"You don't *have* to be. I want to live with you, Dylan. I want us to get along so I can have some stability in my life before I move out for college. I only have a year left."

"I know. I know. I'm sorry. I'll change."

"It's cool." Dee shrugged. "Just lay off the beer."

Dylan nodded. "Hey—here, take this. Knock yourself out. Uh, sorry. Bad choice of words." He took out a wad of cash from his back pocket, holding it out. It was almost two hundred dollars.

"You really don't need to."

"Shut up, bro. Just take the money." He shook the bills in front of him, and Dee warily took them. *Money won't undo my black eye. It won't solve all of my problems. It won't bring my mother back to life*, he thought. But having no money wouldn't do any of those things either. In fact, nothing would. Nothing at all.

21

LIMBO

A few days had passed, and Dee decided to head to Central Harlow to buy a limited edition, custom design skateboard with the bulk of his brother's two hundred dollars. Dylan had been cleaning up his act since his apology, spending more time working out and less time drinking. He was also noticeably more subdued, almost too quiet to be himself. A certain malaise and absence of morale swept through the house, keeping the brothers in bed until one of them mustered the energy to cook up a half-assed lunch at two in the afternoon. They'd dig in and sit in silence, going about their lives before reuniting for a takeout dinner in front of the television. Between that and spending time with Naya, there wasn't much else Dee was up to. Everything was blue, everything was dark, and a little bit of trite shopping seemed like an ideal way to thin out the molasses-like heaviness that cloaked his mind. Of course, the wonders of shopping around near higher-end stores downtown increased the probability of bumping into richer people, like his ex-girlfriend, Vanessa.

"Fancy seeing you around here," she said to Dee as they stood within the perimeters of the downtown plaza. Around them, the district was bustling with tourists and kids hanging out and posing for photos in front of the fountain.

"I just went to Reinvent the Wheel for a new toy," Dee responded, holding up his board. "I take it you've also got some money to blow today." He pointed to the shopping bags hanging off her arms.

"Ugh. My plan was to get an outfit for my party this weekend," Vanessa said. "I kind of went overboard, though. I just can't really help myself." She shook her head.

Dee wondered what it must be like to leave a clothes store with a receipt so long it curled like a scroll. "Nuts. Anyway, I'm gonna head home. Nice seeing you." He nodded.

Vanessa stopped him. "Wait—are you busy right now? Shall we grab a milk shake at Benno's or something? You know—for old time's sake."

Dee paused, shifting his weight. "Uh . . . yeah, sure. Okay."

A few minutes later, they sat in the diner, looking everywhere but at each other. Their reunion had seemed to come out of some semblance of common courtesy and a forced sense of obligation. Things had been up in the air with them, after all; they had ended their relationship on a terrible note, and didn't quite manage to redeem themselves after the messiness of their breakup. Dee felt odd hanging out with Vanessa, couldn't help wondering how

Naya would react. Limbo was opening up again—one of those moments when he was just stuck somewhere in the in-between.

"Pearce and I are over," Vanessa started. "You were right. He's an asshole. I think he's still in, like, ninth grade. At least mentally."

"Yet he looks like he should have graduated when *we* were in ninth grade."

"Ugh, tell me about it. Well, he's leaving for college next month, so I guess his time has come."

"So you wouldn't have worked out anyway."

"I know."

"Sorry."

"Oh, don't apologize." She shook her head. "It's no big deal. Just gotta keep focusing on myself." She took a sip of her strawberry milk shake during the silence that ensued. Everything in the air just nagged at the two of them, illuminating the tension that they tried to hide through small talk. As Dee looked around, a woman a few tables away caught his eye. Before he could fully register who she was, the woman saw him and her eyes lit up. She smiled and waved, standing up to approach him and Vanessa.

"Dee! Hello. Long time, no see!" Jocelyn Begay-Graham hovered beside them. When Dee was fourteen, his mother took him to the Western Navajo Fair at the Tuba City fairgrounds, where there was an array of events spanning over three days. It was his third year attending, but he mostly just hung around his mother's herbal soap stall, helping to promote and sell products to the attendees. It was one of the few times he'd interacted with some of his extended family, like two of his mother's older sisters that she'd had a shaky relationship with over the years. Instead of attending any of the rodeos, pageants, or dances, he tagged along with his cousin Hannah in the evenings. She would introduce him to the teenaged children of other event organizers and attendees, and they would barter for chewing tobacco or weed, and play drinking games on the outskirts of the fairgrounds. Jocelyn was the mother of Shauna, one of Hannah's friends. Dee had never really held a conversation with her for longer than five minutes before. Though knew her well enough for small talk, it almost physically pained him to engage in it.

"Hey. This is Jocelyn, my mom's friend." He turned to Vanessa, then back to Jocelyn. "Jocelyn, this is Vanessa."

"Lovely to meet you. So how're things going? How're you holding up?"

"I'm cool. Just living life. How's the rez?"

"The usual. We're in a *real* dry season—stock ponds empty, but we're doing what we can, making trips while we wait on some more rainfall." Jocelyn stood with her hand on her waist, tapping her foot as she spoke.

"That sucks," Dee said. "Drought isn't fun." He hated himself for being so bad at chitchat. *'Drought isn't fun'? No shit.*

"Indeed it ain't. But anyway, I'll leave you guys. I was just over in Tucson and I thought I'd stop by the Pretty City for some grub. This place has a great menu."

"It does," Dee said, nodding. He shuffled around in his seat, sensing that she had more to say by the fact that she hadn't walked away yet.

"It's a damn shame Yiska closed. It was my lifeline! The *best* shampoos. I'm so, so sorry about your mother."

Dee swallowed. "Thanks. It's okay," he said. Vanessa looked at him, watching him shrink.

"Seriously. She was *so* talented. She raised a good kid too. Bless her soul." Jocelyn gave an endearing smile. "Anyway, I'm on my way outta here. I'll see you around, okay? Keep your chin up."

"Thanks, I'll see you around. Say hey to Shauna for me," he responded. "*'Say hey to Shauna'? Why did I say that? Does Jocelyn even know I know her?*

"Ah, you know Shauna? Lovely! I'll pass that on to her. See y'all later."

"Have a good day, Jocelyn." Vanessa waved as she walked away. "That was cute, wasn't it? You're bumping into a lot of people today."

Dee drank up the rest of his shake and fiddled with the straw. "Yeah, small world. She was my mom's most loyal customer. She always helped us out at the fairs."

"How sweet." Vanessa sighed. "You know, I still have a shit-ton of your mom's soaps and shampoos at my house."

"You do? I didn't know you went there a lot."

"Uh . . . well, I have something to confess." She grimaced, cupping her chin, resting her elbow on the table. "Remember when we went to Lights last year? And how I basically *begged* you to come with me?"

"Yeah, I do." Dee furrowed his brows, intrigued. The Lights Over Phoenix music festival tickets were extortionate, and Dee had backed out of the plans, but Vanessa offered to cover him. He'd accepted the offer, but he wore his pride on his sleeve, so he made sure he would find a way to pay her back. He'd spent the summer working at a bike store in town, eight hours a day, four days a week, for two and a half months. He'd despised every moment of it. Once he'd pocketed enough wages to level the cost of the festival, he'd quit the job and paid Vanessa back.

"The money you gave me . . . I really didn't need it. I meant that. But you wouldn't take no for an answer, so . . . I took the cash and bought, like, half of the stock at your mom's store. I told her not to tell you." She looked down at the table, diffidently sipping on her milk shake.

"Huh. Okay. Thanks. You really didn't have to do that, though."

"I *wanted* to, Dee. When you gave it back to me, it was up to me to spend it how I wanted, and that's where I went. Plus—Jocelyn's right. Those shampoos are amazing. My hair feels like literal silk all the time."

Dee smiled. "My mom was Walter White, turning the house into a fucking lab. She'd spend hours mixing shit together. She really perfected that formula."

"She was the best," Vanessa said. Her eyes watered and she blew out air, composing herself. "Anyway. That's why I still have so many of her products."

"Nice." Dee nodded, smiling softly. He'd always cherished Vanessa's generosity, her willingness to spend her money on others so easily. Even though most of her friends lived in opulent McMansions in Smithson, their wealth often paled in comparison to hers. She found herself being the one providing all the drinks at parties, giving away spare tickets to concerts, and letting friends fly first class with her on vacations, never asking for anything in return. Dee knew when he met her that she could easily be taken advantage of by the kids that wanted a slice of the high life, and he'd never wanted to give her that impression of himself. That was one of the things that attracted Vanessa to him in the first place; he had never shown interest in the flashiness of her lifestyle. He wasn't a freeloader; he didn't want anything from her. Ironically, because of that, she wanted to give him the world.

"So . . . how's your love life going?" Vanessa asked him a few moments later. If Dee knew anything, it was that she must have known about Naya by now. But for whatever reason, his brain told him to lay low about their relationship.

"It's nothing." He frowned.

"Nothing? Really? 'Cause I heard through the grapevine that you've got a little summer fling going on." She raised her eyebrow. "Nadia or something?"

"Naya."

"Huh?"

Dee cleared his throat. "Yeah. Um. She's called Naya. We're volunteering at the nursing home. That's all." He shrugged.

"Not what Evie Anderson told me."

"Hmm. Didn't know she was the oracle."

"It's fine, Dee." She laughed. "I don't care if it's true. We're not together. I just wanna know how you've been doing, that's all."

"I've been fine, honestly."

She paused before reaching out to touch the bruise under his eye, which had shifted into a yellow green, scattering onto his cheekbone. "You sure?"

"Mm-hmm."

"Well, that's all I care about."

"Why?"

"What do you mean?"

"Why do you care about me? You shouldn't. I'm so confused. I screwed you over. You should want nothing to do with me. Ever."

"I forgive easily, I guess," Vanessa said quietly. "Either that or I'm just an idiot. Or I don't like to carry burdens and weights around with me."

"You can just see that I'm fucked up. You've always seen that. You can't hate someone who's fucked up, can you?" Dee's heart was somewhere in his throat all of a sudden.

"That's not true at all." She perked up. "I just feel like . . . I *know* you. I don't think you're fucked up. I don't think you're a bad person, either, just because of everything that's happened. You just taught me that . . . I mean, I don't mean to sound brutal—but you taught me to put myself first. That's a lesson learned. I can't hate you for that."

He looked down at the table, biting the inside of his cheek in the silence that followed. "Well, I'm happy that I gave you that lesson. If anything."

"I'd just like us to stay friends. No awkwardness, no stepping on eggshells around each other. I'm tired of it all."

"Same."

"Awesome." She smiled. "Come to my party this Saturday. It's gonna be a big one. Bring your friends. Bring Naya."

"Was this all just a scheme to add to your guest list?" He grinned.

"Of course not. I don't need your help. I'd just love you to be there."

"Well, okay. Sure. I'll come."

Before they parted ways outside Benno's, Vanessa gave him a quick peck on the cheek. It made him feel all kinds of things but above all, awful. He was always suppressing the truth about *something*. About Naya. About Karina. He knew it would all explode, one way or another. Vanessa didn't like to carry around her burdens, and he probably should have considered taking a leaf out of her book. *Just tell the truth, Dee. Tell the truth. Tell the truth.*

Tell the truth.

◆

"Look to your left a little. No, not that far. Just a tiny bit," Jasmine instructed, squinting through the lens of her camera. Naya stood poised, trying her best to pose naturally as the glare of the studio lights overwhelmed her. Amber and Evie were sitting on the other side of the room, sharing a joint and digging into snacks.

"How many more shots do you have?" Naya asked. "My neck is killing me."

"Sorry! Just a couple more. They're dope, by the way."

"Nice to know," Naya said.

The Girls were doing profile shoots for the summer issue, preparing a spread dedicated to each of them. After Naya's argument with Tori the other week about the zine, they'd held another meeting to discuss Naya's concerns further. She opened up to them about everything, disclosing that her passion for art and fashion probably stemmed from her deteriorating eyesight. She also opened up about Haley, Ampleforth, and her parents, feeling more confident in sharing her tumultuous backstory with her newfound friendship group. It was like a monumental weight had been lifted off her shoulders, and for once she didn't feel like the outsider of the group. She felt like she was being taken more seriously, not like she was just filling up space. And once she told them how she truly felt about Dee, they toned down on the defamatory gossip. They started scheduling zine hangouts earlier in the day so Naya could actually join in without frequently breaking curfew. For the first time since she'd moved to Harlow, she felt the presence of friendship. She felt like she really belonged.

"Wow, girl. These are gorgeous. I swear to God, if you don't move to LA after school and get scouted somewhere, all your beauty is going to waste," Jasmine said. Naya relaxed, walking up to the camera's monitor to check out the gallery of photos.

She was impressed at the editorial flair that a high-quality camera gave her. "I could never model," she responded. "I walk like a baby deer. Bambi has better coordination than me."

"A runway walk ain't nothing you can't learn," Jasmine said. "You've got everything else down. Can't wait to see you at Fashion Week in a couple of years." She winked. "Amber, get your ass up here! It's your turn."

"God, I'm too high for this." Amber groaned. "Can you edit out my red eyes?" She rose from the table, walking up to the photography backdrop.

"First of all, can you keep your eyes open? I think that's a great place to start." Naya and Evie laughed at Jasmine's remark.

Just as Naya went to take Amber's place at the table, she felt her phone vibrate. She had a text from Dee.

Big party this weekend, it read. *Vanessa's house. U n the Girls wanna come?*

How'd u find out? Naya texted back.

Saw her downtown 2day, she told me I can bring whoever I want. U down?

Yeh sure. I'll tell the Girls.

Sweet, he texted. *Cant wait :D*

Naya had butterflies. It was, of course, Vanessa Bailey's party—the girl about town, the hottest in school, the Kylie Jenner of Harlow, Arizona. She had admittedly stalked her social media profiles at one point: eight thousand followers on Instagram, four thousand on Twitter, and a thousand friends on Facebook. Her photos were all stunning, arguably Photoshopped but potentially not. Whether they were snaps of her on vacation in Bora Bora or casual mirror selfies in her gargantuan bedroom, the selection made one thing clear to Naya: Vanessa was good-looking. A pretty, curvy, hazel-eyed girl with bone-straight, sandy blond hair. A jazz musician, an academic achiever, and, worst of all, a seemingly *nice* girl. Dee's ex of over a year, someone who looked like she could be a mean girl, a superficial, shallow, affluent bitch, seemed . . . nice.

Naya wasn't sure what to expect, but she did know that she'd probably need more than just a couple of shots of vodka to make it through the night. She had only broken curfew the one time on her birthday, and had spent that one night away (at Jasmine's, as far as her parents knew), so she knew she had a little bit of wiggle room to figure out another escape plan for the weekend. Ultimately, she was excited, absorbed at the thought of spending a hot summer night in the midst of revelry, wrapped around the arm of the one boy she could never get out of her mind.

22

NOTHING FATAL

"Holy shit. You look amazing!" Tori squealed as Naya came downstairs into the living room. Jasmine and Amber were in the kitchen pregaming, having finished getting ready a half hour ago. The Girls had decided to prepare themselves for Vanessa's party at Tori's place (all except Evie, who was getting ready with Vanessa). Tyler was pregaming at Dee's with the rest of the Guys. Tori wasn't going to attend, because a bash in the mayor's mansion didn't seem like the safest place for someone who was eight weeks along. Instead, she wanted to play stylist and hang around for support and gossip, since she was suffering from an intense bout of FOMO. Naya was given the go-ahead to dive into her closet and find something to wear that strayed from the usual mom jeans and block-colored outfits. Both Amber and Jasmine were wearing skintight minidresses, but Naya opted for a blue floral Bardot crop top and a high-waisted denim miniskirt. Though it was a cute getup, she would never be caught dead wearing something like that around her parents; she was happy they'd even agreed to let her stay out of the house past curfew, though she *had* lied about where she was going. The fact of the matter was, she was Dee Warrington's plus one to the biggest party of the year. This was uncharted territory, and the thought filled her with both terror and excitement. For one night, she'd dress like the rest of the girls in the Pretty City, and she'd have fun in the process.

Amber teetered in from the kitchen in high heels, clutching onto a glass of vodka cocktail. Her makeup consisted of a bold, smoky eye, red lips, and shimmering highlighter on her cheekbones. She had straightened out her kinky brunette hair for the occasion, and it swayed sleekly past her shoulders. "Dee's gonna drool when he sees how hot you look," she said, beaming.

"You think?" Naya responded coyly, crossing her arms over her bare torso.

"Uh, *yeah*. It's about time you made your debut as the coolest new couple in South Harlow."

"We're not—"

"You've spent the last week either hanging around with old people or hooking up with him. We don't even see you anymore. All your precious time is being used on the kid. If you're telling me that it's all for nothing, then . . . do *you*, I guess." Tori rolled her eyes.

"Can we just drink and leave?" Naya turned to Jasmine and Amber.

"Yeah, whatever. Let's just get fuckin' *lit*." Amber threw an arm in the air and spun back into the kitchen, Naya following behind. The drinking progressed, and everything slowly started on a messy downward spiral from thereon in.

◆

The party was mayhem; though there was a guest list, a horde of uninvited kids still found their way in. There was a professional photographer snapping people in the midst of their drug-and-alcohol-filled revelries, which would definitely leave them rolling in regret the next morning when the photo gallery eventually showed up on Facebook. Naya wondered how *the actual mayor of Harlow* would even allow such dissolute roistering in his own home, but the question left her mind once she was taken over by the vodka monster at the party. She became someone she had never been before—boisterous and sloppy. She drew attention to herself and had people wondering who she was and where she came from: the cool, charismatic chick with the kinky, strawberry-blond hair and legs for days; the girl who wouldn't stop talking to anyone about anything and everything, and dancing to every song; the eccentric newbie.

The Guys had not yet arrived when she found herself having a drunken heart-to-heart with Vanessa (who was also extremely intoxicated) in the backyard. She rambled on about how intimidated she was by her, and Vanessa responded with, "What the fuck? How could you ever be intimidated by me—I was intimidated by *you*. You're so cool and unique and confident and edgy in a good way, you're also pretty, and . . . cool." Their conversation was circular for a while, as they rallied compliments back and forth at each other. Things took a turn when Dee became the topic of their talk, which was almost inevitable; they had failed the Bechdel Test. Naya ranted about how he was the first guy she had ever liked, how she'd never expected anything to come from their friendship, how amazing he was, and somewhere in the midst of pouring her heart out, she mentioned sleeping with him.

"He told me you guys were just friends," Vanessa said, heart sinking.

"Oh. When?"

"The other day. He was . . . adamant about it, actually."

"It's fine. It's whatever. I mean, things aren't serious. I've only known him a couple of months."

"So you're together?"

"I don't know. We haven't talked about it."

"Why couldn't he just tell me that?" Vanessa said to herself more than to Naya.

"It's no big deal," Naya slurred, feeling equally upset. For one, Dee was hiding her away again. She could understand from his brother, but not from Vanessa, at least not fully. She just didn't know how to feel about it anymore. In her drunken state, a certain anger brewed in her, but sadness came through most of all. Confusion, disappointment, frustration, sadness. Both of the girls sat in silence, swaying, holding in their own explosions of emotions, trying to keep the faucet of throbbing anger closed tight. Then Amber found Naya and whisked her away from Vanessa. They found a spot in the house to dance without care or coordination, and they took over the floor, stumbling and laughing, yelling along to the music. When "In My Feelings" came on, Jasmine and Evie appeared from nowhere as if summoned, and the four girls broke into the viral choreography that they'd spent time practicing after the zine meetings. It was almost enough to make Naya forget the conversation she'd just had, to let her focus on the fun of the moment with her friends while she attracted the attention of party-going strangers. Deep down, though, she knew if she didn't have the distraction of revelry in that moment, she'd be falling apart.

Everything was a blur for a while after that. Bodies were melding into one another, the music was just a mixture of sounds reverberating across the walls, time was patchy and inconsistent. About a half hour later, Vanessa found herself crying in one of her bathrooms. Dee sat along the wall adjacent to the toilet as she hovered over the sink, somewhere between hollering and weeping. He had only just arrived but had immediately bumped into her and been hit with a barrage of drunken yelling. All she kept wondering was *why, why, why* couldn't he just tell the truth? Once again he'd omitted information; once again he'd lied. He'd pulled her into the closest bathroom in order to stop a commotion from starting in front of everyone. Her makeup was smudged, her hair tousled, her dress wrinkled in odd places. She was a mess.

"Why would you *lie*? Why couldn't you just tell me? Did I do something to deserve this? Ugh, fuck. FUCK. First Karina, now . . . fuck. Fuck. What was I to you, Dee? Was I just the . . . dumb, blond, rich girl you could take advantage of? I really, really . . . really loved you, and I don't know what it was all for," she sobbed, gasping through her words. "You came to me and told me to my fuckin' *face* that you hadn't done anything with Karina, then she goes around telling everybody like a smug little whore. Then you say *maybe* you did, you just can't remember shit. Then you do the same thing with a *new* girl . . . I know you don't owe me shit anymore, but that's not the fucking point. You lied to me again. It was always lies on top of lies with you. It always has been. You're just a fucking liar. It's not fair.

"I know you've been through a lot, I get it! I was there at your mother's funeral. I loved her too. I felt your pain, I cried along with you, I hurt when you fucking hurt. I didn't think you'd ever hurt me like this. This is so painful. I hate you. You *liar*. You're just a liar," she yelled, making less sense as she went along, just flinging anything she could think of at him in an inebriated barrage.

Dee just sat there staring at the floor, seeing his two feet splaying out into four, seeing everything double. He hadn't even seen Naya yet—all he wanted to do was greet her, kiss her, let everybody know that he'd found a girl he really liked, set things straight. In his uninhibited state, he decided he wasn't going to lie anymore; he wasn't going to hide anymore. He was sure of that fact. But then he realized he had to start with Vanessa. He had to let her know the truth, even if it was something he still couldn't quite register himself.

"I bumped into Karina a few weeks ago," he mumbled, feeling nauseated. "We got into an argument. I was trying to figure out what she'd spiked my drink with at that party. You know, the party I went to that weekend. The one you didn't want me to go to after our fight. It was the beginning of the end, Ness. The beginning of one of *many* ends. I just knew for a fact that she had roofied me. I know this because . . . I lied about that night. I lied about not ending up at her place. I lied about not ending up in her room. I lied about not remembering anything too. I do remember things. Like waking up on her bed, my head fucking pounding. I could barely see straight. It felt like I was coming up from general anesthetic or something like that. I felt like I couldn't breathe or speak. I couldn't fucking move, Vanessa. And I was just lying there, staring blankly at the ceiling. Then I started putting the pieces together. I could see Karina getting on top of me. She's not wearing anything, she's saying things but I can't fucking process anything." Dee's voice was barely a whisper at this point, and his eyes were blurred with tears. "I try to move, she makes sure that I can't. She's going down on me. I don't even know if she had me bound to something, but . . . I don't know. I just couldn't fucking move. I generally thought that *this was it for me*. I was gonna be found dead and naked in some girl's house, it would be set up as a weird drugged-up sex game gone wrong, like something that I had agreed to, something I had put myself up for.

"We had just been talking at the party, Ness. I know that seemed hard to believe because I'd had that argument with you earlier that day. She was just an old friend, we were talking about small, trivial, useless shit. We sat at the kitchen counter and she'd refill my cup every now and then, whenever hers was empty, and I thought nothing of it. I didn't think she'd do anything to my fucking *drink*. But then I blacked out, and I was in her room, and I've never been more afraid of anyone and anything in my life. A different kind of fear than that of my brother, my father, even of myself. I'd never been made to feel so small, so exposed, so fucking dispensable before that point. I thought I could just have a friendly conversation with a girl I used to know, and that was how it ended. How the fuck do I tell you that? How do I tell *anyone* that? Who the fuck would believe me? So I just faced the fact. I had nothing to fall back on, no way to defend myself. I'm a fucking *guy*. I can't tell people the truth, nobody would believe me.

"The other week, I asked her what she'd spiked my drink with. She told me 'nothing fatal,' and she laughed it off like it was nothing, like *I* was nothing, and I've felt like nothing ever since that night. I've never felt more alien in my own body. To be honest, I haven't felt normal since I left her house that next morning, going home and throwing up, fevering from whatever comedown I was having. She said those words *'nothing fatal,'* and they ring around my head all the fucking time. *Nothing fatal, nothing fatal,* but I always feel like my fate has been sealed, every day, all the time. I feel like the world is over. I'm just living and breathing, postapocalyptically. The world has been over for me for a long, long time. Do you understand?"

Vanessa stayed stock-still, frozen, staring hard at the marble-tiled floor.

"I recently met a girl who helped distract me from all the shit that has been festering in my mind for all these months, but . . . people kept getting involved, contaminating whatever it was we were developing. I didn't want us to get sucked up into the outer world, the gossip. I wanted to keep what I had with her to myself, keep her close to my chest, because for a while, nothing has just been *mine*. My shitty past life hasn't been something I can hide. I can't even claim my own body as my own. Nothing is sacred for me anymore. That's what I mean when I say that my fate has been sealed for me. I just wanted to protect Naya from all of that bullshit, but I can't. I can't save myself, I can't save relationships, I can't keep anything from fucking up. Shit. I'm sorry. I didn't mean to rant." The silence that ensued was stunning. Dee kept wiping his tears as they fell, and Vanessa just slid down the side of the bathtub, in shock. "I still haven't even found it in me to say the word out loud. To articulate what happened with Karina in black-and-white, because it just sounds too surreal, too *odd*. I still can't say it, Ness. And that's why I lost you. I was too afraid to face it. I'm sorry."

"You were raped," she whispered. "Karina . . . *raped* you." He didn't speak, instead just shrugging and staring. "That's why you freaked out that time I came over," she murmured, trying to catch her breath. "When I was on top of you. That was the thing you wanted to tell me about, right? It makes sense now. Oh my God. No," she cried.

"I'm sorry, Ness."

"No. No, no. Stop apologizing, please," she pleaded, crawling over to him. She lay her head on his lap, sobbing. "Don't ever say sorry again."

"Okay," he sighed, stroking her hair. "I won't."

The activity in the house was increasing as the party got louder, wilder. People were spilling out onto the other floors, and some kids were meandering outside the bathroom door, trying to get in. The ex-lovers just stayed where they were, losing all sense of time. Soon, they both fell asleep on the marble floor, shut out from the mayhem surrounding them.

23

LIFE OVER LOVE

Haley Fawcett was the last person Naya thought she would end up speaking to again. Especially while her head felt like it had been split in two, while she could barely keep her eyes open lying on the makeshift mattress at the foot of Tori's bed the morning after the party. There were bruises all over her legs and scratches on her arms. She remembered close to nothing of last night. In fact, the last thing she recalled was the unexpected conversation she had had with Vanessa Bailey, and the thought made her wish to run off to the closest toilet and vomit. She had never experienced a hangover, and if this is what it felt like, she questioned why anybody would make the rational decision to do this on a regular basis.

Despite feeling worse than horrible, she found herself waking up before Tori and checking her phone to find a text from someone called *Hales*. Haley. Haley Fawcett had texted her.

Hey, Nai. It's been a long time since we spoke. Just dropped by to say hello.

It took almost every bone in Naya's body for her not to go straight to the green button and call her. She stumbled out of the bedroom, wearing Tori's pajamas. Everything hurt everywhere, but the strength that came with the desperation of needing to speak to her first love again had her feeling invincible. She grabbed a glass of water in the kitchen and gulped it down, almost choking, suddenly crying. Dragging her feet out into the backyard of Tori's home, she lay on the deck swing, shading her eyes from the stinging light. She took a deep breath, hesitating before calling Haley's number.

"Oh my God," she spluttered, the second she heard Haley's voice. It had been months, and she hadn't realized how much she missed it. "Hales."

"Nai."

"I don't even know where to start." She sniffed. "It's been forever."

"I know, I know. I've been busy. I'm sure you have been too. How's Arizona?"

"Have you brought your socials back? Facebook? Twitter, all of that?"

"I brought back Instagram. Just for art and photography stuff. I'll hold back on the other ones for a while longer. I still need to hold off from certain triggers."

"Oh. Good. Are you back home now?"

"Yeah. I came back a couple of weeks ago. Just been trying to settle, figure things out here in the real world. It was so weird, knowing that I couldn't knock on your front door, though."

"I know. I'm sorry."

"Oh come on. Shit happens."

"Haley. What was it like in there?"

"It was fucking awful. Then it was just the daily grind, then I felt comfortable, like I never wanted to leave. Imagine that. Not wanting to leave a treatment center. Wow. Says a lot, right?"

"How long?"

"Forever. Months, dude. I did all my schoolwork there. I did everything. I got so used to getting assignments in the mail, writing out math equations while I was feeding through my tube. Obviously, at first I couldn't bear doing that—I just wanted to study. But I was pretty close to death at that point. So whatever. Algebra and nutrition would have to become the OTP of the year."

"One True Pairing." Naya smiled through her tears. "Like we were." She thought back to their obsessions with TV shows and fandoms, and how they'd ended up going around using corny phrases they had found all over Tumblr to describe character relationships.

"All before all that bullshit ensued."

"Do you forgive me?"

"What?"

"You almost died because of me, Hales."

"Do you hear what you're saying?"

"It's true."

"I've gained twenty pounds since getting admitted. I don't exactly feel revitalized, but I'm definitely feeling better. Nai. Have you been blaming yourself this whole time?"

"Of course. I didn't have to confess that it was you I was with.

I didn't have to tell them that it was you that I loved. That was your place, your time, and I took that away from you. And then the Ampleforth church started a dumpster fire, shit just spiraled out of control, and I couldn't do anything about it. You just stopped eating for *weeks* even though you had been fine for almost a year. You fucking had a *heart attack* after the shitstorm that followed me opening my mouth and I'm not supposed to feel awful about that?"

"First of all, my parents are pieces of shit that made the situation worse. Secondly, it was a minor attack."

"It was a fucking heart attack!"

"It was because I wasn't coping, Nai! I had, and still have, an irrational phobia of calorific consumption of any kind. A fear that started while I was young, before I even got to know you, or knew I liked you, or that I loved you. Before Ampleforth found out. I had my own demons—they swallowed me whole and tried to kill me. Nai, we never even got to say good-bye to each other. I was whisked off to a facility before you moved. You don't know the revelations I underwent. You built up a story of guilt and redemption, but I never blamed you, silly. Everything that happened just happened to keep me alive. I spent months in retrospection, self-reflection, missing you more than anyone else in this world. I felt like my world was over when I found out you'd left town. I had my own ups and downs, but they were mine, and whenever you were on my mind, there was a pining I had. My heart was so desperate for you.

"I missed you, Nai! I was sorry for how things ended, and of course I took blame too. That's what happens. We take the blame. It's the only way it all makes sense. I can't blame you, I could never blame you—only myself. And look. I'm better now. If you hadn't

confessed to our relationship, I'd probably still be dividing, plus-
ing, and minusing all the energy I transferred into fat, the energy
I expelled with every step I took daily, like a madwoman, while
acting like everything was all good, like nothing was wrong.
Inadvertently, all that mess got me getting my shit together. I'm
better now, Nai. I'm getting better."

"Are you sure?" Naya snuffled, wiping away her tears. Her
head was throbbing intensely.

"I'm home now. God knows where I'd be if none of all this shit
had happened."

"We'd still be together."

"I might have not been around, Nai. It's life over love sometimes. Life over love."

They spent a long time on the phone, catching up over everything and anything. Naya didn't hesitate to tell Haley about
Salvation Hill, about the mysterious case of Marie Delden,
about her poetry book. She told her about her new friends, Tori,
Jasmine, Amber, and Evie. About Tori getting knocked up by
Tyler, about the rest of the Guys she had come to know. She
didn't have it in her to speak of Dee, so she didn't. Things were
suspended with him at this point. They'd never crossed paths at
the party, and she had no clue if he'd even attended. She needed
a break from him before things got too complicated. He needed
to figure out how he truly felt about her, and she had to do the
same. Besides volunteering, she felt that they couldn't spend any
more time with each other for the moment; an ultimatum was
on the rise.

Naya had been up for over an hour when the house finally
began coming alive with activity. Tori's mother came downstairs to
make breakfast for everyone. She saw Naya on the phone outside,

giving her a smile and a wave when Naya looked over. Tori soon sauntered down afterward, joining Naya in the garden.

"I have to go," Naya said to Haley. "Let's talk later, okay?"

"Sure. Seeya whenever."

Naya chuckled. "Whenever." And the line went dead.

Tori sat and stared at Naya for a long time before bursting into laughter. "Girl. You were a mess last night."

"I'm aware."

"No, like. Seriously. Levi and Ash carried you back to my place at, like, two in the morning. You were fucking conked. The funniest thing I ever saw. Even funnier than that one time Jasmine fell out of the back seat of Tyler's car on Spring Break last year. You've topped it."

"Nice to know."

"You're looking a little rough."

"Great."

"Haha. I'm sorry. Just teasing. Who were you speaking to?"

"Haley."

"Oh my! The girl from back home?"

"Yup. She texted me out of the blue this morning, and we had a little catch-up. We haven't spoken to each other in months. It was well overdue," Naya responded. "By the way . . . have you told your parents yet? About . . . you know?" she asked in a hushed tone.

"Ugh. No, not yet. I keep stalling."

"Tori, you have to. You need a checkup, all of that. See how things are going in there."

"You're right." She sighed, resting her head on Naya's shoulder. "I just still don't want to face it."

"You have to." Naya put her arm around Tori, stroking her hair. "Got no choice."

"I know. I know."

They stayed silent for a while until Tori spoke again. "There was a lot of drama at the party, you know. Fights broke out. Cops showed up after you left. Someone got bottled, some girl broke her arm jumping into the pool—"

"Did Dee show up?"

"Uh . . . so I heard," Tori responded sheepishly.

"What aren't you telling me?"

"Nothing."

"Spit it out."

"I don't wanna spread rumors—"

"Tori."

"He spent the whole night with Vanessa. They were locked in one of the bathrooms for maybe a couple hours, and there's a rumor going around that they . . . hooked up. But I highly doubt it. Nobody heard or saw anything."

"Oh. Hmm."

"Yeah. I mean, nobody knows what happened in there. They were found passed out, completely gone. Apparently people *did* hear arguing, Vanessa yelling, that kind of stuff. I wouldn't jump to conclusions."

"You're right. We don't know."

"This is what I meant all those weeks ago, Nai. When I warned you. I didn't mean any harm by what I said, and he's grown on me since. But the kid still has issues. I doubt he's over his ex. It just be like that sometimes."

"I suppose."

"Don't sweat it."

"But . . ."

"But what?"

"It doesn't make sense. Like. Literally. We were together yesterday. We've been together *all week*. I know you could say that all boys want is a lay, but he could get it anywhere. He's dated a millionaire, like, Jesus. And he's telling her we're just friends. How can he just show me one thing and then tell Vanessa another?"

"I don't know, Nai. I just don't want you to get hurt."

"Too late," Naya mumbled. "Always too late."

She thought back to Haley and how much she really missed her. She thought of her eyes, teal green, her chestnut brown hair that was always styled into a bob with bangs, clothes like she was a character straight out of the set of *Moonrise Kingdom* or *Juno*. She'd always stroll through Ampleforth's church pews wearing something baggy, something that engulfed her petite frame.

It took a few weeks after Haley's fourteenth birthday, and five months into their newfound friendship, for her to finally admit to Naya the secret she had been keeping: that she was petrified of food. She strived for her own sense of control, feeling like she had none under the roof of her family's home. Naya related all too well, even though she didn't exert her frustrations in the same way Haley found herself doing. Eventually, she started getting help, as well as dealing with somewhat of an intervention from the church. And the Stephenses held their arms open to the Fawcetts. Haley had been better for a long time, never quite perfect, but she was eventually back to a healthy weight, she got her period along with all the other girls, her hair was getting thicker again, her arm hair was growing less fervently . . . She was getting better.

Things were smooth sailing for a while. Then one day, the cat was out of the bag, all hell was let loose, no heaven, no salvation. Naya came out to her parents, the Fawcetts were informed, and the families fought. Haley went into relapse. Naya hated herself, hated everything, hated the world but still wore colorful flared pants and quirky gold-rimmed glasses; she held her head high and thought of the future, a new life in Arizona—a chance to start new, fresh, with a blank slate. Then a boy came and painted something anew. Something she couldn't erase. Something she didn't want to. Something she was also afraid to look straight at. He was a masterpiece, a disaster. A disaster-piece. And she was in love with him.

24

THE ICEBERG

"What are you doing here?" Naya stood just inside Tori's front door. Dee was on the front lawn, shifting his weight awkwardly. He kept balling and stretching his left fist, something Naya noticed him do whenever he was stressed out.

"You weren't at Ty's. I didn't think you'd be at Jasmine's or Evie's. I knew you wouldn't have gone home yet. A process of elimination, I guess," he responded.

"That's not what I meant."

"Well, I'm here to see you. I want to talk to you. You probably heard about last night, right? Some bullshit about me getting with Vanessa. Rumors always go around all the time after parties."

"I really don't wanna talk right now. I don't feel too good. I feel awful, actually."

"Nothing happened," he said. "We fought, then we patched things up. Then we passed out in the bathroom. I drank too much. Way too much. I heard you did too."

"Seriously, Dee? Do you expect me to believe that? Honestly?"

"No, I don't. But it's the truth."

"You told Vanessa we were just 'platonic' friends." She signaled quotation marks with her fingers. "You acted like there was *nothing* going on between us. Do you know how stupid I felt?"

"I . . ." Dee choked. He looked at the ground, putting two and two together. The girls must have spoken to each other at the party. "I was wrong for that, I know."

"So you expect me to believe that you're telling me the truth about you and Vanessa? Right. Right, okay. That makes sense."

"I'm sorry. I really don't want to get into the details about last night. But all we did was talk. What we talked about was something important. Something that we needed to talk about. That's all I can tell you. I hate that I can't say more, but I just can't. I wanted to see you last night. I was hoping I'd see you at the party, and I could show you off to everyone, tell everyone how much you mean to me. But I bumped into Vanessa, and she was upset. She was angry at me for the same reason you are. And she brought up something from the past, back when we were together—something she thought I'd lied about, and I had to set the record straight. And I'm here to do that with you as well."

"But if you can't tell me what you spoke about, that still makes you hard to trust. You could be lying to me right now."

"Well, I'm not. And I'm not lying when I say I like you. I really do. I don't know how else to prove it. I don't know what else to do."

"There's nothing left for you to prove, Dee. I get the picture now. So . . . I think we should just stay friends. Platonic friends. I think we've made things complicated."

"Things don't have to be. We can start fresh now," he pleaded.

"Look. If you're going to tell your ex that we're just friends, then you stick by it. You don't get to choose when we are and when we're not. And if you're telling her that, then that's the truth. That's that."

"Nai, come on. I just want you to hear me out." He moved in closer, taking her hands into his.

She could feel a lump rise in her chest. "My head hurts. I can't deal with this right now."

"I'm sorry. I'm such a fucking idiot. I don't know what else to say."

"It's almost like you don't want to be liked," she said, unlatching her fingers from his.

Dee sighed, shaking his head. "Of course I want to be liked. But I really don't think I deserve it."

Naya looked at him and could see the sheepish dejection in his eyes. She tried her best not to cry. She briefly closed her eyes and pressed her fingers into her temples. "I'm really hungover. I'm going to go and take a nap. I think you should just go home. I'll see you on Tuesday, for Salvation Hill, all right?" She turned back to Tori's house, went inside, and closed the door behind her.

Dee stood unmoving for a few seconds. He'd felt a sense of relief that morning after finally coming clean to Vanessa about what Karina had done to him. But now Naya was retreating, and he had no idea how to make things right. He had dug himself into a hole that he may never be able to get out of.

Dylan was sitting in the living room when Dee arrived home shortly afterward. His eyes were on the television, but it did not seem like he was really watching it. He turned to look at Dee and smiled awkwardly, sitting forward and scratching his neck.

"How's it going?" he asked.

"Fine."

"You don't look too happy."

"I'm just hungover. I'm gonna get some rest. Is there any weed left?"

"I have about a gram. Take it all if you want."

"You sure?"

"Yeah. I'm heading off to Mia's tonight, for the night. I'll be back tomorrow, okay?"

"Did you make up again? Are you back together?"

Dylan nodded, leaning back onto the couch. "It's fucking complicated, man. A lot of things are."

"Do you think maybe it's because you're not really meant for each other?"

"No, it's because I've got a lot of hang-ups. I'm a dumbass." He chuckled. All Dee could hear was himself in his brother—the self-deprecation, the self-hatred. It was almost like nobody could really despise the brothers as much as they despised themselves. But where did they go from there?

"Well, you can change. You know that. If you want to keep Mia around, you've got to at least try."

"Dee the love guru," Dylan responded, picking up a packet of menthol cigarettes from the coffee table and lighting one up. *No, I'm being a hypocrite*, Dee thought. He bit the inside of his cheek, sinking into himself. If he couldn't even follow his own advice, he must be just as broken as his brother.

"Anyway, I hope the best for y'all. I'm gonna go to my room. Thanks for the weed."

"No problem, kiddo. It's Stardawg. The best of the best." Just as Dee turned toward the stairs, Dylan stopped him in his tracks. "By the way . . ."

"Yeah?"

"Uh . . . I'm leaving in a couple hours, so I might be gone by the time you're awake."

"That's cool. I'll see you tomorrow, then."

"Also . . . uh, I hope you're doing okay. I mean it." Dee found Dylan to be acting off, but he couldn't put a finger on it.

"I am. I'm okay. I hope you are."

"I'm good, I'm cool. See you tomorrow."

◆

"I think Zoe Schaffer started the rumor, you know. About you and Vanessa. But then again, it was a pretty easy rumor to start. Locking yourself in a room with your ex at a party is gonna look pretty suspect. It's not like y'all would be arm wrestling or talking about politics or something," Tyler said as he mindlessly played video games on his phone. Dee had awoken from his brief nap to find his brother gone, and he'd skated off to his best friend's house to vent about everything. He sat on Tyler's desk chair, swiveling left to right as Tyler gave his two cents.

"Everything I do always looks suspect. It's so fucking annoying."

"It's just because you keep shit to yourself. Which is cool—like, you don't gotta be telling everybody your business and nobody gotta be in it. But people will find ways to fill in the blanks. Especially at school. That's just the way it is. But don't sweat it. Nobody's gonna be talking about this in a week."

"I don't think Naya's gonna talk to me ever again."

"She will. Don't worry about it. Time heals all wounds."

"Do you believe me? That I didn't get with Vanessa last night?"

"You're my homeboy. I've got no reason to doubt you. But I do think you're stuck in two worlds right now. You're switching the lights on and off." He chuckled. "You're light switching two different girls. Been doing it all summer."

"Ha. And my baggage carousel just keeps going around and around." Dee leaned back in the chair and looked up at the ceiling.

"Deep shit. You know, when Tori got dumped by Jay Newman last year, she was so hung up about it. Amber would always be over at her place, being there for her and all that. And sometimes, on our first few dates, when we were talking, she'd bring him up. Not in an obsessed way, but enough for me to notice that he was probably still on her mind. It took a while for her to move on. But I don't know. I never felt like I was just a shoulder to cry on, or a rebound. I felt like she was genuinely interested in getting to know me. But also, she's pretty fucking hot. And she speaks her mind. There's a lot of shit to like about her. She told me how she felt about me, and I felt the same way, so I asked her out. And now here we are. So if she did have any baggage, she definitely packed light. And I think you should probably do the same."

"I want to. Shit's just hard. I just feel so lost. I keep tripping over myself. I should have asked Naya out a long time ago, but I didn't. I missed my chance."

"Do you *really* want to be with her? You know. All committed and shit? Is that really what you need right now?"

"God, I don't know. All I know is that she makes me happy. And she's a great kisser. And she's beautiful. And she's fun to be around. And she's wise. And superclever. But . . . I'm just a killjoy half the time."

"So it's not her, it's you. A classic."

"Maybe I'm just not compatible with love. Maybe it's not for me."

"That's some bull if I've ever heard it. Love is what keeps us all alive. It's what keeps us reproducing, in theory. It's an evolutionary advantage. Survival of the fittest, you know. If you ain't got love, you ain't gonna survive very long."

"Well, I guess that's why my mom died."

Tyler paused, then shook his head. "No, no. That's not what I meant, Dee."

"Well, it's true, isn't it? My parents didn't really love each other. Well, I guess my mom loved my dad. Some Stockholm syndrome shit."

"I'm sorry. There's nothing I can say. I mean that. It's so fucked up you had to go through this. But I'm telling you, all of that, that ain't a question of whether she had love or not. She obviously loved you, and your father at one point. But abuse . . . man, that's a whole other beast. You got a whole lotta love in your heart, but you've been through it, man. That kinda shit will fuck anybody up. Give yourself more credit."

Dee thought about how his best friend didn't know about his worst secret, the reason he and Vanessa had broken up, the reason everybody thought he was nothing but a heartbreaker who couldn't stick to one girl at a time. Tyler had no idea about what

Karina had done or what she was capable of. All of these awful things had happened to him, and he kept them in a small but perilously heavy box in the inner corner of his mind, and he didn't know what to do with it. Whenever he looked in the mirror, he could see damage that nobody else could see. His actions were just the tip of the iceberg.

"I really want Naya to talk to me again."

"I told you, she will. But if you wanna talk to her, you gotta make it clear what it is you want. If you're not ready for anything serious, just tell her, dude. You just gotta be honest. And you know she's not exactly gonna key your car." Tyler laughed. "She might be upset but she'll understand. She's a cool girl."

"Should I message her?"

"I'd say give it a couple of days. Then say something. Think hard about what you want to say."

"Okay. Got it. Thanks, dude."

"It's nothing," Tyler said.

The pair continued talking for a couple more hours, breaking into more jovial and lighthearted conversations while they took turns playing songs on Tyler's speaker. They shared a joint and made up rough freestyles to boom bap classics. The music was loud enough that Dee almost didn't notice his phone ringing, but when he did, he saw Mia's name appear. Confused, he stopped the music and answered. Tyler looked on.

"Hello?"

"Dee? Where are you? Can you come home soon?" The timbre of her voice sent Dee's heart skipping.

"What's wrong? Is everything okay?"

"Just get here when you can. Please."

"Is Dylan with you?"

"Dee. Just get here *now*."

When the line died, he quickly stood up and went to grab his jacket from the desk chair. Tyler didn't even have a chance to ask him what was wrong before Dee told him, "I think something bad has happened. I need to get back to my place. I'll see you later."

◆

He saw Mia's car parked in the driveway when he arrived home. Inside, she was pacing around the living room, and another woman was sitting on the couch. The two of them looked strikingly alike, and then Dee remembered that Mia had a sister. When Mia saw Dee, she broke into tears.

"Where the fuck is Dylan?" Dee asked sharply, but his voice faltered slightly.

Mia's sister responded. "He's in the hospital. We've called your uncle and let him know. He should be here first thing in the morning." There was a gravitas in her tone that sent a chill down his spine.

"Hold on. Why? What happened?"

Mia had collapsed onto the couch next to her sister, still sobbing. "Lana, don't say too much."

"He has to know, Mimi."

"Fuck." Mia wiped her eyes and composed herself. "Dylan came over to Phoenix today. He seemed okay. I thought he was. But then he locked himself in the bathroom, and he left a bunch of letters outside the door . . ."

From that point on, Dee couldn't hear anything except the

blood rushing in his ears, and his vision blurred. His chest tightened, his skin red-hot. He could not stop scratching the side of his neck. Before he knew it, his eyes were watering, his head heavy.

25

THE OPPOSITE OF SIMPLE

"Oh my God," Naya breathed. "I . . . is it really serious? Like, an accident, an injury or something?"

"Like I said, we don't know much else right now," Amber said over the phone. "Dee kept it short and just said his brother was sent to the emergency room. Could be anything, really. It could go either way. But judging by the call he got in Ty's room, I think it's probably pretty serious. And also judging from his brother . . . being his brother, it probably is."

Naya's heart sank. She could not begin to imagine the state Dee was in, with everything that had occurred in the last twenty-four hours. She thought back to the last conversation they'd had and she felt sick with regret, a wave washing over her. "Amber, can I come over? I don't really feel like being on my own right now. I think I'm going to spiral if I'm alone." She felt short of breath, as if her chest was slowly squeezing inward. The early signs of panic were becoming hard to ignore.

"Of course. Our front door is always open."

She immediately switched out of her pajamas and into jeans and a T-shirt, leaving her room hastily. When her mother asked her where she was going in such a hurry, Naya told her that her friend Amber was in a bit of a crisis and needed help over at her house. A white lie, of course; it wasn't Amber who was in the crisis.

◊

Amber was home alone; Tyler and their parents were over at Tori's house discussing the pregnancy, which had become news to the families the previous evening.

"I'm just about to make some pancakes. Do you want some?" she asked, leading Naya into the kitchen.

"Sure. Do you need any help?" Naya sat at the island counter on the other side of the room as Amber prepared the batter, melting butter and sprinkling a generous amount of sugar into a ceramic bowl.

"No, I'm good. I've managed to perfect my pancake formula. How are you feeling?" Amber asked, adding eggs before whisking.

"Slightly better. I just rushed here because I could feel an anxiety attack coming on. I don't know why, but the second I saw that text you sent about Dee, I started freaking out. It felt as if *I* was the reason he's in this situation. I know that doesn't make sense."

"No, it really doesn't, Nai." Amber paused, looking at her.

"I don't know. I think I just . . . I wish that we were on good terms. Literally on the same day I ask him for space, something like *this* happens. Like, Jesus. And now I feel even guiltier because I'm not actually freaking out about the fact that his brother's in the hospital and it could be life or death; I'm just upset that I cut him off too soon—"

"It's okay that you wanted space from him. It's okay that you asked for that. I think anyone in your position would have done the same thing. Or considering how idiotic he's been acting, I think most people might have done worse. Like, I don't know, keyed his car or something." She chuckled. "But you asked him for space and to just stay friends, and there's nothing wrong with that. If he wasn't such a doo-doo head, you'd probably be on speaking terms right now." She sighed, going back to whisking the batter.

"But I still feel guilty, Amber. I can't shake the feeling. A part of me just wishes I'd taken his word for what happened with Vanessa."

"Okay, but even if you did take his word, you're allowed your own space. You're entitled to that. Whatever happens afterward has no connection to that decision you made. Especially *this*. Now, this is just astronomically bad luck. It was so unpredictable."

"I dumped him on the day his brother probably nearly died. Five months after his mother."

"You set boundaries with someone who has broken your trust on the same day that some unfortunate shit happened."

"Stop it. I'm a Cancer. Let me find a reason to cry." She wiped a tear away as Amber laughed, sieving flour into the bowl.

"We need to wait for more information. We don't know if it's life or death yet, so we can't come to any conclusions on how Dee's feeling right now."

"Should I call him or message him or something?"

"I wouldn't if he hasn't said anything. Maybe he'll let you know. Or, I mean, a short message won't kill anyone. Just like a 'hope everything's okay' kind of message. But nothing more than that. Just think about what you want from the interaction. And if he's going through something right now, he might not really be present. And we know what he's like when he's not present."

"God. This sucks. Really, really bad."

"Look. You remember the whole Ash thing, right? When you first got here? It was all Jasmine and Evie teased me about. And they did tease Tori for getting with her best friend's brother, but I definitely got it worse. And it wasn't just because it was juicy gossip. It was because whatever we were doing . . . we were forcing it. I wanted to one up my brother because he was winning at breaking a pact that I'd broken first. So I was willing to make a fool of myself to make it work with a guy who was nothing more than a friend. I just want to make sure that you're not doing the same thing, because it was bad enough to go through it myself. I can't watch you fall into the same trap." Amber picked up a pan from the dish rack and placed it on the stove, ready to fry the batter.

"Yeah. I get that. I totally do. You're right. I don't want to try and make something work that won't. But he lives rent-free in my mind and that's the problem. I'm always thinking about him."

"I mean, I probably shouldn't tell you this because he did tell my brother in confidence, but . . . three weeks or so after Dee and Vanessa broke up, they hooked up. He basically booty called her. Then they got into a fight at the Fourth of July party over Pearce Wilson. Oh— and remember the day you guys hooked up for the first time? Well . . . first of all, I'm going to apologize because I can't keep shit to myself and I told Tyler after you told me. He told me later that day that

Dee was with him at No Man's Land when he found out. He could have just told you he was going to No Man's. Why lie? Did he not want you to join him? God knows. There's a lot of shit that's piling up against him, Nai. He doesn't have a good case, even if we don't consider the whole Karina thing. I'm just telling you this so you can maybe see things a little differently."

"He had a fight with Vanessa about Pearce Wilson at the Fourth of July party? You're kidding. That was the same night he kissed me for the first time." Her heart sank.

"My point exactly." Amber shook her head before attempting a pancake flip—it was only inches away from a fail when she caught it on the edge of the pan. She grimaced, then swiped her hand across her forehead, mimicking relief.

"Oh God. I'm such a fucking clown. Every time I don't think it can get any worse, it does." Naya sighed.

"I just think you should consider all things before you feel superguilty about everything that's happened and then go running back."

"I get that." Naya bit her nails. "I want to say something to him, though. I mean, just in case it's really bad. I just want to know if he's okay."

"You can do that. But keep it simple, Nai. No questions or apologies. Keep it simple." Amber poured more pancake batter into the frying pan.

"Ugh. Nothing in this world is simple. How will I ever cope?" Naya lamented theatrically, resting her forehead on her hands with her elbows on the counter. Nobody was simple. Dee wasn't a simple person. Nobody was.

26

MISSING OUT

"How are you feeling, buddy?" Uncle Jared asked Dee. They sat in Dee's backyard in the early afternoon, around a half an hour after his arrival from the Navajo Nation. He'd driven four hours south to Harlow that morning, and Mia had been there to greet him when he got there, thanking him for making it as quickly as he could. For Dee, his arrival turned his stomach into a ball of trepidation. He'd never seen his uncle much, but in recent years the only time he did was when something was wrong. Like when his mother was first hospitalized after his parents' final fight all those years ago, and again when his mother died. His uncle's presence was a stark reminder of the constant instability in his life.

"I'm not great. But I'm happy that Dylan's okay."

"You have Mia to thank for that. If she'd acted any later, things could have been much worse. He may not be here right now."

"Okay, but Mia shouldn't have been put in that situation in the first place. And clearly he didn't want to be here. He lied to me. He acted like he was just going to Phoenix for a night, but he knew what he was going to do, and he knew he was planning on never seeing me again. He wanted to leave." Dee's voice shrunk to a whisper. He frowned, looking down at his thumbs as he twiddled them. He could not stop thinking about his last interaction with Dylan: the awkward air in the room, how Dylan had seemed like he had a lot to say but he ended up not saying much at all. It all made sense to him now.

"Your brother needs a lot of help, Dee. He's not well. But my goal here is to make sure you're in safe hands, no matter what happens. I know we're not extremely close, but you're a member of my family, and we look out for each other. Your well-being is important to me. I'm here to help in any way possible."

"Thank you. It means a lot."

"Judging by the looks of things, Dylan's set to make a full recovery. He'll be back home soon. How do you feel about that?"

"I just want to beat the shit out of him for trying to fucking kill himself. I want to kill him for wanting to die. I know that sounds so stupid."

"No, I get it. There are a lot of emotions that come with something like this. There are gonna be a lot of feelings, and you're justified in your anger. But do you think you'll still feel comfortable living with your brother in the immediate future? Do you think you'll be able to cope? Because the way we see it, it's not a healthy setup."

"I'm not sure what other choice I have."

"But if you did have a choice, what would you want to do?"

"I honestly don't know. It depends on a lot of factors."

"Well, the real reason I asked is because you do have a choice. I got a job in Tuba City. My wife and Hannah and Christina— we're moving there in the fall. You're free to move with us if that's something you'd consider."

"Oh, wow." Dee looked up at his uncle. "Really? That's a huge commitment. For you, I mean."

"It's probably an even bigger commitment for you to stay in an unstable household. I don't know how well you've been holding up since March, but I'm guessing it's not been very easy for you, has it?"

"Not quite." Dee bit the inside of his cheek, then took a cigarette from his hoodie pocket and lit it.

"I never knew you smoked," Jared told him.

Dee shrugged. "I don't need a lecture on that right now."

Jared chuckled, shaking his head. "Your mother said the same thing to me when she started smoking, before you were born. I told her it was a habit for idiots, and she told me that she didn't have any plans to take a Mensa IQ test anytime soon."

"Haha. I don't either." Dee smiled softly. The funny thing was, she could have passed an IQ test with flying colors if she'd really tried. A self-taught cosmetic chemist, his mother spent months reading university-level books and attending skincare tutorials, perfectly blending her knowledge of sacred nature with science. She had her vices, her weaknesses and addictions, but her strengths trumped them. In Dee's eyes, she was a genius.

"Speaking of tests, how was your junior year? Did you stay on track, even after March?" Defining Dee's mother's death by month, and month only, seemed to be the best way to go about it.

"I don't get my finals results until next week, I think. They weren't really that easy. I had quite a few distractions. Mainly Dylan and Vanessa, besides Mom."

"The girl who came to the funeral with you, right?"

"Yeah. We're not together anymore. And school was not great after we broke up. It was pretty hard to concentrate. But I don't think I've failed my classes or anything. I don't know."

"Well, no matter your results, I can guarantee you a senior year transfer to the school I'm going to be working at. If you didn't do too well, you can retake some subjects, and if you did, you can just continue your studies."

Dee took a long drag. "Tuba City isn't near here. And I'd be a new student, right at the end of high school. That's going to suck."

"Well, lay out your current situation to me. Is being the new kid in a new town fundamentally worse than staying here, where you'll most likely be seeing Vanessa around for the next year, for example? Where you'll be staying with Dylan? Is there something you'll be missing out on that you can't form or create somewhere else?"

"I'll be missing out on my friends."

"That's true. I get that you don't want to let that go. But you should consider that in Harlow . . . you barely see anyone around here that looks like you. That's got to be isolating. You could make more Diné friends and connections."

"I don't know. I don't think that would make me feel like I belong there."

"Do you feel like you belong here?" With that question, Dee thought of his high school experience: the jokes, the microaggressions, the nicknames he'd been given, the ignorant comments other students made, the awful Native American

Halloween costumes he'd witnessed time and time again . . . He was safe around his friends, and he'd once felt safe around Vanessa before she'd shrugged off Pearce Wilson's insensitive ignorance, but he realized that that was as far as it went. He thought about his brother, who constantly struggled to relate to him. Being safe around people was not the same as being understood by them. Deep down, he knew that to be true. He'd probably not have to explain himself and his maternal culture to anyone if he was surrounded by it. But he knew it wouldn't be that easy.

"I've been to the rez, what, like, ten times in my whole life? I don't know shit. I don't know the language. Maybe a couple of phrases, that's it." He stubbed the butt of his cigarette with his shoe.

Jared paused before responding. "Your mother . . . she was a funny kid. She was wise beyond her years, but she was also very naive. You should understand—your circumstances aren't your fault, Dee. Culture is taught. You didn't get that luxury. I know your mother tried to relearn everything when your father was out of the picture . . . but she was so young when she left the rez. She did what she could, but it's never too late. You're still a kid, you can learn a thing or two. Maybe this is your chance."

"I suppose," Dee responded. He'd never truly known the depth of his mother's rebellion—her desire to break out of the world she grew up in. She'd been young and impressionable, a typical teenager. Hating where she was from was just a part of the package. Being her older brother, Jared had tried so many times to tell her that she didn't need to lose herself to find something bigger. But then she met a man who charmed her, groomed her, led her astray; a man who couldn't care less about where she was from, and didn't care to know about her background. And then she had a child with that man, and that child had been suspended in mid-air since the day he was born. Not quite here, not quite there. Dee's uncle had given him an offering to find his feet, place them firmly on the ground. The choice was his to make, and the clock was slowly ticking.

◊

Naya spent the rest of the day fighting off the urge to double-text Dee. She'd agonized for nearly half an hour on the first one, drafting the most concise text possible, deleting and rewriting it over and over again until she gave up and eventually pressed Send. Afterward, she went through their text chat, looking back at old conversations. It hadn't even been two days yet, but she already missed him dearly, felt restless in his absence. She was restless, and she wanted Dee to know about it. And though it had only been a day since they had held a real conversation, she was itching to feel something more than dread, to abate the intense separation anxiety. Amber's advice played over and over again in her mind—a reminder that she may have been investing all of her attention and care into the wrong person. She was at odds with her own intuitions, her own proposition that Dee was deep down an honest person with nothing to hide, and she didn't know what to do with how she felt. She thought, *It wouldn't kill me to pick up my phone and call my ex-girlfriend, my first love, instead.* She was losing the memory of Haley, and she realized that she'd never wanted it as tangibly as she wanted it right there, right then. To her surprise, Haley answered her call.

"What's up, buttercup?" Haley's lighthearted voice boomed on the other end of the line.

"Hey. I'm doing good. How are you?"

"Physically, I'm good. I'm doing good mentally too. I've mainly been reading a lot of mystery novels and watching old episodes of *The X-Files*. I've come to the conclusion that I'd literally die for Gillian Anderson."

Naya laughed. "I don't know why I could never get into that show. I think the theme song spooked me too much. And I don't want to entertain the possibility that aliens exist."

"You're the one who theorized that that mysterious old lady at your nursing home was abducted by them."

"True. But I obviously didn't mean it."

"What other theories did you make up? I can't remember."

"Uh . . ." Naya had to stop and think for a second. "We thought she might have just run away and wanted to start a new life. Or maybe she was abducted by the CIA for mind control experiments. Or maybe she joined a cult somewhere."

"You and who?"

"Huh?"

"You said 'we.' I thought you volunteered alone."

"Oh. Uh. Yeah, no, I don't. I have a partner. He's my friend, actually. Well—sort of. He's my friend's brother's best friend."

"Oh. I swore you told me about all your friends the other day. Let me see if I remember—Amber . . . Taylor, Tori, Jasmine or Yasmin. Uh . . . Ashley? I can't remember the rest."

"Close. Amber's my closest friend here, yeah. *Tyler* is her brother. Tori is Tyler's girlfriend. It's *Jasmine*, and there's also Evie. You're right about Ashley, but it's just Ash. Then there's a couple more guys. This guy called Wallis, he's superfunny; then there's Levi. Then there's . . . this guy. His name's Dee. He's the one who volunteers with me."

"So you just happened to forget to mention the one friend who you probably spend a considerable amount of time with? That's . . . interesting." Naya could hear Haley's smirk.

"Ugh. I'll just be honest. I didn't bring him up because he's been a real headache recently."

"Hmm. Is that the only reason?"

"Yes."

"Lies detected."

"Fine. Okay. I'll just tell you everything." And that was exactly what she did. She held nothing back—telling Haley about their friendship, how it had escalated into something more but now they were stuck in some weird purgatory. She told her about the recent loss of his mother, his entanglement with Vanessa, and the most recent course of events—his brother's emergency hospital admission. The same brother that Naya was intimidated by and afraid of. The same brother that had dared to lay a finger on him. By the end of her disclosure, Naya was crying.

"Oh, Nai. That sounds like a lot of shit to be dealing with. Being the new girl isn't always so easy breezy, is it?"

"No. It sucks. All I want to do is get over this *one guy* and move on with my life."

"I didn't know you were bisexual," Haley said quietly. "I mean, I guess I never asked. I was secretly hoping you were only Haley-sexual."

Naya chuckled. "I thought I was too."

"Are you out? Does everyone know over there?"

"Oh, everyone knows. Also—imagine thinking someone who handcrafts their own jewelry and wears silver Birkenstocks could possibly be one hundred percent straight."

"You've got a point there." Haley laughed. "Does Dee know?"

"Yeah, he does. He knows about you, as well. My girl friends all do too."

"Oh. That's awesome. Well, great, now I feel like I'm missing out on all the fun over there! It'd be nice to formally introduce myself to y'all. My friends here are great and all, but it's been a pretty uneventful summer all around. You know, recovery and all that. I could do with a little more action."

"I wish I could see you," Naya found herself saying. "I wish you could visit for a while. I miss you."

"Okay! I'll visit. Just for a few days," Haley said. Another surprise. Naya wasn't expecting such a statement from her, but she didn't know *what* she'd expected.

"You sure? What about . . . your parents? How will that work? Would they let you come and see me . . . after everything that's happened?"

"I can figure something out."

"It's okay if it's not possible. But it would be nice." *It would be amazing*, Naya thought, feeling her heart race and her smile grow wider. She tried her best to conceal her excitement at the thought of seeing Haley Fawcett again.

27

LOST

Later that day, the proposal Dee's uncle had presented to him was still hanging suspended over his head. Jared had driven back to the rez after telling him that if he needed time to think about it, he had it. He was of two minds about everything, fatigued by decision making. That evening, it was just Mia and Dee in the house, and they sat with each other in the living room watching *Dazed and Confused* on television. The windows were open, the air conditioning on full blast. Dee was hungrily inhaling a joint, but no amount of stimulant/depressant hybrids could shake away the desolation and disquietude that hung about in the warm, sticky air.

When he offered a hit to Mia, she declined. A few moments

later, she spoke. "I went to this open cinema with Dylan once, back in college. We went to watch this film. I didn't remember *any* of it because we were parked right at the back and it was so hard to see. And if my memory hasn't failed me, I'm sure we were both on acid." She laughed.

"That's so funny. How long ago was this?" Dee asked, keeping his eyes on the television.

"I don't know. Probably, like, seven-ish years ago? A very long time."

"I would have been ten years old back then."

"*Un pequeño chico*. A little ol' boy."

"After Dylan moved out, I don't think I ever saw him more than once or twice a year. Maybe on Christmas if he felt like it. It was just me and my mom. I'm not complaining. I remember him being a piece of work at times. Pissing my mother off when he came home late from parties in senior year. Stealing her car. Shit like that."

Mia looked at Dee. "He never spoke a lot about his family life when we first started dating. He was very secretive about it. I think it took him over six months to tell me that both of his parents were in prison, and I guess it's because he was ashamed. He told me he lived with his stepmother and that he had a little brother, and that he felt like the black sheep of the house. He never got to know his own mother, his father was not a great role model, and he wanted to feel like he belonged somewhere. I could tell he was very lost when we first met."

"I don't think there's really been a time when he hasn't been," Dee said quietly.

Mia continued. "I have a *huge* family. Three sisters, four brothers, and both of my parents are larger than life. My extended family is even bigger—I have so many aunts, uncles, and cousins back in Medellín. I'd invite Dylan to family dinners and functions, and I'd watch him retreat once the party was over. He was so taken aback by my family when he first met them, and I knew that he must have been missing something.

"He loved your mother very much, Dee. He really does love you. I just think . . . he didn't know what to do with all the anger and all that abandonment. All of that abuse. The two of you don't look alike. You look like your mother, he looks like his father. You're not the same race. He doesn't know jack shit about your world. It doesn't excuse his ignorance, but . . . I guess I'm trying to tell you that . . . Dylan's lost. And if you're lost for too long, you can't identify real love. You don't know how to treat people. You live in your own reality. That's how he ended up here."

Dee killed the joint and left it in the ashtray on the coffee table. Then he sat back, sighing. "I always thought he hated me. I was so confused when my mom put his name in her will. When she made him my legal guardian. I guess she thought she'd still be around by the time I turned eighteen, so it wasn't exactly part of the plan. But I just don't understand why she chose Dylan over, I don't know, my uncle."

"Your brother left a bunch of notes outside the bathroom door last night. One was addressed to me, there was one for you. I took the letters, and I read them over and over and over again until it clicked in my head that they were real, he had actually written them, he was actually going through with ending his life." She was talking through tears. "I still have them, and they're weighing down my soul, Dee. It's so, so heavy. But if I took anything from these letters, it's that I think your mother's trust in your brother didn't come from a vacuum. There was so much love in the words he wrote down. So much pain, but so much love."

"Can I read my letter?"

"Do you really want to?"

"If Dylan had succeeded in his attempt, wouldn't you want me to read it? Does it matter that he's still alive? He wrote it for me, and I want to see it."

"I'll give it to you at some point. But there's no turning back once you read it. And I don't want you to ever let him know you saw it. Understood?"

"Of course I won't."

"Okay. Good." She wiped her eyes. They both pretended to watch the TV for some time. Then Mia asked, "So are you going to move out with your uncle?"

"You know about the offer?"

"I do. I think it sounds like a good idea for you. A change of scenery."

"What about Dylan? Is he going to live here on his own? I don't think that's a great idea."

"I'm moving in here. Permanently. We're going to live together. He doesn't know that yet, but he will soon."

"Why? Just because of what happened?"

"Not just. *Estoy embarazada.*"

"What?"

"Your brother is going to be a father next spring. I found out a couple of days after the fight in the kitchen. I felt the ground give way beneath me when I saw those two faint pink lines, but *Dios*, I knew it was a turning point. I knew a lot was going to change from that point onward."

"You're *pregnant*?" Dee blinked at Mia. She nodded. "So you're moving in with my emotionally unstable brother? Because being pregnant is not a good enough reason to do that."

"My plan was to tell him and give him an ultimatum—become a better person for this new life, or stay out of mine forever. No access to his child allowed. I was mustering up the courage to tell him, and I was going to tell him last night. I was waiting for him to finish showering so that we could eat dinner and I could break the news. But I was waiting for too long, and my impatience got the best of me. I couldn't wait anymore, so I went to the bathroom door to tell him. I called out his name and heard nothing, then I looked down and saw the papers, and I realized what was happening, and the whole world stopped."

"Wow. That's rough. I'm sorry."

"It was hard. But he's safe now, and that's all that matters. And my ultimatum still stands. I'm going to tell him as soon as he comes back. Wednesday, I think."

"And you're sure he'd be okay with you moving in?"

"If I hadn't seen the note he'd addressed to me, I probably wouldn't. I'd probably just stay in Phoenix and try and figure things out on my own." Her voice wavered. "But I know he would be okay with it. And don't get me wrong—I acknowledge the toxicity and the abuse. I swear to God, I'll run for the fucking hills the second he starts acting up around me and my kid. I won't take any of that bullshit. But I want to give him a chance to heal from his own traumas, and I feel like this is an opening."

"That makes sense. I guess it could all work out if he actually sobers up after this."

"Exactly. He has one more chance. And besides . . . he's a hard one to get rid of. I love him too much. I've gotten many tattoos under the influence, but I was stone-cold sober when I got his name on me, because that's where he lives. Right here." She pointed to the left side of her chest.

Mia continued, telling Dee about her plans to open up a tattoo parlor. She had been working as an artist in Phoenix, crowd-sourcing clients through friends and on social media, practicing her ink work on other tattoo artists, and designing a lot of Dylan's pieces. She had been refining her craft for years since getting her art degree from Arizona State University and was ready to start earning a better living. She told Dee that the thought of opening up a parlor in downtown Harlow was exciting for her, and with some fundraising help and a little bit of digging into her savings, she could make it work. The pregnancy posed a financial chal-lenge, but her family would be her safety net. Dee thought about the empty retail spot in town, the one that used to be alive with his mother's herbal skincare products. Five months later, it was still waiting to be rented out. He told Mia about it, and she raised her eyebrows in intrigue.

"Maybe I could change that," she said.

Before Dee went to sleep that night, he clicked on the message notification he had gotten from Naya a few hours earlier. There was a sudden lump in his throat, and he wanted to call her, but he had to respect her wish for space. He put his phone down on the dresser beside him, stared at the ceiling, and tried not to think about the cavity inside of him, ever growing.

Hey.

I heard about your brother. I hope he's doing okay and that it's nothing too serious, and that he'll be well soon. Please stay safe, and stay sane. It's a rough world out here. Take care of yourself. You deserve to be loved. You just have to want it.

x

28

THE BREAKING OF A DAM

The following evening, Naya and her parents were eating at the dining table. Ever since the aftermath of Vanessa's party, she had been struggling to maintain her morale. She poked and prodded at her food at dinnertime and spent more time in her room than she usually would. Her parents suspected that something was wrong, but until she said something, it seemed that they weren't going to be quick to address the stillness in the room.

"I've started speaking to Haley again," Naya said. Both her mother and father paused, looking at each other, then at her.

"You have?" her mother asked. "How is she?"

"Still living in Ampleforth, so . . . not the greatest."

Her mother stepped over her remark. "Is she still at the treatment center?"

"No. She got discharged a while back. She's doing a lot better. Um . . . can she come visit this weekend?"

"That's a little too soon, don't you think?"

Naya sighed, rolling her eyes. "Forget I even asked." She stood up from the table and beelined for her bedroom upstairs. She was tired, exhausted, of her parents' inability to reconcile with her happiness. Naya didn't want to believe in a heaven or a hell because she wanted to live without limits. With just three color receptors, the human eye constructed its own reality, a scattering of light at different frequencies. Different shades of violet, blue, green, yellow, orange, and red formed the basis of how one walked through the universe. There was no such thing as pure black or pure white. No such thing as right or wrong. Everything was a spectrum. Everything. The mistake was thinking that there was good and bad. That there was a heaven and a hell. There was only life, which was both, and neither. It was just life.

Just as she was about to put in her earbuds and mope, the sound of her parents arguing downstairs caught her attention. She knew it was probably about Haley. Stealthily sneaking into the hallway, she eavesdropped from the top of the stairs.

"You can see she isn't happy, Rachel."

"It will pass. She's young! One day she'll understand. We don't need to revisit the past. It's not good for her," her mother rebutted. "That town drove us out. They treated us like dirt. We don't need that energy here."

"So it was the Fawcetts' daughter's fault, huh? A girl the same age as our own is the problem? Because I think that's where you've been focusing all of your anger."

"It's not about the girl, Terrell. It's about greener pastures. She hasn't even *tried* to make friends at the HECC the whole time we've been here. She hasn't put herself out there in this community."

"If you don't think Naya has been trying to put herself out there, you're mistaken. She's just not doing it the way we expect her to. But we know her more than anyone else does. Her intentions are earnest."

"So that's it? You just want her to turn her back on the church? Lose her way to nonbelievers?" Naya could hear the pointed fear in her mother's voice. For the first time, she truly pitied her parents.

"All she needs in her life are good influences. People that help her strive to become a better person. We can't demand anything more than that. We can't choose her social circle, Rachel. She's a teenager. If we push her any harder, she'll never come back. I'm telling you."

Naya wanted to cry, and she also wanted to scream, and laugh, all at the same time. Nothing was black-and-white, nothing was simple. Even her parents weren't on the same side. Though their intentions were pure, they had different approaches. It was a relief to know that, even if it broke her heart. Haley was never the problem. It was the fear of the unknown, the uncharted. That never worried Naya. It was the unknown that made her feel safe. She hoped her parents would one day understand that.

About an hour later, her father knocked on her door. She let him in.

"Hey, Yaya. How's it going?"

"Fine," she muttered, sitting up as her father sat on the end of the bed. "I heard the fight."

He smiled, forlorn. "It's never good to hear your parents fighting," he said. "It's been tough for your mother, Naya. The move. She wanted to rise above it all, back in Ampleforth. She wanted to prove everybody wrong about you. Because she loves you. She really does."

"It's like I'm a prize possession or something. It's like I'm an award. She just wants to put me on display."

"We're both so proud of you. How you handled the situation. You dealt with it better than *I* could have. I hate to say it, but if your mom was in your position, I don't know how she would have taken it. She saw your fearlessness and it made her scared. Trust me, it's terrifying seeing your only child break free. It's a hard pill to swallow."

"I just don't want you to *worry* about me all the time. I'm *fine*. I'm seventeen! I've had a long time to figure myself out, but I'm not done. I haven't even ruled out going back to church. It's just . . . if I want to go, I'll go."

"I understand," her father said. "You're a good girl, Naya Grace. You mean no harm. If I don't know anything else, I damn sure know that."

Naya smiled. "I'm glad to hear that, Dad. Thank you."

"It will take some time for your mother to adjust. Ampleforth— that was her whole life. Her mother lived there. Her grandmother lived there. A lineage of headstrong women. That was her home. *Our* home. We're still grieving that loss, that sense of belonging. Your friend—Haley—she's a sensitive topic. A reminder of the past. But there's no point closing it off. If you want her to, she's free to visit."

Naya blinked. "Really?"

Her father nodded. "If that's what you really want."

"Thank you," Naya breathed. "Thank you so much."

"No worries." He stood up to head back downstairs. When he was gone, Naya lay back on her bed, staring out at the dusky sky outside her window. She put her earbuds in, took a long, deep breath, and cried happy tears.

◆

Dee was sick with anticipation at the thought of seeing his brother again, especially since the last time they'd spoken had almost really been the last time. What would he say? What *could* he say? There was a line drawn between that evening and everything that occurred afterward. But his fear and anxiety dissipated as soon as his brother came through the front door.

"Hey, kiddo."

Dee stared at him. "Fucking idiot."

"I'll take that." He smiled sadly.

"You lied to me."

"I couldn't tell the truth, could I?" Dee turned around and stormed to the back door, and his brother followed him outside. "Can we talk?"

"Say whatever it is you've gotta say. I've got nothing." They sat down on the plastic garden chairs on the patio.

"Well . . . first and foremost, I'm going to rehab. Next week, for three months. I need to get sober. I'm an addict, and that's the fact of the matter. Going cold turkey's going to be hard but it'll be worth it. Because if I don't, I'm gonna keep fucking shit up, hurting people, lying to the ones I love. I don't want to have to lie to you again. I just want to get my head straight. So, yeah. I'm going to rehab. I signed all the papers, everything."

"Oh. Have you spoken to Mia? Does she know?"

"Yeah. She knows." He looked back at the house. "I noticed that she threw away all the alcohol. Not one bottle or can in sight. All the weed's gone too."

"And the cigarettes."

"Yup. Everything. She's moving in this week, with Lana. When I'm out of rehab, Lana's gonna move back out. It's all being arranged."

"So you know she's staying here?"

"Yeah. I know about the baby too," Dylan said. "She told me this morning. Damn nearly lost my mind because I almost never knew. I would've died not knowing. That's the scariest thing." He seemed smaller and meeker than usual. There were dark circles under his clear blue eyes, and he appeared to have lost a few pounds over the last few days. It was like he was now walking the world without armor, without a piece of himself that was robust and loud, as if he'd cut it away and become lighter. "I'm not just getting better for myself. I'm doing it for Mia, for you, for the kid. By the looks of it, Mia'll be in her third trimester by the time I get out. If I'm not ready by then, I don't know if I ever will be. Otherwise, I'll probably end up just like Dad."

Though Dee was grateful that his brother had finally seen the light, he wasn't going to let him off the hook so easily. "You always defended Dad. No matter how much I tried to tell you it wasn't healthy, it wasn't right. You stuck to your guns. You never listened to me."

Dylan looked down. "I should've known better, Dee. He made our lives a living hell. He hurt us. He hurt your mom. I defended him because I thought it was the right thing to do, to put him before you. He spent the first eight years of my life treating me right. He gave me all this attention when my mother wasn't around anymore, when it was just me and him. Then he met your mom, and he had you, and . . . he just turned into this huge ass-hole and I . . . I guess I thought it was normal. He was just being the man of the house.

"I think reality sunk in when I hit you. I knew that if I didn't realize then, I'd never stop. And I didn't want to keep going." His eyes twinkled with moisture as he looked at Dee. He scratched the back of his neck. "And I've still got a lot of shit to learn. You know, like, how to treat people with kindness. Who knows? Maybe they do sensitivity training in rehab," Dylan joked.

"Sheesh. Is there a hate crime on your record that I don't know about?"

"God, no. I just don't remember half the dumb shit I say when I'm eight beers down. No excuse for any of it, though. Anyway, why don't I save all of this self-analyzing for my one-on-one sessions at the Tucson Greenwood Treatment Center?"

"Sounds like a plan." Dee smiled softly. He hated his brother for everything he had put him through in the last seventy-two hours—hell, over the last five months—but he couldn't stay mad at him forever. He just didn't have the energy for that.

"I've been told you're moving to Tuba City," Dylan said.

"I haven't decided yet. But I guess with Mia being pregnant and all . . . you probably wanna try and live as a real family and stuff, right? You'll need some space for that."

"Cut the bullshit, Dee. This house has three bedrooms and there's plenty of space for you. Whatever we got going on over here shouldn't affect the decisions you make."

"All right, all right. I got it."

"Besides, I'm gonna be mailing y'all letters from rehab. I'll need a permanent address for you, so you better pick one."

That evening, Dee sat down on his bed and read the letter Mia had given him. Like the breaking of a dam, he broke into a torrent of tears. He read it three times over as he cried, until he'd had enough of reading it and enough of crying about it. He looked over at the framed photo of him and his mother and wondered how long the grief would last—how long that Tuesday morning, the morning his mother had died, was going to hang over him. It still felt like yesterday. And all this time, Dylan had felt that grief too.

He ripped the letter into minuscule pieces and let the paper cascade into the trash can under his desk.

◆

I've never been much of a writer. Everybody knows that. I keep shit short n sweet, I do. Almost failed English, what can I say? Anyway, I'm stalling. Sorry. I've been stalling all damn week. But I had to write this. I couldn't leave before I did. I owe it to you. I owe it to Mia, to my friends, my family. But you above all. Cause you're my little bro, my only ~~broter~~ brother. I ain't felt quite right since Freya died, Dee. And I know you haven't, either, but I've disappointed the fuck out of her. I had one job! One job, and that was to look after you, and I couldn't do it. I couldn't just lay off of the fuckin coke and the beers and the parties, even for you, even for your mom, God bless her fuckin soul.

I wanna believe that I can be better, but this shit must be genetic. You said it yourself. Both of my parents are locked up and statistically, I should be too. Your mom saw that I hadn't been yet, and she just wanted to keep it that way. She gave me the responsibility of taking her place, but nobody can take her fuckin place, Dee. Nobody can take your mom's place.

I've disappointed you. I've disappointed my step-mother, Mia, everybody I care about. I'm twenty-six: how much longer can I keep disappointing people for? I don't know. I don't know. I'm just faulty. I can see myself turning into Dad, and I don't know why I can't help it, but I can't. I'm a shitty person. But you, you're fucking amazing, you're a great kid. I don't deserve you, I never deserved Freya, I don't deserve anybody. I'm sorry this is a ramble. I didn't really plan it out.

I still remember the first time I met your mom. My dad told me that I had a new baby brother, and I had never been more ~~pchs~~ psyched. I saw you when you were a few months old, in your mom's arms. She was your age at the time, which is so hard to believe, right? She seemed fuckin millennia older. Just the way she held herself, the way she spoke, it was insane. You didn't move in with us until a couple of years later, when you were a toddler, and I still remember so clearly this one time when Frey left us in a video game store while she quickly went to buy something next door, and she told me, "Stay here and look after your brother. If you even think to step an inch out of this store with him, so help me God." It scared the shit out of me at the time, but it instilled somethin that I should have held onto, to this day. But I fuckin failed to, Dee. I failed to look after you.

Yes, I was out partying the night that Dad almost killed Frey. I wasn't in town the day she had her first seizure a couple of months after that. I wasn't in town when she died either. I left you to deal with these things alone. And I'm so, so sorry. About everything. I have been a huge burden on you. I'm telling you this right now, your life is only gonna look up from here on out. Cuz I'm like that odd number you gotta get rid of to balance everything out.

So I guess you can see where I'm goin with this.

I want a cremation. Keep the day short and small, don't invite too many people. Give all my assets and whatever to your mom's side of the family. Take it all to the rez.

I love you. Forever and always. I'm sorry. I'm sorry. I'll rest easy knowing that you're okay. There is new shit on the horizon. Seize it.

—Dylan.

29

FORWARD

"Good morning, Nai!" Haley kneeled at the foot of Naya's bed, popping her head above the bed frame.

"Geez, are you trying to scare me?" Naya sat up, stretching her arms and rubbing her sleepy eyes.

"No, I want you to get up so you can give me a tour of this place. I'm a visitor. A tourist, if you will. So come on. Let's get outta here."

"Okay, give me a minute to wake up," Naya responded, reaching for her glasses on the dresser. "I can't believe you're already dressed. It's eight thirty."

"The sun rose, like, three hours ago."

"And it's not setting for another fifteen." Naya rolled her eyes, getting out of bed. "Okay. So we're going to go to Benno's Diner for breakfast. They have the *best* waffles. And I mean the best. Then we can do some thrifting, maybe walk around Silver Rock, all that. Then we can bus it back to New Eden and head off to No Man's, and you can meet my friends. Sound like a plan?"

"Yup. I'll just follow you where you lead me," Haley said.

Though things were not the same between her and Haley as they once had been, there was still a feeling of familiarity, of home, that she gave Naya. She did not know whether love was the right word for it, but it was something that she could not just ignore. There were old wounds being opened with their reunion, but the fact of the matter was that they were just two girls trying to find out who they were in an unrelenting world. Naya never knew where she fit in, never knew where she truly belonged. She had always been trying to figure it out, and she guessed that this was just a part of growing up. She was still young; she still had the future laid out in front of her. She was still on a forward trajectory into the future, as one always is. Just as Marie Delden was, until she hit a wall—one where the future was always the present, and the past was always the past. Naya was lucky to remember her own past, to be able to soak in the present moment, and to anticipate what was coming.

◆

Naya and Haley found most of the Girls and Guys hanging out at No Man's Land. Tori and Tyler were nowhere to be seen, but Amber, Evie, and Jasmine were sitting over on the edge of the skate pool while Dee and Ash practiced gazelle flips, and Levi and Wallis had a one-on-one going at the basketball hoops.

Naya's heart stopped at the sight of Dee in the distance as she got closer. When the Girls noticed the pair, they yelled and waved. Amber stood up and strode toward them, giving Naya a hug and turning to Haley.

"I see you've brought company today, Naya! Hi. My name's Amber. Haley, right?" She smiled.

"Right," Haley responded. "Just passing through the Pretty City, as y'all call it."

"I love your outfit!" Amber said as Jasmine and Evie approached them. "Where did you get this T-shirt?"

"Aw, shucks. It's actually Naya's. She gave it to me. It's already my favorite." She looked at Naya, smiling softly.

Naya was introducing her to Jasmine and Evie when the Guys approached to greet the new guest. Only the Girls had known that Haley was coming over for the weekend, so it was a slight surprise to Dee when he saw that Naya had a companion with her that he was unfamiliar with. But when he exchanged names with her, it all made sense. Her ex-girlfriend was in town.

"Nice to finally meet you! I've heard a lot about you." Haley smiled.

"Good shit, I hope," Dee said, balancing his skateboard horizontally across his palms.

"Sure," Haley responded. Naya felt the tangible awkwardness in the air. By now, the rest of the Guys and the Girls had left the trio on their own. "So . . . what's the scoop with this old Marie chick?"

"She's a wild one. Full of secrets," Naya said. "It's really sad, but also really cool, trying to fill in the blanks. Right, Dee?"

His eyes flitted between the two girls as he nodded. "Yeah. She's a real character. Has a notebook of all these cryptic poems.

I haven't read anything in a minute, but there's something about that book. I can't stop going through the pages."

"He's always the one reading the poems aloud to Marie, out in the garden. It's so adorable." Naya beamed. "You're selectively passionate. You'll read *The Anatomy of a Worried Heart* or nothing at all."

"What can I say? She sold me."

"Dramatic name for a book, don't you think?" Haley chimed in.

"This woman stayed under the radar for forty years—I wouldn't expect anything mediocre from her," Naya said.

The time span since Dee and Naya had last spoken had been the longest since they'd first properly met, back in Mr. Walters' office. She had been dreading seeing him again, and was not expecting the Guys to be at No Man's Land with the Girls. Though it had been possible, it had seemed unlikely. When the Girls invited her to play a game of ball at the park, they'd somehow omitted Dee's presence. Maybe they wanted drama to unfold, to get their popcorn ready for the show. But there was no animosity in the air.

"Oh. So *that's* the guy she's been crying over?" Haley muttered jokingly into her shoulder when the Girls sat on the ground in a circle, watching the Guys as they returned to their skateboards.

"Don't embarrass me in front of everyone." Naya blushed as Amber and Jasmine giggled. "I only cried once, by the way. I'm over it now."

"Join the club!" Amber raised her hand. "I also learned the hard way that the Guys are totally out of bounds. There's more emotional intelligence in a sea sponge than all of my brother's friends combined."

"Aren't guys like that in general? That's the vibe I get.

But I'd never know, and I don't plan on finding out either," Haley responded.

"Teenage boys are stupid. I think Tyler's probably the only mature seventeen-year-old within a twenty-mile radius out here," Evie said. "Pearce Wilson's going to college soon, and he's probably still going to end up in blackface or something at the next costume function."

"Oh goodness. Don't remind me about the 'Chief' costume from last year." Amber sighed. "The fact that Vanessa dated him after that says . . . a lot."

"Wait—there are too many names being flung around right now. Pearce? Vanessa?" Haley narrowed her eyes.

"It doesn't matter who they are," Naya quickly interjected. "Let's change the subject, shall we?"

"Don't you want Haley to know about your little *love triangle*?" Jasmine smirked.

"Do we really have to go into the minuscule details right now? Is it even possible for us to go three seconds without talking about boys?" Naya huffed.

"You're right. We should keep it even and talk about all the genders. That's real equality," Jasmine joked.

"Haha," Naya said.

Jasmine stood up, grabbing her DSLR from her backpack. "Y'all look so cute. And you've color-coordinated your outfits. I'm gonna take some photos of you. For the zine. Stay there, I'll take one from above. Just look up at the camera." Naya and Haley obliged, staring into Jasmine's lens with smiles on their faces. Amber and Evie were in the periphery of the frame, with Naya and Haley directly in the middle. The sun shone down on their heads so intensely that they had to shield their eyes by the time the third photo was taken. Jasmine then reached for her Polaroid and squatted down to their level, taking two more photos—one for her collection and one to give to them. "You can decide between yourselves who wants to keep the photo."

"It's all yours, Nai," Haley told her.

"You sure you don't want it?"

"I already have your T-shirt. That's my souvenir."

"Aw, you guys!" Amber gushed. "So cute. I could implode. Please invite us to your wedding. I know it'll be so much fun."

Naya laughed. "Bold of you to assume we'll be getting married when we're not even together anymore."

Haley looked at her and said, "We never officially broke up, you know."

"Oh damn. I guess it's time. Wait, let me just think of a nice way to put it. *It's just . . . you know, the distance. I'm so busy, I don't have enough time for myself. It's not you, it's me . . .* Does that work?"

"I'm dying of a broken heart," Haley delivered ironically. "How will I ever get over this?"

"I don't know. Maybe *The X-Files* and ice cream?"

"That sounds more like our plans for the evening."

"You're going to *make* me watch *The X-Files*?"

"It's the least I could do to get back at you for officially dumping me in front of your friends."

Naya laughed. "Touché."

Dee watched as the Girls took photos with each other. It was impossible to ignore the laughter, the warmth, the chemistry that emanated from Naya and the girl she'd once loved. It was at that moment that he realized that he'd lost Naya, and that there was probably no turning back. They were back to square one—mutual friends, volunteer partners, nothing more, nothing less. He was on his own again. But maybe it was for the better, he thought. Maybe he needed time to breathe, to start fresh. He could have a new life soon, meet new people, start over. No more complications. He could Violet-Winslow his way through the world, leaving everything behind him as he ran into the future.

But there was someone he couldn't leave behind just yet. Not until he truly processed the night that had changed everything.

◊

Vanessa emerged from inside her house holding a bottle of Jack Daniels and two small glasses. She sat opposite Dee on her garden deck, sparking up a cigarette before handing Dee the lighter. She'd been surprised to get a text from him earlier that day, asking to meet up for a talk. He didn't specify what about, but she wasn't going to decline. There were still many words left unspoken between them.

"I'm sorry about your brother. Last weekend must have been tough," Vanessa spoke.

"It's okay. He's doing a lot better. Yeah, it was pretty rough, I won't lie. But I'm good now."

"You know I don't want to have to ask, 'Are you *really*?' But . . . are you, really?"

Dee shrugged, staring out at the swimming pool ahead. The turquoise water swayed and rippled, illuminated by the pool lights. "Of course not. But I'm still breathing. I'm healthy. So I'm fine."

"I didn't think I'd hear from you again after the party."

"Do you remember much? From that night."

"It's all a little bit hazy. I was pretty fucking drunk." She broke into a grin before immediately sobering up. "But I definitely remember the conversation we had."

"About Karina?"

She nodded in response. After taking a deep drag, she shook her head, biting her nails. "What she did to you . . . you don't understand how badly I want to beat her to a bloody pulp. I'm fucking furious. I can't stop thinking about it. I'm sorry I didn't message you soon after the party. I was going to reach out eventually, but I got into deep shit for wrecking the house, and I'm technically supposed to be grounded right now, but my mom's on a business trip and my dad's at some boring town conference, so I took advantage. Sorry, I digress. I didn't message you the next day because I . . . I was trying to think of the right thing to say to you. Then I found out Dylan was in the hospital, and I didn't think you needed any more shitty reminders at the time."

"It's cool. Don't worry about it. It's not like it's your responsibility to look out for me. I've got to look out for myself."

"But I'm angry, Dee. I'm angry at Karina. I'm angry that you never spoke sooner. I'm angry at myself for not believing you when you said you didn't cheat on me. I believed the rumors. I believed *Karina*. But I didn't believe you. It hurts to come to terms with that."

"Don't blame yourself. Shit happens."

"You could have told somebody. Anybody. Even if she wasn't charged with . . . rape, she could have had some form of punishment for fucking drugging you. That's not cool. At all."

"It doesn't feel comfortable."

"What doesn't?"

"That word. I don't want to hear it."

"Rape?"

"Yes."

"It's true! That's what she did. It's not rocket science."

"I'm a guy, Ness. Why don't you get that? I'm a fucking guy. Things like that don't happen to us."

"You're so wrong. It happens all the time. You didn't want to sleep with her, you never planned on sleeping with her, and yet somehow, you did. And you didn't even know it was happening until it was happening. It's so crystal clear what it is. She took advantage of you. Only God knows why she did it, but she's clearly fucked in the head."

"Vanessa. What do you expect me to do about it?"

"I didn't want you to keep it to yourself," she muttered, crying. "You've been through so much. It's not fair to you. You could have told me. I would have understood." She realized that this was the fourth time since their breakup that she'd found herself in tears while talking to him. It couldn't be a good sign; things between them would never be like they once were.

"If I'd told you at the time, it would have just sounded like a slimy cop-out."

"There's no way on earth I would have assumed that. You'd never lie about something like that. That's not who you are."

"It was her word against mine, anyway. And I just know for a fact that it wouldn't have changed anything. We weren't working out. We were always fighting, Ness. We were going to split up eventually. So I took the fall."

"We could have made it. I know we could have gotten out the other side, and we would still be together right now. Karina broke us up. She broke us up, and she enjoyed doing it." She wiped a tear away, sniffing.

"I don't think she had a great home life either. I don't know the specifics, but I'm guessing there was probably some abuse. Maybe that's why we gravitated toward each other. We had been through things. I thought she was so cool and hardheaded. I was so intrigued by her. She was also really secretive—she never told me anything about her life. Nothing ever became personal to us. I'd just sneak her into my house a couple of times a week, and she'd leave immediately afterward. No conversation, no pillow talk, nothing. For a while, I thought that was an okay setup. I was just about to turn sixteen, and I had this smoky-eyed, enigmatic seventeen-year-old girl climbing through my bedroom window whenever I called her. I thought it was normal, to not feel connected to somebody but give them your whole body. When I met you, I realized how wrong I was.

"Karina didn't take it well, you know. When I stopped calling her over. When I told her I wasn't feeling it anymore. It wasn't that she blew up in anger or anything, but she blocked me on everything for a few weeks. I thought it was weird, since it had never been that serious. I didn't really care at the time. I'd only realized a couple of days after my first date with you, before we'd even kissed. I don't know, maybe she was jealous. She probably saw me growing closer to you and she was angry about it. She was probably just trying to get back at me, and she waited for the perfect opportunity. When she found out I was going to the same party as her. And then . . . what happened happened, and I'm not with you anymore. So maybe you're right. Karina *did* break us up. But I really don't think there's any turning back."

Vanessa sighed. "Okay. You might be right. I'm going to have to get over you one way or another."

"You're not over me?"

"Of course not. It's only been three months. We were together for a year. But I get that you're moving on and you're trying to heal from everything. I'm going to keep putting myself first. Making myself happy. Focusing on the jazz band, maybe picking up another hobby while I'm at it. I need to start looking at colleges. There's a lot of shit to look forward to. It's not always about looking back."

"Exactly. It's onward and upward."

And for Dee, moving onward and upward was starting to feel less and less plausible in the sleepy suburban town of Harlow.

30

WITHIN

"Where's William today?" Marie asked Naya as they lounged in the garden. She had also asked this question the other day, the second shift Naya had attended without Dee. There were more pressing issues he had to deal with before returning to Salvation Hill, so it meant Naya going to the nursing home by herself. Haley's older brother had taken her back to Texas the previous night, and Naya was overwhelmed with a sudden sinking feeling, an unshakeable loneliness. She'd found it hard to get out of bed in the morning before her shift; it was her father who'd had to make sure she got up and dressed so he could drop her off in time. She didn't have the energy to entertain Marie, and she had lost the motivation to keep coming up with theories as to where she had spent the majority of her life. Between sorting out the library and fetching Marie drinks, Naya flipped back and forth through the poetry book, getting lost in it. It was the only thing giving her hope. As Marie's life was lost in her memories, her notebook was the only tangible thing left, a reminder that she'd once been full of love, zest, and a certain magical profoundness.

"Will's not here today. He's sick," she lied.

"What's wrong? You look upset," Marie crooned, rubbing Naya's back warmly. "You shouldn't be upset, dear."

"I'm okay. Honestly." Naya choked, holding back tears. It would be embarrassing if she fell into a sob at that moment, in the middle of a nursing home. She sucked in her breath and sighed, twiddling her fingers. In reality, there was a multitude of things bothering her. She was also anxious because she had an upcoming ophthalmologist appointment that would determine the speed of her eyesight's deterioration. There might not be a huge difference, but she was terrified nonetheless. She may need to get stronger lenses before school started again, and she may have no choice but to sit at the front of the class, potentially having to use binocular-like glasses to read. Her peripheral vision was not as good as it once was. Naya recently found herself stumbling over things in dim light and sleeping with her bedroom lamp on. She was having trouble sleeping, having nightmares about the future, fears about how she'd cope ten, twenty years down the line. She'd never be completely blind, but she wouldn't be far from it. She felt like that might be worse—*almost* seeing, still registering some kind of light, but not enough, never enough to go about her daily life without struggle. She wanted to live daringly, without thinking, without looking ahead. But she'd always be looking ahead, until she no longer could.

"I don't believe you. You're upset. I'd always tell my husband I was fine, even when I was hurting. I can see it in your soul that you're hurting. You're usually nothing but a ball of energy, but . . . it's gone today." Marie took Naya's hands as they sat side by side.

"I know." Naya sniffed, nodding her head. She wiped a tear away. "I'm just really sad. I'm just worried about a lot of things. It's all so much to handle sometimes."

"You can worry. You can be afraid. But one thing should be mandatory—that peace of mind depends on nobody and nothing besides you. It has to come from *within*. Do not depend on anybody. You need to be adaptable, to uproot from marred soil. People constantly change. Everything is transient. The only way you can get through anything is to remember that it is a transition. Every emotion is. From A, to B, to C, all the way to Z, and then back to A. That is what the heart is. It is a vessel of change. You can only worry for so long."

"Thank you. That means a lot to me." Naya squeezed her hand, smiling through wet eyes.

"It's no problem, darling."

After a moment of silence, Marie spoke again. "My little Charlie," she gushed. "She was such an adorable girl. I wonder what she's up to now. I think she'd be in her forties now, right? I wonder when she last came to visit. Anyway, the last time I saw her, she was sitting in the back seat of our car, all gigglin' and happy. She had these beaming, gorgeous eyes—very blue, like yours. We were originally going to spell her name as though it was a mixture of mine and my husband's: C-H-A-R-L-E-T. But Charles wasn't too keen once she was born. He just wanted to keep it traditional, and so that's what we did. Oh, Charlie. You'd love her. She's older now, maybe in her early forties. I hope she comes to visit one of these days."

Naya remembered how Marie's daughter had only come by once, and it was just to give the home some of her long-lost items, including the poetry book. She wondered if she had even read it—if she'd been willing to give it back to Marie, chances were that she hadn't. If she'd seen the poignance in those words, she'd never have wanted to part with the one tangibly beautiful thing that her mother had created. But it made sense—if Marie had disappeared when she was just a child, her daughter probably had no connection with her. It would have been like keeping hold of a stranger's possessions.

When she got home after her shift, Naya decided to do some research of her own on the family Marie had left behind. She started off with a Google search on Charlotte Winslow to see if she could find who she was looking for. It didn't take long to end up on the LinkedIn page of a Charlotte Winslow-Ellis, a real estate agent based in California. She couldn't be sure it was the right woman, but there was an undeniable resemblance, and she fit the age range, judging from her photos. Naya opened up a new tab and searched through Facebook for Charlotte Winslow-Ellis, and she hit the jackpot, finding a profile that matched the LinkedIn one. It didn't take long for her to find a gallery of family photos; by the looks of it, Charlotte was a mother of three—one daughter and two younger sons. The daughter, Madeleine, looked college-aged, or at least no older than her midtwenties. As Naya dug deeper, she wondered how she'd never thought to do this level of sleuthing much sooner, but she also felt like a certified stalker. It didn't stop her from going through Charlotte's profile as she was taken over by an ever-intensifying curiosity. Through a tagged post, she found herself on Madeleine Winslow-Ellis's Facebook profile.

When she scrolled down to her education and occupation section, Naya's jaw dropped.

Marie's granddaughter was a poet.

The cogs in her brain began whirring. She had to say something—to reach out, to let Madeleine know about the poetry book her own grandmother wrote. Maybe she already knew and didn't care, but on the off chance that she didn't know, Naya felt it right to say something. Before she could begin formulating a message to send her, her phone lit up with a text. It was from Dee.

Hey, Nai.

Sorry I didn't respond sooner.

Thanks for the well wishes.

I'm out of town right now. I left for the Navajo Nation with my uncle last night for a few days.

When I get back, I've got a lot to tell you. I owe it to you.

I miss you a lot.

I can't wait to see you again.

31

HOPE

"*Yáát'ééh*, Yiska. Good afternoon." Hannah Stone waltzed into the kitchen. "How are you doing on this sunny day?"

"You're such a cornball." Dee chuckled as his cousin embraced him from behind. She looked a lot like her father, and so had his mother. Although they weren't raised together, there was an instant familiarity in their interactions. She was so magnanimous and welcoming, and her infant sister, Christina, was a pleasure to spend time with. Though he didn't mean to, he sometimes found himself resenting his mother for her estrangement from the reservation; he hated feeling like he had missed out on something, thinking about the many years lost.

"I'm not corny. I'm just happy. You should be too. What are you making?"

"Eggs and bread. Do you want some?"

"Sure, thanks. Wanna head out hiking later?"

"I'm down."

"Awesome! I'll show you this cool trail that I love taking."

"Is it superlong?"

"Don't worry, Dee. We won't get lost out in the desert. I could walk back with my eyes closed."

"All right, show-off. Let's do it, then."

"Ready when you are."

There was a trail just outside that ended on a cliff overlooking the Little Colorado River in northwest Cameron. It took the cousins around three and a half hours to make it there, under the unrelenting sunshine and permeating heat. They collapsed upon reaching the edge, desperately swallowing down gulps of water from their bottles as the sun began to set. Hannah stopped to take photos of the view before lying back on the red soil.

"You know your clans, right?" she asked Dee.

"Yeah. Red Running into the Water. Grandma was from the Blue Bird People, right? Grandad . . . Deer Spring."

"Yup. Táchii'nii, Dólii dine'é, and Bįįh bitoodnii."

"That's pretty cool."

"Your mom ever talk much about them?"

"No. I think she felt like she couldn't, and that was probably my father's fault. I just had to embrace my 'American' side, which was always weird. I didn't know what that meant. On both sides, I am American. But both sides still clash with one another. It's wild."

"It's all part of a bigger story." Hannah sighed. "It's more than just your mother and your father. It's more than my parents, our family, our hometown. It's centuries old, Yiska. You know the narrative, the ideology, all of that BS. It's about our ancestors. It's about the bloodshed, the survival, the hope, the tenacious-ness. It's about the Long Walk. Hwéeldi. It's about everything that brought us to this moment in time, right here, right now. We're still alive! We're still here, even though we were told we shouldn't exist. Forget about everything else, like family feuds and identity crises that you shouldn't be having. You belong here, with us."

"I'm finding it hard to wrap my head around the fact that you're only sixteen." Dee chuckled. "You're too damn wise."

"I'm not wise. I just know who I am, and who I want to be. I want you to have that too. I know Aunt Freya would."

"Fuck. Hannah, I miss her so much. It doesn't get easy, you know? I thought it would, but it doesn't. It doesn't help that I feel like I'm responsible for her death."

"How, though?"

"I was asleep when she died, in the middle of the night. It was SUDEP. A complication of epilepsy. There was an alert system in my room, and I was fucking conked out, man. I didn't hear it."

"There is *no* way that could have been your fault. She already had that condition. You didn't give it to her, or make it worse. It was a sudden death that nobody could have predicted."

He sighed heavily. "I always knew my dad had fucked her up. I knew it was brain trauma. That's how she ended up in the hospital all those years ago. I mean . . . I vaguely remember it *happening*, back when I was a kid. The fight. The ambulance and cops turning up. And I know that's how she got epilepsy. And I watched her take all these fucking pills for years. I'd watch her have episodes, I'd rush to help her every time. But I wasn't by her side the last time. I wasn't there, and she's gone." Hannah rested her head on his shoulder, rubbing his back in consolation as they looked ahead. The sunset illuminated his glazed, wet eyes. "I . . . I just vividly remember how I was gonna ask her where my washed-out gray jeans were so that I could wear them on that day; I knew they'd been in the laundry. I could feel the silence in the house, and I knew something wasn't right at all. And I was right. I ended up walking in on my *dead mom*. A great fuckin' way to start a Tuesday morning, right?"

"Oh my God, Dee. Bless your fucking heart. You know . . . I still don't really understand what happened with your mom and the family. But I overheard my dad on the phone the other day, to Aunt Lindsay and Aunt Kayla. I think Aunt Freya's will really ruffled some feathers. You know, refusing a traditional burial and all. I think our family knew that it would, and they tried convincing her otherwise. I'm just putting the dots together, though. I could be wrong. Maybe it was a zero-sum game kind of thing. If they didn't want to respect her wishes to have her own chosen send-off, she didn't want the family in the will."

"Shit. Well, that makes a whole lot of sense. She was kinda cutthroat like that. I think it's scary being so young, staring death in the face like she did. Even having to write a will must be so fucking weird, like you might be jinxing yourself," Dee said, staring up at the clear orange sky. "After the coma, she wanted more control over her life. She set the rules and she didn't want them to be compromised." Dee didn't tell Hannah how his mother's near-death experience must have left her jaded, causing friction with the family's traditions about the afterlife. She had spent a total of two weeks submerged in shuttered blackness, in a state where time and space no longer existed. At the time, Dee was too young to understand what had happened and where she had been, but she eventually told him about her experience in the hospital. That feeling of nothingness, that taste of what may be on the other side, had her managing her expectations. Only the dead knew what death was. Ironically, it meant that nobody really knew at all. Not only that, but she was still in frequent contact with Dee's father, and her sisters couldn't forgive her for that. Freya was a complicated woman, unpredictable and contradictory in her actions. There were things Dee had to accept that he'd never truly understand about her, as much as he was desperate to. The grief and confusion ate away at him, leaving him helpless and frustrated. There was no end to it.

"Nothing has been the same, Hannah." Dee frowned, eyes watering. "I feel like I've been floating in limbo for the past five months. I haven't been anchored to anything, or anyone." He then thought of Naya and felt his heart break a little. Of course, somebody had been holding him down, giving him a slight sense of purpose. His pain had obscured that, but it would have been wrong to overlook her. He had spent the whole summer doing that, and he was riddled with regret—for all the times he'd tried to hide her away, deny her respect, treat her like nothing more than a rebound. He still had a lot to answer for, and he knew he had to do it soon.

◆

Later that evening, Dee tucked into a meal prepared by Sandra, his aunt, after his uncle had taken a trip to Flagstaff for a hefty grocery run. The family sat at the dining table, dipping into blue cornbread, lamb stew, and frybread tacos, sharing hearty stories and jovial quips as they ate. Dee couldn't remember the last time he had felt this full since the dinner at Naya's house, and the thought of indulging in home-cooked meals on a regular basis was tantalizing. His mother had never been an amazing cook, but there was heart in everything she'd made, and it trickled down from the recipes she knew and loved in her childhood. Today, Dee could taste the heart on his tongue, and as satiated as he may have been by the time the meal was over, he dreaded returning to any meal made without it.

After dinner, the family lit up a small fire in the backyard, framed by plastic chairs for them to sit in. His uncle broke into stories of his childhood with Dee's mother, and how as the eldest child, he had never had a hold on the baby of the family. She loved to press people's buttons—whether by defacing her grandmother's walls with rainbow Sharpie pens, or skipping classes to go hiking or play ball games with the older kids, or stealing her parents' car for joyrides, or coming home still buzzed after a three-day bender. Dee and Hannah listened intently to Jared's anecdotes while Christina sat on Hannah's lap, attempting to throw stray twigs into the fire. After a while, Dee's uncle went back into the house, returning with a battered acoustic guitar.

"This was your mom's, way back when," he told Dee. "She was convinced she was the next Tracy Chapman for a long time, but me and your aunts—we'd tease her a lot, tell her she didn't have the vocal range. It never stopped her from trying." He chortled.

"That's funny." Dee smiled. "I think I'd hear her singing 'Fast Car' in the shower at least once a month or something. Yeah, she wasn't exactly the best singer in town."

"Hey, it's the passion that counts, right?" Sandra interjected. "That's all that matters. And she had tons of it."

Dee reached over and took the guitar from his uncle's hands. He examined the scratches and dents, even noticing what looked like cigarette burns. When he turned it on its back, he could see some words carved into the surface. Under the dim light of the fire, he got a closer look, squinting:

PROPERTY OF FREY

DO NOT FKIN TOUCH

GET UR OWN

He smiled, returning the guitar back to his uncle. "Supercool that you kept it this whole time," he said. "Even when she got a new one."

"We thought one day she might want it back. Or that she might return to the rez and give us hell for giving it away. You saw what it says on the back." Jared chuckled.

"I guess you could give it to me," Dee responded. "I could learn to play it or whatever. I know it's rundown, but I could get the strings replaced."

Hannah's eyes lit up. "We could start a band or something. I could learn the drums or the bass."

"Let's not get ahead of ourselves." Dee shook his head, grinning.

"It'd be so cool, though. You know it would. Right, Chrissie?" Hannah turned to the toddler on her lap, who nodded like she could comprehend the conversation. Dee paused, trying to envision it: him and his cousin practicing their instruments and jamming out to songs in the garage. If he actually got good at playing, he could keep the hobby up while he studied at college. In that moment, a small bud of hope bloomed from somewhere within him, and it pointed him to the future, to a multitude of possibilities. He leaned back in his chair, looked up at the sky, took a deep breath. What happened next in his life was his choice to make.

32

IT IS GOOD

Dee rapped on Naya's front door in the late afternoon, the same day he had returned from his trip to the rez. When she opened the door, her heart stopped.

"Hey. You're back."

"Like I never left," Dee said, smiling softly. Physically, he may have not been around, but he'd not once left her mind.

She folded her arms, leaning on the door frame of the house. Looking behind his shoulder, she spotted the old pickup truck he used to drive parked on the side of the road. "What's that doing here? I thought you got your car fixed."

Dee turned to look at it. "Mia was using it to transport her things from Phoenix. So I thought I'd seize the opportunity for a desert drive. I came over to invite you to join me."

"Oh. I guess I can take time out of my hectic schedule. What's the plan?"

"I want us to talk. It's been a couple of weeks since we last spoke and . . . I really do miss it. I miss our friendship."

"I do too," Naya responded softly. "Yeah, let's talk. Let me just grab my jacket—it's kinda chilly today. Give me two minutes, okay?"

Dee nodded. "Take your time. I can wait."

On this sleepy evening, Harlow was caked in a soft orange incandescence from the setting sun. There was a cool breeze that suffused the air. The rock formations in the distance glowed bright red, and the pinyon pines, alligator juniper trees, and fiery soil were tinted with the shade of a fuchsia dusk. During the drive, not a single word was exchanged. Instead, they played some songs from one of the records they had bought at the music store. The silence between them was no longer awkward, but peaceful. Like they both knew that they had a lot to say to each other, and that there was no rush to say it. Summer was ending soon, but everything they had built over that time was not going to fade as quickly.

Once Dee found a spot to park in the red soil, the pair sat in the back of the pickup truck, staring out into the horizon. Their conversation started off light; he told her about his time on the rez, going back and forth between Cameron and Tuba City, helping run errands with his uncle or following his cousin around. They'd spent a few hours at the local flea market, where Hannah bought jewelry and they shared slushies and hot dogs, and then met up with Hannah's friends in the evening as the stars slowly surfaced. As he gazed up at the constellations, he could see the ones that his mother used to point to, and felt solace in the idea that she was never truly gone. Every element of her being was birthed from the stars, millions of years in the past. She was still a part of the universe; an energy that never dissipated but had merely transformed.

"Have you seen any of the Guys or Girls yet?" Naya asked, wrapping her hands around her knees and tucking her chin atop them.

"Not yet. I just got back, and I came straight to see you. Like I said, I've got a lot to say."

"What about?"

"About how I fumbled the shit out of everything," he sighed. "You know, with us. With what we had. I don't really think I was truly over all the shit that happened to me before you moved here, but I was so excited at the prospect of . . . of, I don't know, starting fresh with someone new. I completely ignored the problems that I was still having. I made them your problem. I lashed out when I shouldn't have. I retreated when you didn't deserve that from me.

"You're the only person who didn't judge me harshly, besides Tyler and the Guys, and the whole volunteering thing . . . it was so refreshing. But I was still the same Dee that wasn't over Vanessa when I met you. I was still the same Dee that was acting out and doing things for my own gain. I don't know why I expected all my problems to dissipate, but I didn't feel them as strongly when I was around you. I don't want to call you a distraction because that's definitely not what you are to me. I really did feel something. I still do, if I'm honest. I wouldn't have slept with you if I didn't. But I treated it like some gigantic secret, like something scandalous. I treated *you* like a secret. That has to be impossible. You're so hard to miss. You're too special to hide.

"But at the end of the day, I haven't been in a great place these last few months, and I just sidestepped all the collateral damage I'd caused from my grief. I tried convincing myself that the toxic household I was living in didn't have any effect on my attitude, but it did. My brother was being an asshole, and so was I. I watched him in this vicious cycle with his girlfriend and I looked down on him for it, but I was doing the same thing. I was just being hot and cold. I should have been more understanding. Woe isn't always just me. Other people have shit going on too."

"Dee . . . it's okay. I don't blame you, I really don't."

"Wait. Listen. I know you won't blame me, and you won't hold it all against me, but you can't say that it doesn't matter, that it's all okay, because it wasn't okay. I acted like I was embarrassed of you. Of course, I wasn't. But it's not about how I felt, it's about what I did."

Dee thought back to his first interaction with Vanessa after their breakup—the drunk call at three in the morning, the desperate lamenting, the effect his words still had on her; she was still willing to drop everything and run to his aid, even when she was under the impression that he'd intentionally broken her heart. Even at his most vulnerable, he still had the power to suspend her self-control. In a way, he'd used his vulnerabilities as a tool for relief, but it was other people who administered that relief to him, and he gave nothing back in return.

"We shouldn't have hooked up with each other the first time. Not because it was inherently wrong, but it wasn't really appropriate.

Not at the time, anyway. I offloaded all of my shit onto you and I stalled when things got complicated. I did the same thing to Vanessa. And I'm sorry. I'm sorry I did all of that. That's not how you treat a friend."

"I don't regret what we did," Naya said. "I don't regret anything I've ever done for you, or anything we've done together. But you're right. You've been trying to heal since I first met you. You didn't notice your blind spots. Hell, neither did I. I needed Amber to speak some sense into me after Vanessa's party for it to click.

"I just wanted to keep everything as a blank slate, before. I wanted so desperately to just start afresh, in a new town, with new friends. So that's what I did, and I treated you like a mystery to crack, instead of just a person. I was still healing too; I was healing from Haley, from everything that went down before Harlow. I've still been trying to figure out my identity, you know. Grappling with the future. Just a lot of stuff. I'm working through it. I'll get there eventually. I'm just happy we're still friends. I don't know if I could continue walking the halls of school or hanging out with the Guys and the Girls if we had bad blood."

"Well. There's another thing I want to tell you. I've made the decision to leave Harlow and move to the rez. So I won't be returning to South Harlow in the fall."

"Oh. Really?" Naya responded after a prolonged pause, eternity thrust into four seconds.

"Yeah. Really."

"Hmm." She looked down at her feet, feeling her chest tighten. She had the sudden urge to scream into a void, but she also wanted to disappear. She wanted him to disappear, for having the ability to crush her into pieces in just a couple of sentences. "That'll be great for you. It's exciting news." Her voice wavered and she wiped away the moisture in her eyes, wondering if everything that had happened over the summer was nothing but a vivid dream. She hoped it was, because the thought of him actually leaving suddenly felt like a visceral fracture that her heart could not take.

"Are you okay?"

"I got sand in my eye," she said, her voice wobbling. "Speaking of my eyes. I'm getting them checked out soon. Not looking forward to that. They're probably gonna make me wear tinted glasses to protect me from the intense sunlight out here. I already look funny enough. I don't need to walk around looking like one of the three blind mice."

Dee laughed. "You'd definitely rock three blind mice glasses. I can see it already. You'd look ice-cold."

"I don't want you to go. You're my best friend." She looked at him, his brown eyes glinting in the fading evening light.

"It fucking sucks. I don't want to leave everyone behind. Tyler, Amber, Tori, Jasmine, Evie, Wallis, Ash, Levi. Hell, even my brother. You're my best friend too. I don't want to make new friends. At least not right now."

"You will, though. In no time. You're a social butterfly, Dee."

"I'm more like an antisocial caterpillar. Let's be honest."

"Everywhere you go, people love you. You have that energy. I don't think you quite get that."

"Hmm. What color am I right now?"

"Huh?"

"Remember? You told me you describe people in color. Try me."

"I haven't been doing that much lately." She shrugged. "It seems silly."

"To me, you give off . . . yellow. Bright-yellow. Kind of like a fire. A lantern. Sunflowers. Buttercups. A canary. A cornfield. Like butter. Like a bee. A daffodil. A lemon. Banana. A raincoat. Macaroni. Pineapple smoothies at Benno's."

"You're just listing off a bunch of yellow things."

"Exactly."

"So . . . *cheesy*. I love it."

"I see what you did there." He laughed.

"I can't assign a color to you. When I see you, I just see light. Which is technically every color there is. You're like the eight minutes between the sun and the earth. You're brighter than anything I've ever laid my eyes on. It's a blessing and it's a curse, because you're a compass. Wherever you go, I want to follow. But you just keep getting brighter and brighter, like a dying star. So when you're gone, you're going to leave behind a black hole. I don't know how I'll be able to fill that."

"That was beautiful." He wove his fingers in between hers. "I miss you already."

"I miss you more."

"I miss you the most."

"Don't try and one up me here. You know I'm the sappy one in this friendship."

"Okay, okay. But listen. We gotta stay in touch. I'm only a three hour drive away. I can always come back for weekends and vacations. Probably once a month at the least. I won't be completely off the radar. Maybe we can take road trips together or something. You can drop by whenever you want. So it's not good-bye. Don't be a stranger."

"I wouldn't ever dream of not knowing you. The word *good-bye* just doesn't compute in my brain either."

"In Diné, you say *hágoónee'*. I know I butchered that

pronunciation, but whatever. You can also say *yá'át'ééh*, but that's usually a greeting. It means 'it is good.'"

"Wow. It has a cooler ring to it, I must say."

"Exactly. I'll have a glossary of new words I've learned from my cousins in no time."

"That's the spirit." She rested her head on his shoulder and they basked in a tranquil silence.

"What are your plans for senior year?" Dee asked a few moments later.

"I don't know. Working on *Black Glitter*. Applying for college. I want to study fashion and get into textile art. Create a portfolio, all that."

"That makes sense. You've got a dope wardrobe, so why not use it to your advantage?"

"Yeah. I want to design stuff myself, not just mix-and-match secondhand clothes. Though I'll still be doing that. But yeah, I want to really develop my creativity, my love for visual art. Maybe deep down I just don't want to accept that there'll be a time when I'm visually impaired. There'll be a time when my world will just be hazy, when light retention will be near impossible. Damn, I might even go color blind. I want to embrace what I can see while I can still see it."

"I can see it already: NAI, the clothing label."

"Haha. I'll give you the discount code on anything in my first Summer Collection. I'll design a bright-blue Hawaiian shirt just for you."

"You should design your own prom dress for senior year. Maybe that's what you could work toward."

"Yo, that's a cool idea. Maybe I should!"

"And you should make Haley your prom date."

"You think? She doesn't even go here," Naya joked, repeating the line from *Mean Girls* with the same intonation in her voice.

"She doesn't have to. I think you'll be able to submit a guest form or something. You can definitely make it work. If that's what you want, of course."

"I'll keep it in mind." She smiled at him.

The pair then broke into a conversation about Marie, about the theory game they had been playing. She'd given them both something that they did not know they needed: she'd given them hope. When her thoughts weren't vacant, she was full of a zest for life; she had so much going on between her ears. It was just all tangled up like tape, like tumbleweed in the desert. But there was a life inside of her. As long as she was still breathing, she was a story in the making.

Naya told Dee how she'd done some of her own research, and in doing so, found out about Madeleine Winslow-Ellis—a Literature student at Loyola Marymount University, California, who was making moves in poetry circles, according to her social media presence. The evening Naya had found Madeleine, she'd spent a long time watching videos of her performing at slam poetry events, and she was enthralled. She told Dee everything, and he was just as shocked as she was.

"Why don't you reach out to her and tell her about the poetry book?" he said.

"Well, I was going to. But then I kinda stalled. I didn't know how to start the message. It's a bit of a weird thing to do. Message a stranger about her long-lost grandmother."

"When you put it like that, it sounds weird. But I think there's a missed opportunity here. And who knows—maybe it could help us find out about what happened to Marie all those years ago.

Just do it, dude. What's the worst that could happen? She either responds or she doesn't."

"Yeah, you're right. Okay, I'll send her an email or a DM tonight. Give her a rundown of everything."

"Whatever you do, don't mention the theories we came up with. She probably won't take you very seriously if you do."

"Alien abduction is a *very* serious thing. Whether it's real or not, that's a different conversation. But I took *my* theories seriously."

Dee laughed. "So did I! I meant what I said about MK-Ultra. If the CIA really was that good at concealing it all, then who knows? I think there's still a chance it's real."

"I'm going to rank the alien abduction theory as the best one."

"I sense a bias here."

"Well, I've gotta rep myself before I rep anybody else. And as scary as aliens are, you've got to admit it'd be pretty damn cool."

"Haha, that's fair. Okay. I think that's settled. The aliens have won."

EPILOGUE

Fall, 2021. New York, New York.

"For a long time, I was fascinated by my grandmother's disappearance. I was *obsessed* with it—I thought about it all the time. About how I'd never got to know who she was. How my mother never got to know her own mother." Madeleine stood at the podium of the conference hall, her eyes flitting between the speech in front of her and the sea of faces watching and listening intently to her every word. "My mom never really talked much about her, and she never really wanted to. As I grew older, I accepted that she was a painful memory for her, a loss that she never really overcame. So I stopped pressing for answers and I just got on with my life.

"I fell in love with poetry in high school, and I never looked back. But everything changed—everything escalated in my senior year of college, when I found out something incredible. I got this message from a girl in Arizona one night, three years ago. She told me that she'd been volunteering at the nursing home that my grandmother was at with a friend of hers. She told me about *The Anatomy of a Worried Heart*. When I got to read that book, my whole world changed. Then my grandmother died last year, and it broke my heart. I'd never even met her, so I was mourning the loss of what could have been. It was a painfully bittersweet feeling. Her poetry helped me so much in so many ways. It spurred me in my goals to perfect my craft, and to keep pushing for the recognition of my grandmother's work.

"I learned that the good you do for yourself will inevitably come to affect the people you reach. Goodness inspires goodness. Love feeds love. Art feeds art. But you have to start somewhere. You have to find calm within yourself. You can't be restless and jittery, or you'll waste your energies. So whatever screams to you in the silence, listen to it. Embrace that little white light in the dark. You never know what may come of it.

"After she died, I got to working. I acquired the copyright to her poems so that I could help to distribute them, to perform her work at slam functions alongside my own stuff. When I found out I was a finalist for this award last month, I couldn't believe it. All I kept thinking was, *Violet would love this*. My grandmother was the sole inspiration for *Gone but Not Forsaken*, and I have to dedicate this award to her. It's a no-brainer. Thank you to the National Poetry Fellowship for seeing something in this collection of work; you're helping me to keep Violet's legacy alive." She clutched the bronze statue tightly, holding it close to her chest. "Before I return to my seat, I'd just like to recite to you an original poem from my grandmother's notebook.

It's called 'The Birth and Death of Andromeda,' and it means the world to me. I hope you enjoy." She took a lengthy pause and cleared her throat in the weighty silence of the room.

"Cassiopeia gazed down on her daughter,
struck by the beauty she beheld.
She loved the girl,
exclaimed of her perfection
at the top of her lungs,
holding the child high
to the disdain of the world
in which she was born.

She was rescued,
spared by Perseus, who killed her demon.

She is a princess.
She is a constellation.
She is a galaxy.

She glimmers
two and a half million light-years away,
two and a half million light-years into the past,
we stare into the abyss,
an inconceivable scale of time and space.

Andromeda was a Greek myth,
a cluster of stars that the Ancients pointed to
in the night sky.

REST EASY

Andromeda was a figment of our imagination,
a history worshipped,
a slice of the universe observed.

From the other side of the dark matter,
billions of light-years ahead of her,
they may see the same thing,
from a different angle.

They may see the same constellation,
but we might be a part of it
a billion years from now.

We are not separate from the things we conceive.
We are in the universe,
we are space and time,
we are stars and galaxies,
we are princesses and gods,
myths and legends;

We are Out Here, just as They are Out There.
We are Andromeda to Them, as They are to us.

As They come in peace, we will welcome Them.
We will leave our front door open,
we will fix Them some coffee as the Mothership lands.

We will wave Them off, back to Andromeda,
and we will know that They named our galaxy
after a story that They told."

ACKNOWLEDGMENTS

First of all, I'd just like to mention how hard I'm pinching myself right now—I've always dreamt of a moment like this, so getting to write out acknowledgments is just another reminder of how far I've come since deciding at age fifteen that this was a dream I wanted to dedicate my efforts into coming true. But it has also reminded me that of course I didn't achieve this goal completely on my own, so without further ado, here are some of the wonderful people I'd love to thank.

First of all, thank you so much to Wattpad for initially picking this story up in the sea of submissions (over three hundred thousand!) in 2018 and giving me my first Watty Award. I remember back then that the winners were narrowed down from a longlist and a shortlist over the course of a few months, and at each stage I waited with bated breath, like a contestant on a TV competition, though I was still intimidated by the numbers and I managed my expectations every step of the way. Finding out I'd made that year's Winners' Circle really encouraged me on my writing journey; I initially wrote anonymously under a pseudonym, as I wanted my work to speak for itself, and I can proudly say that it did. I have Wattpad to thank for that burst of self-assurance in my writing career.

At Wattpad Books, I'd love to thank, in particular, Deanna for giving *Rest Easy* a chance to be shared with the whole world. It's a story that covers a multitude of difficult but important topics, and there's always the risk of potential misrepresentation or ill-informed depictions of serious life issues, so I'm grateful that I could join the multitude of Young Adult books that aren't afraid to tackle the big, scary, and dark things in life. I'd especially love to thank my editors, including Whitney, for helping me to elevate the story while still staying true to my vision, and for teaching me a lot about myself in the process. Thank you to Robyn, Irina, Meghan, I-Yana, and everyone at Wattpad Studios and Wattpad Books for your support as well.

I have to give a special thanks to the readers—especially the day-ones on Wattpad, including Brianna M. Belle (XxBriannaMariexX), a Black and Indigenous writer whom I'm just grateful I got to provide representation for through this story! I'd love to thank my fellow Changemakers category winner (and now publishing housemate!) Matthew Dawkins, who showed support and love for *Rest Easy* in its early days on the platform. Thanks so much, and I can't wait to see what you do in your writing career. I'd also love to thank Nadirah Ashim (cupofsass), Francesca (the-war-veteran), Immanuel (Mr_me-sterious), Genesee (siren-philocalies), Ray (jesus-saw-u-twerking), Lunathi (umvemnyama), Aaron (A_M_Giovanni), Michela (midiros), Chelsea (Chelseaburke2), Layla (llmattison), alyxcath, beehoyeh, Jessie2708, princessofbrightness, and lemontoji, to name just a few of the wonderful people who supported *Rest Easy* on the platform.

My friends and family have been a huge support network during this, and I can't ignore the immense influences they have had on my writing journey. I have to acknowledge the people in my life who gave *Rest Easy* a chance before it even had a platform anywhere—when I was just a law student with a hobby that I couldn't give up. Thank you to my bestie, Elysia, for being one of the first people to read *Rest Easy* before I had even finished it—going through the opening chapters and giving me really helpful feedback. I'd also love to thank my friends Per, Kamala, Giulia, and Daria-Nadège, and my cousins Tshepi and Dollah for reading the original drafts of *Rest Easy* and giving it their stamps of approval! Thank you to my friends Emma, Paris, Hasan, Lucy, Sakina, Marya, and so many others who've been there for me during my writing journey and/or given me such helpful feedback. I'd also love to give a shout-out to Molly Looby, one of my first-ever writing friends, whom I had the pleasure of meeting through the shortlist of the Sony Young Movellist of the Year Awards in 2013—it's been inspiring seeing how much work you've put into your writing since then, and it subliminally drove me to keep at my passion for storytelling.

I named Vanessa after one of my closest friends, who I met during my year abroad while I was writing this book—she was a breath of fresh air, and inspired the fun-loving and generous sweetheart we see throughout *Rest Easy*. I named Haley after my two best friends from home, Leah Haley and James Fawcett, who have been a special part of my life for nearly fifteen years. Jasmine was named after one of my closest university friends, who has been one of my cheerleaders from the beginning, and I named Madeleine Winslow after my closest year-abroad friend, Maddy, who has continued to support me in everything I do and has given me invaluable feedback on some of my work. I'm grateful for the great company I was in during the writing of the first draft, particularly to my flatmates in Hong Kong, who witnessed my crazed writing sessions in the living room on my broken MacBook keyboard. The naming of Hannah was inspired by my fellow law classmate and flatmate, and Marie's name was inspired by my endearingly kind roomie Mary.

Finally, it would be a crime for me to not acknowledge my family—especially my parents, who have rallied behind my passion for writing since the beginning. I still remember them giving me a day off school after I submitted my first-ever novel to a competition; I'd been writing nonstop, and was completely sleep-deprived for an entire week straight, to reach the deadline. It was completely my choice, and they had no idea how seriously I took writing up until that moment, but they've taken me seriously ever since and have always supported my endeavors. Thank you to my dad, who has been my cheerleader and on many occasions has offered to market my work or help me self-publish when the chance to be published traditionally seemed bleakly unlikely. I don't know where I would have been without such supportive parents, so thank you again. Even though Alanah and Evie are too young to read *Rest Easy*, I have to acknowledge their unadulterated love and support for me, and I'd also love to thank my sister Angela for rallying around me. I love you all so, so much. I can now rest easy knowing I've made you all proud.

ABOUT THE AUTHOR

Warona Jolomba's lifelong passion for storytelling was further ignited by her first writing accolade, aged sixteen. Since then, she has won two Watty Awards and was a finalist in Penguin's WriteNow editorial scheme. Her debut novel *Rest Easy* has garnered over 350,000 reads on Wattpad. When she's not working on her PhD in creative writing, she's reading or painting portraits in her home in South East London.

There are some friends you never forget.

The Invincible Summer of Juniper Jones
by Daven McQueen

Get your copy today!

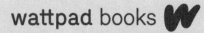

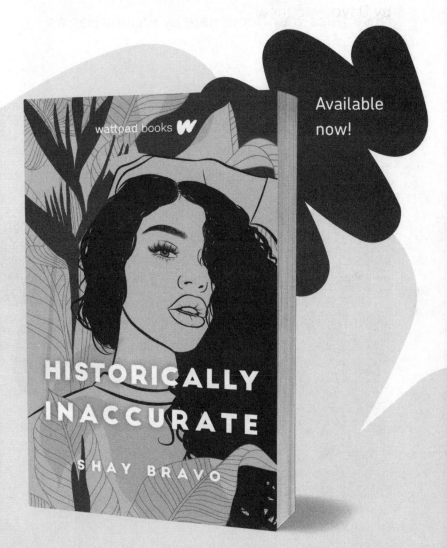

If hookups and scandals were subjects, they'd be straight A students.

Never Kiss Your Roommate by Philline Harms

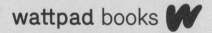

 premium

Supercharge your Wattpad experience.

Go Premium and get more from the platform you already love. Enjoy uninterrupted ad-free reading, access to bonus Coins, and exclusive, customizable colors to personalize Wattpad your way.

Try Premium **free** today.